LUTON LIBRARIES

Renewals, online accounts, catalogue searches,
eBooks and other online services:

www.lutonlibraries.co.uk

Renewals: 01582 547413

**Luton
Culture**

Interviews with an Ape

Interviews with an Ape

Felice Fallon

CENTURY

1 3 5 7 9 10 8 6 4 2

Century
20 Vauxhall Bridge Road
London SW1V 2SA

Century is part of the Penguin Random House group of companies
whose addresses can be found at global.penguinrandomhouse.com.

Penguin
Random House
UK

First published by Century in 2021

Quote on p. xi taken from *The Ultimate Quotable Einstein* by Alice Calaprice.
Archives call number (AEA 45-702) © The Hebrew University of Jerusalem.
With permission of the Albert Einstein Archives.

www.penguin.co.uk

A CIP catalogue record for this book is available from the British Library.

ISBN 9781529135343

Typeset in 14/17.75 pts Fournier MT
by Integra Software Services Pvt. Ltd, Pondicherry

Printed and bound in Great Britain by Clays Ltd, Elcograf S.p.A.

The authorised representative in the EEA is Penguin Random House Ireland,
Morrison Chambers, 32 Nassau Street, Dublin D02 YH68.

Penguin Random House is committed to a sustainable future for
our business, our readers and our planet. This book is made from
Forest Stewardship Council® certified paper.

MIX
Paper from
responsible sources
FSC® C018179

For Jesse, Grace and Zidane.

And in memory of Sudan, the earth's last male northern white rhinoceros. Born 1973, Southern Sudan. Died 19 March 2018, Kenya.

Dear reader,

In the following pages you will find a series of interviews conducted over a period of three years by myself, Dr Graciela Sadiq, and my colleague, Einstein, a male silverback mountain gorilla.

I met Einstein in the capital city of the land of my birth, a city that was soon to be at war. I'd arrived to take up my position as head vet at the city's principal zoo. Einstein had already been an inmate there for several months, serving his time along with six hundred and fifty other non-human inmates. Together they represented a broad spectrum of the animal kingdom. I use the term 'inmates' because that's what they were – prisoners detained against their will. But unlike most prisoners they had committed no crime. They were innocents. If one were forced to level an accusation against them there is only one that would withstand any sort of reasonable scrutiny and it is this: they were not human.

I cannot honestly say that Einstein was the favourite destination for the 1.5 million visitors who flocked to our zoo every year to gawk at him and his fellows.

Far from it. He was much too disagreeable. A few who came could see past this – I remember one young girl in particular called Amal – but once word got out about 'the angry ape', most of those who visited him were inspired by a kind of perverse curiosity. Confronted with the reality they soon lost interest, chased away by his aggression or bored by his indifference. Those who persisted came in order to contemplate the largely unacknowledged connection to themselves that Einstein so clearly represented. Having satisfied their urge, they would wander off to engage with some of our less sullen inmates, and there were many of those to choose from.

Einstein was, however, my favourite, and the reason for this was simple: he was the most interesting of all our prisoners. Why? Because he could communicate. He spoke the language of the deaf, by which I mean he knew and could use sign language. More than this he was fluent, and his vocabulary was wide-ranging, nuanced and sophisticated.

A signing ape, you ask? Preposterous. Perhaps, but true all the same. When he was gifted to us we were well aware of the rumour that he possessed a singular talent, but neither his patron nor any of his previous owners had ever witnessed it. Einstein was determined to keep his alleged talent a well-guarded secret, and I was equally determined to verify or disprove the rumour surrounding him once and for all. If it was true that he could sign, the possibility of gaining insights into the mind of one of our closest cousins was simply too tempting to ignore. If it was not, I had nothing to lose. And so began what was at first a challenge, then a collaboration, and finally a friendship that was to change my life – and his – for ever.

The result of our collaboration is the book you hold in your hands. Within its pages you will embark on a journey that many among you will claim is fantastical, bizarre, ridiculous, possibly even blasphemous, and you would be right on all counts but for one thing: each of the stories in this book is true.

Over the past three years Einstein and I have travelled the world. We've visited every continent and all the earth's five oceans. Together we've met and interviewed creatures of every kind – human and non-human alike. In the case of the humans, I recorded their stories and testimonies exactly as they were given to me. With regard to our non-human subjects, Einstein used his own judgement and understanding of human language to render their voices and personalities as representative of the individuals as he was able. In this formidable task I had the considerable privilege of assisting him, and we ask the reader to trust that together we have done our best. In every case both he and I have learned much from all of them. More than we ever imagined. What follows are their stories. And ours.

Dr Graciela Sadiq BVM&S, MSc, PhD, DipECZM (Wildlife Population Health), MRCVS
EBVS® European Veterinary Specialist in Wildlife Population Health

International Union for the Conservation of Nature
Gland, Switzerland

The love of living creatures is for me the finest and best trait of mankind.

Albert Einstein

Part 1

THE GORILLA

I am called Einstein. How I came by this name will be revealed to you in due course. For now, suffice it to say that it is the name by which most humans know me, and so, to avoid confusion, I will stick to Einstein.

I was born in the mountains high above a valley in a land that is known by humans as the birthplace of humanity. I have since learned that this is not entirely true. It is the birthplace of one species of human – *Homo sapiens*. But this is another matter.

Earliest memory. My mother's smell, musky and ripe, enveloping me as I suck on her teat. Nearby my father rests while my older brothers and sisters play, their joy as soothing as the sun that warms my face. I half-listen as they tumble and squeal and chase each other among the trees. I do not dream. There is no time to dream because I am barely asleep when I feel my mother's muscles tense. Suddenly, violently, she erupts. Then a crack, like a tree splitting, and from behind closed eyes I see a silhouette of mountain ridge that forms the backbone of our forest home spewing liquid fire.

When I open my eyes a murderous creature with three arms stands before me. One of his arms spits sparks that kill, and he points it at my mother. A second later I tumble from her grasp only to be snatched up and thrust into a bag. Now his companions surround us and several more cracks follow the first. I cannot see what is happening but I can hear all too well, and then it is over as quickly as it begins.

To this day memories of my family are vague, for I was very young when they were killed. Even now I cannot tell you what I felt when I lost them, for there are no words in my language, or yours, which can convey my grief. I was spared simply because I was worth more to the poachers alive than dead.

Another memory. A town. Everywhere I look there are these creatures called humans in all shapes, sizes and colours. I am mesmerised and terrified. I stare. I cannot help myself. I see that, like us, they have only two arms and two legs, ten fingers and ten toes, two nipples, eyes that face forward, and no tail. They stand and walk upright and their legs are generally stronger than their arms. And though their scent is different from ours, it is not so different. But as I study these first humans I encounter, I wonder most at their skin. Apart from their heads, they lack any hair worth mentioning, and so cover themselves in bright colours and textures called clothes. All of this fascinates me, but it does not lessen my terror.

It is morning when we arrive in town, and already it is hot and windless. The humans that live there are packed together like ants, but unlike ants they live in squalor and chaos. The streets are crammed with cars, each one blaring its horn into a din which is already deafening. We stop and start and stall amid the traffic, the fumes choking me, until we reach a large central square. Everywhere humans jostle and shout while their ragged children dart and swoop among the stalls, vying for scraps of discarded food like vultures over a carcass. Squabbles between stall-holders and customers pass for conversation, yet in the midst of the chaos many things are exchanged. So many unfamiliar objects, so many different scents, so many vivid colours and sounds. My senses are overwhelmed, but I am not alone. There are other young animals like me who have been stolen from their families. Even so, we are not the only victims.

In the middle of the square, unsheltered from the sun, humans sit cross-legged, their heads bowed. A few brave ones raise their eyes to stare at the hard-faced men who guard them, and for this act of defiance they are struck with the butt of a gun. I watch as the men are separated from the women and children. It is the latter who are sold first. Buyers raise their fists and bare their teeth, pushing and arguing among themselves as they prod and examine each female and child in turn.

One young female in particular is sought after by many and there is much haggling over her price. When she is sold she refuses to follow her new master, and he punches her with such force that she buckles and falls to her knees. Then he grabs her by the hair and drags her until, crying and screaming, she struggles to her feet. When all the females and children are sold the men are auctioned, and the buyers bid fiercely for the youngest and strongest among them.

A human arrives who has nothing to exchange. He is easy to spot, and I watch him as he weaves among the various stalls casting hungry looks here and there. Soon he sees his opportunity, and he grabs the thing he desires and runs. He is cocky and swift and I think he will escape, but the square is teeming with merchants and the one from whom he has stolen cries out. Before long the man is grabbed by a furious crowd, beaten, and set alight. Afterwards, the stench of his burning flesh lingers in the air like a threat.

When the commotion dies down signals are exchanged. Now it is our turn, and I and my fellows are brought out in our baskets and cages and stacked – one on top of the other – like the carpets and rugs that lie in piles behind us. Among us are bright green snakes, exotic birds with feathers as vibrant as tropical flowers, chimps, monkeys, even baby tigers and lions. Eager buyers approach, pushing and shoving one another while deals are quickly struck. Afterwards the buyers depart, and later, when the market is spent, we are delivered to our various destinations.

I am one of the first to be sold to a human called Middleman. He lifts me roughly from my basket and inspects me carefully, lifting each arm and leg in turn, checking my eyes and mouth, my teeth and ears, turning my head from side to side and finally, flipping me onto my stomach and running his hand along my spine. When he is satisfied he hands my trader a wad of paper called money and leaves. Many hours later I am delivered to his house where his children prod me with sticks, shrieking and laughing and baring their teeth in hideous grins while their mother sits in a chair sucking on a pipe and blowing smoke from between cracked lips.

***

I remained at Middleman's house for several weeks, tormented and desperate, too frightened to sleep and too tired to stay awake. Finally, he sold me to another man. This other man lived far away and it took many weeks for me to travel to his land. I do not recall much of the journey. My guards stuck needles into me and afterwards I slept. But when I was awake I was hungry and thirsty and very frightened, so frightened that by the time I arrived at Circus I could hardly remember feeling anything else.

THE ELEPHANT

The morning you were born, says my mother, *the sun rose late and the sky wept for joy.*

Her gaze shifts from me to the herd, and obediently the herd nods. Before I was born we had the longest dry season any of them could remember and, like me, they sense that her words are more than just a reminder.

Listen, she continues. *My son brought into the world life and luck. For this reason I have named him Bahati. Look well and remember.*

A few of the younger ones turn away. I have other names, you see, names they've given me. Newby, Flatfoot, Patch. Before that Speckles, Spotty, Pink. As long as they play with me I don't care, but my mother has grown tired of their teasing and so she's laid down the law. She can do this because she's the matriarch of our herd.

She turns and motions for me to step in behind her. We're off, the two of us at the head of the herd. I grab her tail while the others fall into line. She's leading us to water. Always to water. No one questions whether she will find it, even though each day we travel further and further. We settle into a steady plod. There's no hurry. We'll keep going until we find it, and if we don't, we'll keep going anyway.

***

There used to be a river nearby. It ran fast in the winter and in summer it wound long and cool. We drank from it. Splashed in it. Not now. Now it's an oily sludge lying still as a bloated snake.

Dust swirls and fills my trunk. I drop my mother's tail and blow to clear it. All around us the earth is parched, the rains that welcomed my birth a brief reminder of what once was. I blink. Through my mother's legs I catch glimpses of the horizon. A snow-capped mountain strains to grab the rising sun. But there's something else there now. Before there was nothing, and then skeletons appeared, and those skeletons grew, and very quickly they became solid, angular and immovable, as if saying to the surrounding landscape, *We are here and now you must go.* My mother calls them 'the hills that spit poison'. They huddle beneath our mountain, nibbling at the sky and spewing fumes the colour of sunbaked earth.

A bump from behind. I stumble and turn my head. My friends run past me, trunks raised, ears catching the wind. They've broken ranks. It's time to play. *Wait for me!* I hurry to join them. I'm the youngest and always the last to catch up. Kesi stops and turns to wait for me. She's older than me – only a few months, but because of this she likes to pretend she's my mother.

We reach the others. They swirl and run circles around us. Kesi charges, breaking the circle. Now the others follow and soon it's a game of tussle and tag. Squeals and grunts fill the air. Not for long. My mother trumpets softly and we quickly fall into line.

Hours pass. Each grows hotter and dustier, and all around me I feel fatigue stealing over our herd. It's late afternoon. We've been travelling since dawn. I'm tired and I want to rest. I pull on my mother's tail, but she ignores me. We carry on, the sound of our plodding like fat raindrops.

Finally, we stop to lie down, all of us in our mother's shadows. When it's time to go my mother reaches out her trunk and caresses my head, but I don't want to get up. Not yet. She signals to the others to go on ahead and with her trunk points the way. I open one eye to watch them leave. Then I go back to sleep.

THE SOW

You'll have to forgive me. I'm a bit short of breath. It .... oh dear, here we go .... it comes and goes. Are you in a hurry?

Good. Then bear with me and, well, I'll begin.

I woke early. I'd slept – you could call it that, I guess. I'd slept on my chest, same as always, my hooves poking through the metal slats. Once I woke up and tried to sta .... stand, but my hoof was caught. Caught so that I twisted it. There's no room in my stall to turn around, no room in any of our stalls, or to lie down on my side. That's the model now. *More efficient,* Boss says. *More economic.* Too much trouble to put us outside is what he means. But it wasn't the pain in my chest and joints that woke me that morning. Or the cold steel pressing against my legs and sternum. Or the smell of my own feces wafting up through the slats from the pit beneath me. Or even the agony of my sister sows. I was used to that. What woke me was something else. It was farrowing time.

The day before the one I'm telling you about a new face appeared in our shed. Not unusual. No, not

12

unusual at all. The humans that moved among us, they .... forgive me .... they changed often. What was unusual was the expression on this one's face. At first I was frightened. Yes, I'll admit I was frightened, and then just plain curious. This was unusual. Shouldn't have been. Shouldn't have been unusual to be curious, but I hadn't been curious about anything for a very long time.

The new face was being shown around by Boss, and none of us *ever* looked at Boss. Why? For fear of drawing his attention. You didn't want to be singled out by Boss on any account because you could guarantee that it would be unpleasant. Sometimes fatal. Boss's wife, she was .... you could say she was even worse, but she rarely made an appearance. The smell of our waste was more than she could bear. There were a thousand of us crammed into that shed. A thousand. The smell was more than any of us could bear, but we were stuck. Each of us confined for life in a six-by-two-foot metal enclosure. Imagine that. Go ahead. I'd like to see you try.

When he entered the shed the first thing the newcomer did was lift his blue bandana from around his neck and cover his nose. Covered his nose and just stood there. He seemed confused. No surprise there, because as soon as he stepped inside it took his eyes a moment to adjust. Not to the light, mind you. To the sight of a thousand sows crammed together like piglets in the womb; a womb made of steel bars and slatted floors. As soon as he got his bearings his confusion gave way to disbelief. Disbelief then disgust, and disgust to sheer wonder. None of these made the least impression upon me. I'd seen it all before. What caught my attention was his look of pi .... pity, I guess you'd call it. It pushed all other emotion from his face until he stood there wide-eyed and speechless and near to tears. We could hardly believe it. The only time any of us had ever seen a human cry were the times Boss and his wife argued. The boy tried to wipe his eyes before Boss noticed, but he was too late. Too late, because right away Boss said, *Pull yerself together, Billy.*

I watched the new boy called Billy. He straightened and tried his best to look tough, but it was no use. He caught me watching him, the boy did, and when our eyes met I could see that he wasn't going to be like the others that came and went. He wouldn't grow hard after a few short weeks, and then later, after a month or two, join in the abuse and cruelty we endured daily. He was different. How did I know this? I can't say. A sixth sense. An animal sense. A sense that humans have long since lost.

Boss looked at Billy, and at the same time gestured a hand down our row. *These here are ready to farrow,* he said. *They'll be moved tomorrow morning. We start at six. Don't be late.*

Billy nodded and followed Boss as he made his way down our row. The sister sow on my right lost her first litter. Premature. One by one they'd fallen into the manure pit below. Wasn't the first time that'd happened and wouldn't be the last. Boss was furious and fired the shift worker for not noticing she was in labor. So the shift worker beat her. He beat her, and now five months later she was ready to give birth to her second litter. Her number was branded on her rump just like the rest of us. Hers was 889, but she called herself Ina, and she bore the scar on her head where the shift worker struck .... oh dear, I .... forgive me. I need to stop for a minute or two. I'm having troub .... trouble breathing.

There, that's better. Where was I? Oh yes. He struck her with a metal rod. I was there when he did it, and I remember it like it was yesterday. The boy Billy noticed her scar but said nothing. Wasn't anything to say.

When they'd finished their rounds Boss took Billy's arm and moved him out of the shed. He wanted to show him the farrowing crates, he said, and the nurseries, and the grow-out barns, and introduce him to Mrs Boss. And so they disappeared beyond the shed doors to the place where the light was different from the cold, harsh light of our shed. Brighter and fresher and fierce in summer, but somehow kinder even so. Sometimes the doors would be left open and we could, some of us, we could see that there were times when there was no light at all in that unfamiliar place beyond the doors, and we told this to the others, and all of us thought it must be soothing now and again to have darkness like a soft blanket thrown over one's eyes. We'd never experienced it, but we knew. We knew instinctively that it would comfort us.

THE ORCA

Mad. Unpredictable. Psychotic. Violent. Stubborn. Depressed.

All of them have been used to describe me by the humans that know me best and by others who don't know me at all. Am I all of these things? Some of these things? None of these things?

Do I know? Do I care?

At one time I would have said yes.

But not now.

The park vet came to see me today. He said I have a bacterial lung infection and I'll be dead in a year.

Do I believe him? Do I care?

At one time I would have said yes.

But not now.

Now there is only one thing I know with certainty. I am bored. Bored to death.

***

I suppose you've heard the rumors. Of course you have. Everybody knows that I'm responsible for the

deaths of three of my trainers. The first two I dis-
patched with the help of my harem. The last one?
That was *all* me.

But I'm jumping ahead of myself. *Jumping the gun*
as my trainers would say. What's the hurry? Start
from the beginning. Give the folks the whole picture.
That's what they paid for, right? The whole picture.
The whole shebang. The whole enchilada.

Are you ready? Ready, everyone? Clap your hands
if you're ready. That's it. Come on, folks. Let me see
*eeeevery*body put their hands together and give a great
BIG welcome to the star of our show. Ready? Oh,
jeez. That's pathetic. I know you can do better than
that. Come on now. What's that? I can't hee-*earrr*
you. All right then! Give it up for the greatest! The
one and only! Our *VERY* own killer *whay*-luhhh …

TUPILAK!

Excellent. Now let the show begin.

The Foxhound

I'll start by describing Sir Robert, shall I? What's that? Yes, why not indeed.

He presented a dashing figure, Sir Robert did. He knew it too. One could tell by the way he admired himself in his dressing-room mirror: scarlet coat, black-brimmed cap, white breeches sleek against muscled thighs, and black boots with tan tops freshly polished. When he readied himself for the first formal hunt of the season I alone was permitted to attend. Because of it the others referred to me as the butler. I took no notice. I knew their remarks were born of envy. *Small minds,* as Sir Robert used to say.

I looked forward to the hunting season. We both did. The thrill of the hunt was, quite simply, exhilarating. But there were the social events as well: the picnics, drinks parties, dinners, balls and, of course, plenty of admiring young women. Sir Robert – or Robbie as he was known to his friends and Sir Rob to his staff – was invariably the centre of attention, and this meant that I, Major, was also the centre of attention. A role, I don't mind confessing, I relished as much as Sir Robert did, and one which I exploited for all it was worth.

It may interest you to know that I can trace my ancestry back to the late 1700s, a fact which, in spite of everything that's happened since, I'm still rather proud. I learned of this through Sir Robert. He often bragged of it to members of the hunt, referring to me as the *other* aristocrat. Among his hounds – some forty by last count – I was the undisputed favourite, and Sir Robert was frequently approached by breeders asking if I might be available to stud. On these occasions he was all too willing to recount for them my rise to top dog, a position that brought with it many privileges and much praise.

He would begin the tale with the story of my first cub hunt when, as a young hound, I was taken with my siblings and other juniors for trial. It was in early September of the year following my birth. The kennelman roused us just as the sun breached the horizon. Upon waking we were, as usual, famished, but on the morning of the hunt our ration was withheld in its entirety, and we wondered if we were being punished. It even occurred to us that the kennelman – silly old chap – had got sloshed the night before and had simply forgotten to feed us. It wasn't until we joined the hunting staff, horses and members of the hunt on that chilly October dawn that I understood something out of the ordinary was about to take place.

After being roused from sleep we were marshalled into the courtyard where Sir Robert, mounted, awaited us. On either side of him, also mounted, were the master of hounds, the huntsman and the first whip, and behind them the second whip, the field master and mounted field. The spectacle nearly overwhelmed me. Each member of the hunting party was dressed informally, as befitted the occasion, in standard ratcatcher attire: black hunting caps or brown bowlers, tweed hacking jackets tailored and vented, and light-coloured shirts. Some opted for ties, others preferred stock and pin. Sir Robert wore buff breeches while the others wore tan. All wore black or brown leather boots with spurs worn down and carried whips with thong and lash removed. It wasn't as flamboyant a sight as that of the formal colours worn for the season's opening meets, but it was impressive nonetheless, and over it all hung an aura of giddy expectation. Around me my pack swarmed, singing and wagging their tails, while men and women struggled to contain mounts eager to set off. While we waited several of the men laid odds on various hounds. My name came up repeatedly, and I could not help but notice that Sir Robert was paying me close attention. This gave me a sense of importance but also added to the pressure I was already feeling, and so made me more determined than ever not to disappoint him.

At a command from Sir Robert we held hard. A moment later the huntsman blew his horn. This was the signal we'd been waiting for. By then a few more experienced hounds – old buffers, we called them – had joined us, and as the huntsman and first whip moved off, I and my pack and the other whips followed. Then came Sir Robert and, finally, the field master followed by the field. Soon we youngsters took the lead, forcing the huntsman, first whip, Sir Robert and field to follow at a gallop.

What's that? Yes, you're quite right. It was up to the huntsman and the first whip to prevent us from rioting – chasing prey other than fox. The old buffers among us had been seconded to keep our attention focused and our curiosity from getting the better of us, but I needed no such reminding. I was the first to pick up the scent. I opened, alerting the hunt and my pack (I have the good fortune to possess a distinctive baritone), and as soon as Sir Robert heard me speak he concentrated his full attention on me. I also boast an exceptionally cold nose. I can pick up a scent, no matter how faint, in grass, fields, brushy woodland, roads, puddles, ditches – what have you. Even the widest streams did not prevent me from tracking my quarry. While others struggled to keep the line I never faltered, and it wasn't long before the pack honoured my lead.

Earthstoppers had been active the night before blocking the foxholes on Sir Robert's estate, and the poor sod whose scent I owned had nowhere to hide and so took refuge in a covert. At the huntsman's command I cast in to flush him out. He was quick to break, and the hunt began. We chased him over the countryside, my fellow hounds and I at full cry, eager to get our teeth into our first kill until, once again, we had him surrounded. At a command from the huntsman we held hard. I had only one thought – to go in for the kill before the others – and upon the huntsman's command I cast myself once again into the covert where he was hiding to draw him out. The fox fought back valiantly despite his tender age. He was still shy of adulthood and had not yet left his family group, but he fought like a trooper. I went for his nose, and grabbing his muzzle between my teeth, I shook my head violently from side to side. He sank his claws into my neck, but I wouldn't let go. Still, he fought to the bitter end. A courageous chap, I'll warrant you that.

When he was dead I released him and watched as the first whip sliced off his brush, pads and mask to distribute as trophies. Afterwards, what remained of his carcass was thrown to us. We needed no encouragement. We hadn't eaten properly since the previous evening.

I can admit to myself now that, despite an eventful career, nothing which followed my first cub hunt was ever quite as exciting. Afterwards, when we returned to Sir Robert's manor, the others were shown to their kennels while I was kept aside. I was tired and thirsty and, once watered and fed, wanted only to lie down among my pack and doze. But Sir Robert had other plans. From that day forward I slept in his private quarters, and though at first I missed the companionship of my fellow hounds, I don't mind confessing that the attention, affection and privileges lavished upon me more than compensated.

The Gorilla

At Circus any hope of finding myself delivered to a kinder fate was soon dashed. It was a barbarous, filthy place where everything was unfamiliar, even the air I breathed. Many animals were imprisoned there. All were new to me, and all were suffering.

I was put in a cage with another orphaned animal called Joey. It was much too small for the two of us, but there was no other place for me, and it was better than sharing with one of the great cats. Joey was very young, like me, and like me he had lost his mother – not to poachers but to something called a cull. When I asked him to explain the meaning of 'cull' he turned away. For days afterwards he barely spoke, sitting silently in a corner of our cage, scratching the fur on his stomach until the skin underneath was raw and red. He had never seen a gorilla, and I had never seen a kangaroo, but, in spite of this, we became friends.

When winter came it was bitterly cold. Frozen water fell from the sky, covering the ground like a thick white fur, but unlike fur it was brittle and bright and provided no warmth. Those who had seen it before called it snow, but for Joey and me it was new, and we were not used to it. We gathered the straw strewn on the floor of our cage into a corner where we tried unsuccessfully to build a kind of nest, but the straw our keeper gave us was as sparse as the hair on his head and provided little warmth from the freezing metal floor of our cage.

The weeks and months that followed were unbearable. We shivered constantly and slept little. I became very sick. My body burned and my limbs caused me unspeakable pain. Days and nights passed, and in that time I became so ill that I was unable to eat. Joey tried his best to comfort me, nudging and grooming me, and attempting to keep me warm by pressing his body close to mine. Finally, the leader of Circus, a man called Vicios Crood, arranged for Old Man to come and tend to me.

By then I was so unwell I hardly bothered to look up when Old Man entered our cage. I lay on a bed of thin straw, my head resting on Joey's flank, but I could feel Old Man watching me. I raised my head and opened my eyes. He had an enormous red-and-purple nose and was covered in wrinkles like an ageing elephant. And he stank. It was this, not his manner, that caused me to shrink from his touch.

All the while Crood stood watching. When he saw me shy away from Old Man, he entered our cage, came forward and made to strike me. Old Man put up his hand. He never looked at Crood or uttered a word, but Crood withdrew. Then Old Man whispered to me and at the same time crouched and again reached out a hand. Joey recoiled and retreated to a corner, but after some moments I allowed Old Man to touch me. Slowly, gently, he began to stroke me. It was the first kindness I had ever experienced at the hands of a human, and I have never forgotten it. We remained like that – face to face – until Crood began to grumble and mutter to himself. Then Old Man reached into his pocket, withdrew a small brown bottle and held it to my mouth. It tasted as bitter as it smelled, but I drank it, and the next day I began to recover.

Our cages stood atop trailers attached to huge round wheels, and when it was time to move we rolled away in a great line like a python uncoiling from sleep. We travelled all day and all night, stopping only to allow our drivers to rest. Some journeys lasted for days during which time we were left in our cages with no exercise and nothing to distract us from our misery and boredom. When, finally, we arrived at our destination Crood and his family wasted no time. They put up great tents, airless, shabby affairs – yet in spite of this many humans, big and small, male and female, came to gather.

When a great crowd was assembled Crood changed his clothes and put on what he called his costume. The white of his trousers was grey and his black boots sagged. His red coat was faded and frayed, and the yellow braid on his shoulders hung like an afterthought. Even his top hat was a size too big so that he was constantly pushing it back from his forehead. The whole sad ritual was intended to impress, and upon entering the tent he would lift his hat, introduce himself with a flourish, and blow on a whistle that sent a shrill noise through the bones of his audience until they fell silent and all eyes focused upon him. Only then would he begin the show, and he opened it by making the older animals perform.

At first I did not understand what this meant, only that those animals that Crood selected were whipped if they refused or if they performed badly or if they were slow to obey. Among us the bears were by far the most pitiful. They were toothless and clawless and, denuded of any means to protect themselves, forced to fight with dogs trained specially for the purpose. By comparison, the rest of us were lucky. Fit for neither battle nor show, we were put on display. Sometimes the humans laughed at us. Sometimes they taunted us. Sometimes they felt pity for us.

None rescued us.

***

One day Crood found two young boys. Roma, he called them. Like us, they had no mother or father and nowhere to go, and I wondered about this often. Both of them were thin and dirty and had the look of hungry hyenas – cunning, curious and wary. Crood told them that if he caught them stealing he would cut off their hands and feed them to the lions. They nodded and took no notice. There was nothing they would not steal, but in spite of Crood's warning they never got caught. It was their job to clean our cages. They hated the work, and so they hated us.

By then I had learned to recognise one human face from another, but these Roma were identical. Apart from their scent it was impossible to tell them apart. For reasons I failed to understand at the time, they did not speak. Yet they never stopped waving their hands in the air and making endless shapes and signs with their fingers. I watched them, trying as best I could to understand what their gestures meant. When they finished cleaning our cage I waited for them to leave and then imitated what I had seen. Poor Joey looked at me as if I was mad. It so disturbed him that he turned his back and for hours afterwards kept his distance, refusing to engage, one eye alert for any sign that my fits, as he called them, might resume.

After many weeks I began to wave my hands and make shapes with my fingers whenever the Roma approached. This amused them greatly, and at first they mocked me. Then, for lack of anything better to do, they began to teach me to sign. I was a quick learner. This delighted them, and the more fluent I became the more they confided in me. As I suspected, they had been abandoned by their parents and left to the mercy of the streets and the gangs of ruffians who preyed on them. On the verge of starvation, they hung around the perimeter of Circus hoping to beg a living from the crowds that came and went.

One day Crood spotted them and called the police, but the police ignored him. They told him that the streets were full of orphans, and if Crood wanted rid of them he should call an exterminator.

What are police? I signed.

Thugs who chase us off the streets when we have nowhere else to go. They threaten us and arrest us and sometimes they kill us, said the older one.

Why? I asked.

Because they can, said the younger.

And exterminator? I signed.

They kill pests. Mostly bugs and rats.

Again I asked why.

Because they're dirty and dangerous, said the older one.

And annoying, added the younger.

I thought about this. It didn't take me long to conclude that at times I was dirty, and though still young, one day I could, if I chose, certainly be dangerous. But was I annoying? The two glanced quickly at each other before simultaneously signing their reply.

Yes, they said.

Why? I signed.

Because we have to clean up your shit, they replied.

This is not my fault, I signed. *If you humans had left me in the mountains where I was born and where I belong, my shit would not be a problem.*

I could see they understood the truth of what I was saying. Afterwards, I determined that my best chance of avoiding death at the hands of the police *or* the exterminator was never to be dirty, dangerous and annoying all at once.

Looking back, I believe Crood seriously considered ridding himself of the twins, but in the end he hired them, and his decision changed my life. Though I did not appreciate it at the time, they did me a kindness for which I will always be grateful. They taught me to understand and to communicate in human language using my hands.

***

My first summer at Circus was as brutal as the winter that preceded it. Temperatures rose with little or no rain to cool the air and no breeze to provide relief from the heat. In desperation, Crood moved us to the coast and onto a campground near the sea. Once again we were left without food or water for our journey, though Crood always had plenty to drink – a clear liquid he kept in a bottle that dangled from the end of his arm. This liquid transformed him from a man who was cruel into one who was murderous. By the time we arrived at our new campground he was in a foul mood, yet even he could see that we were close to dying from thirst and something needed to be done.

Nearby lay what looked like a coiled yellow snake, and to my surprise he marched over, grabbed it with his free hand and dragged it to our cage. Joey and I shied away as Crood made to hold it between our bars, when something miraculous happened. It began to spout water, and before I could raise myself to my feet Joey hopped over and began to drink. I am ashamed to admit that I was so thirsty I could not wait for Joey to finish. I grabbed Crood's hand and wrenched the rubber snake from his grasp, causing him to drop the bottle containing his precious liquid. I hardly had time to drink when in Crood's empty hand appeared a blade. Reaching through the bars he grabbed my wrist, and with one swipe sliced off the end of my thumb. It dropped onto the floor of our cage where it remained for many days.

Shortly after this he separated Joey and me.

THE ELEPHANT

Our trek to the river is hot – hot and dusty – and my mother and I fall behind the others so that by the time we arrive they're already gone. My fault, I know, but I'm not worried. I know we'll catch up. Right now I'm tired and thirsty, and all I want is to plunge into the river. I drink greedily while my mother fills her trunk and douses me with jets of cool water. When I finish I snort up a great gush, arch my trunk over my head and blow it out with all my might.

Behind me a sound, shrill and unannounced, blasts forth with such force that I trip and tumble face forward. I right myself and turn to see an enormous old bull elephant standing over me. He glowers, his face and ears dripping, and immediately I back away. When he sees the look on my face he grunts and reaches out to stroke me. I glance at my mother, and in response she raises her trunk and touches the old bull's head in a gesture that's both familiar and welcoming. We stand together like that, the three of us, while he cools me with water snorted up and sprayed from his trunk until, finally, he turns and trundles away.

I want to ask her who he is and why he's come, but she's already wading from the river onto the muddy bank. She walks barely ten steps up the slope to the cover of the bush when her head swivels, her ears shoot forward, and her body stiffens to attention. Lifting her long, ridged trunk high above her head she sniffs the air in all directions. I follow her lead, swinging my head from side to side, extending my ears to capture every sound, and thrusting my trunk as high above my head as I can reach when my mother descends into the river and gives me a violent push.

Run, she bellows. I climb from the river onto the bank and run as fast as my legs will carry me, my ears pressed flat against my head, my trunk extended before me.

***

I hide nearby under cover of a willow, its branches sweeping the ground, and through them I can see my mother. She's standing on the muddy bank, her trunk raised, and with it she blasts her fury so that I can almost feel it come roaring through the bush like a violent gust of wind. Closing in to the right and left of her are two humans. I know instantly what they are after. My mother has warned me of them repeatedly, and when my older siblings and cousins play poacher they trumpet warnings and charge, locking their tusks in a rough-and-tumble before one or the other is defeated. It's fun. A game. One I join only to be pushed out of the way. But not now. Now is a scruffy collection of rags and tattered fatigues and faces warped with greed. When they see my mother with her long, graceful tusks, I know there's no hope of mercy.

I want to call out, to warn her, but I'm too afraid. I watch her look right and then left. The poacher on her left is tall and as mean-looking as a hyena. The other is short and bears a jagged scar along the length of his arm. Thrusting her ears forward until they are stretched taut, she raises her trunk, lets out another mighty blast and charges.

The mean one kneels and raises his arms. In his hands he holds a rifle. I know this thing. My mother has told me about it. As I watch him take aim the old bull elephant reappears from the bush. Extending his ears, he raises his trunk and bellows. The scarred one stands his ground, calmly raises his arms, aims at the bull and fires. An instant passes before he realises that his rifle has jammed, but by then it's too late. The earth shakes with the old bull's charge, and with his tusk he flings the poacher into the air. When he lands the bull is upon him. With one violent stomp of his leg he crushes the poacher to death before turning and vanishing into the bush.

I look for my mother. She doesn't fall with the first bullet that penetrates her hide. Her momentum and rage continue to propel her forward. Then she stumbles, and a moment later she's down, her chest heaving as she gasps for breath. Now her killer stands over her, listening and waiting for any sign that the old bull might return, before raising his rifle a second time. I hear a splintering sound, bullet against bone. After that she's still.

I watch as he bends to touch my mother's tusk. His smile is wide, revealing a gaping hole, and I wonder if other poachers have taken *his* teeth, and if so, how he's managed to survive. He remains bent over my mother as if he can't believe his luck, ignoring his companion lying only yards away on the bank, so that he doesn't hear the bush behind him part.

The old elephant's fury is boundless, and it doesn't cease when the poacher is dead. With his tusk he flings him into the air, trampling him again and again as he comes to land upon the muddy bank. By the time the old bull's rage is spent the killer is recognisable only as a toothless puddle of rags, bones and flesh.

From my cover I watch the bull stretch out his trunk. Rumbling softly, he strokes my mother's body, all the while sniffing and nudging her gently as if to wake her. Soon he raises his head and calls out to me, but I'm afraid to give myself away. I rumble as quietly as I can, and when he hears me he leaves the riverbank and the body of my mother and comes to lead me away.

THE SOW

Yes, I'm better today. Some days are worse than others. Today's not so bad, so let's begin.

The next morning Boss and the boy called Billy and the fat one called Gordo and the painted one called Hank arrived in the darkness to move us to the farrowing crates. I was awake and badly wanted to stretch, but I quickly banished the thought from my mind. Not to stretch, ever, was just one of a hundred frustrated urges we sows endured every day, and to hope for a better life was, well, it was madness.

As soon as they entered I prepared myself to stand. This took every ounce of effort I could muster. We were obese, every one of us. I guess that sounds funny to you because nobody thinks of a pig as being lean. But if you can't move more than two steps forward or two steps back for the whole of your life, well, you figure it out. The extra weight made our joints ache so much that the pain .... oh dear, here I go .... the pain was, well, it was hard. Hard to endure. While I struggled to rise, 887 on my left began to rub her snout against the concrete floor.

Poor thing was trying to prepare a nest, and she rubbed the concrete floor until her snout was raw and shreds of bloodied flesh hung from it like strips of torn cloth.

But like I was saying, it was hard to breathe in our shed. All in all we had plenty of ailments, and so Boss fed us a constant diet of what he called antibiotics. They were supposed to cure our ailments. Even so our lungs ached. One day a man came round and explained to Boss that all the antibiotics he fed us went straight into his customers. Boss stayed silent, but his face grew redder and redder. After the man left Boss started in on one of his rants claiming it was propaganda spread by a bunch of animal-loving do-gooders hell-bent on ruining his business. We didn't understand what he meant, only that it made him angry whenever he spoke of it.

While we waited, Ina, the sow on my right, began to gnaw on the bars of her stall. The first time it drove me to distraction, but like everything else in our lives there was nothing I could do about it, and so I did my best to ignore it. But that morning the sound seemed to grow louder until I thought my head would explode. Took me a good while before I realised it was the sound of my own fear.

Boss and his two hired hands, Gordo and Hank, went up and down the aisles checking which of us was ready to farrow. After that they went straight to a corner of the shed where a pile of rusty iron prods lay in a heap. There were electric prods to hand as well, but Hank and Gordo preferred the irons. Said they had more bang for the buck. Each of them grabbed one and held it in his hands.

Gordo was obese, like us. He was always sweating and his breath was sour, and I reckoned it was the beer he drank from the moment he arrived until he left, though he was careful to hide it whenever Boss was around. Hank was covered in blue-and-red patterns as if every vein in his body had burst just under the skin. He called them tattoos, and every now and again another one would appear. Finally, Billy arrived. He took off his jacket, hung it on a peg, and turned to face the others. He looked sleepy and anxious and keen to prove he was neither, but it didn't fool us and it didn't fool Boss. Soon as Boss saw him he called him out.

Billy? Get over here, he said.

Billy took a step forward.

You deaf, boy? he said. *Get over here.*

Billy moved forward until he was standing beside Boss.

Where's your prod?

Billy shrugged.

Hank, give him yours, said Boss.

41

Hank stepped forward.

I don't need it, mumbled Billy.

Speak up, said Boss.

I said, I don't need it, he repeated.

Yeah, you do, replied Boss, and he shoved his own electric prod into Billy's hands.

Billy said nothing. Just stood there looking at it. Boss reached forward and opened a stall. The sow didn't move. She was confused and frightened. Course she was. Bad as our confinement was, we all knew any change was likely to be worse. A shout and a jab from Hank's prod and off she went. One after another our stalls were opened. Some of the sows came out willingly, others stumbled or hesitated, one or two lay down. As if that would make a difference. A whack with an iron prod soon saw them off.

Then Ina started to squeal. The sound was so shrill several of the sows panicked and bolted for the open doors. Hank and Gordo raised their prods and began striking them until they stampeded back toward the farrowing shed. Boss's voice rang out – *Close the damned doors!* – and right away Hank lunged for the doors, grabbed each of the handles, and pulled them shut with a loud clang.

Shortly after that all hell broke loose.

THE ORCA

Here she comes. My trainer. She's very fond of me. More than fond. She *luuuves* me. Hah! Funnier still, she thinks I love her. I need her. No doubt about that. I need her because she pays attention to me. She focuses on me. She sees that I'm fed and cared for, such as it is. The fact that her idea of care is as far from what I need as the distance that separates me from the ocean of my birth is beside the point. Or exactly the point.

Still, it hasn't been easy for her. My first trainer had very different ideas. He was old-school. When in doubt – punish. As if being separated from my mother and my pod at eighteen months wasn't punishment enough. What do I remember most about that hideous event? My mother's cries as I was loaded into a canvas sling and winched aboard a ship.

But I digress. Where was I?

Ah yes. My first trainer. He paired me with an established orca. A female. She knew all the tricks and was there to guide me. I was willing, but I didn't catch on quickly enough for her *or* my trainer's liking. As a result he often deprived us both of food. Then there was hell to pay. As soon as our session was over and our trainer departed my companion would rake me with her teeth from head to foot until I was bleeding and raw. Can't say I blamed her. She didn't want to be in that bathtub they called a tank any more than I did.

But he left. Yep. Now you see him, now you don't. Maybe he got fired. Maybe he got fed up. Who knows. Who cares? And then there was Sharon. Dear Sharon. Sharon's first order of business was to convince the powers-that-be to ditch the punishments and concentrate on positive reinforcement. I love that term. Positive reinforcement. Do a flipper wave? A handful of thawed fish. A tail slap? More thawed fish. Ever tasted thawed fish? Maybe it's different for humans, but for an orca it's – well, imagine a raw fat juicy salmon caught fresh from the sea and then substitute it with a wad of saltwater-soaked cardboard. Thirsty? Have a nice cool slug of gelatin. Anxious? Have a benzo cocktail. Chill you right out. Meanwhile, the chlorine level in this tank is killing me. Mucus is streaming from my eyes. My skin is peeling from my back and sides and …

Hello out there? Is anybody home? Anybody paying any attention at all?

Sharon. Sharon pays attention. Sharon rubs my skin with black zinc so that my fans can't see just how sunburned I am. They wouldn't like that. Or maybe they wouldn't notice. But there's no hiding my sagging dorsal fin. Sharon tells the honking crowds that it's normal. It's normal for an orca to have a sagging dorsal fin. About as normal as a human with three legs. But hey, who's counting.

So Sharon doesn't punish me. Okay. No punishment. Sharon is very earnest. Very conscientious. She wants me to know that she cares. I appreciate this. I do. I'd appreciate it even more if she'd open the goddam gates and let me out of here. *You want appreciation? Free me. Get me the hell out of this concrete paddle pool before I ... before I lose my mind.*

Oops. Too late. It's already gone. Ah well, better luck next time, baby.

***

A typical training session? Sure, why not.

We start with tank circling. I hug the perimeter while rapidly gaining speed and then leap from the water at a designated spot. Sharon runs along the edge of the pool watching and coaxing me on. I do this several times. At a sign from her I stop, swim to the edge and open my mouth. Mushy fish treat, then on to the next trick. Circle tank once and propel forward onto shallow shelf so that my entire magnificent body is out of the water, and when it's showtime Sharon calls out, *Look at that. Isn't he magnificent, folks?* And from their gaping pop-eyed stares I can tell they agree. Then flip tail up and bow to audience. This one's always a crowd-pleaser. Lets them think I'm oh-so-happy to be here. More mushy fish, and all the while I watch Sharon carefully. There are several arm, hand and whistle signals. I'm pretty confident now that I know them all.

Next up – twirl and spy hop. Essentially sticking my head vertically out of the water to have a look around. We do this in the wild so it's not exactly a leap into the unknown. The difference is that out in the open ocean there's actually something worth looking at. A few rolls, then twirl, flipper wave and tail slap. Splash audience before executing a backflip. Back to shelf where I do a belly slide ending in a full 360-degree spin. Standard stuff. Working up to the grand finale. But first, stand on tail and spit water at the audience. They love this. Being irreverent puts them at ease. We don't want them thinking we aren't having fun. We don't want them thinking at all.

Sharon stands at the edge of the pool. She signals to let me know that she's coming in to join me. I'm ready for her. She dives in. I dive, too. I find her. Propel her upward by her feet, and when I surface she's balanced on the tip of my nose, my power alone lifting us both clear of the water. The audience goes wild for this one. As we disappear below the surface I find her again and this time she faces me, her arms hugging me, a foot on each of my outstretched pectoral fins. With my tail flukes I power us up from the depths of the pool until we break the surface of the water and, to use Sharon's description, 'freeze like a tableau suspended in air'. We're face to face. Body to body. Woman and orca in perfect harmony.

Alas, I wish she'd dim the din. At least while we're training. I can't hear myself think. Sharon calls it music. I call it torture. Like a thousand ships' propellers stifling all thought, all feeling, until the only option is to bash my head against the tank's concrete walls hoping for a few moments of sweet oblivion. Now she bends to clasp my chin. Rubs my head. Then she's off to fetch my reward. Buckets of the stuff. Fish muck to sate my hunger. Gelatin to quench my thirst. More pats and strokes and kisses from Sharon. Our training session has gone well. Her bosses will be pleased, and I can see in her eyes that she feels exhilarated by our contact. Contact with a wild creature. But there's nothing wild about me here.

Here I am simply a prisoner held against my will with no hope of parole.

THE FOXHOUND

Once entered I quickly established myself as the leader of my pack. In some ways it was a rather unenviable position and one which entailed considerable responsibility, and so I took it upon myself to learn as quickly as possible. I knew that my tender years might be perceived by some as a sign of weakness – or worse, ineptitude – and I was keen to nip this impression in the bud. I strove to set an example and to execute my duties with dignity and as much humour as one can muster in the face of what is, admittedly, a bloody sport.

Sorry? What was that?

Yes, it's true. In the beginning I had to deal with a certain amount of resentment. But I was careful not to flaunt my position, and as a measure of my largesse I often shared among my pack the spoils of the hunt. And so months passed and season followed season, and over time I became admired far and wide. By all accounts Sir Robert delighted in my success as much as I did, and I think it wouldn't be a stretch of the imagination to suggest that he might even have harboured a tiny element of envy. You see I had by then become something of a stud. The ladies in the pack flocked to me, and more than once I caught Sir Robert watching me with a certain, shall we say, wry amusement.

One particularly bitter winter's evening I was curled up in the kitchens with the huntsman, kennelman and first whip. Sir Robert was out for the evening, and I fancied a spot of company. When I joined them the chaps were arranged in a semicircle before the hearth, drinking and chatting. The fire was lit, and I lay upon the rug soaking in the warmth, glad to have a quiet evening in with the lads, half-dozing and half-listening to their banter.

In a corner of the room sat the television, the sound muted. Now and again I cast an uninterested eye towards the screen when, suddenly, the huntsman turned up the sound. A cacophony of barking and whining and cries of terror filled the room. I jerked up my head and focused my eyes. By now the huntsman, kennelman and first whip had fallen silent and the four of us stared, still as pointers, at the images unfolding before us. It had something to do with the dog trade and it was all happening in a faraway place.

Until then I'd never heard the terms 'dog trade' and 'dog festival', but the footage I saw needed no explanation. Dogs were being beaten and hung before their throats were slit, their skins stripped from their bodies, and their carcasses butchered. Some were skinned alive. When it was finished there was a long silence, but by then they'd been hitting the whisky hard and their tongues were loosened. The first whip piped up.

Savages is what they are, he said. His voice was full of disgust.

We're no better, replied the kennelman.

I swivelled my head. He had my full attention.

Mind, when their hunting days are over, he continued, *where do you think they go, eh, lad? Up to London to the palace for an MBE and then off to tea at the Ritz? Some are adopted or kept on like faithful servants, but the others take a bullet to the head, and they're the lucky ones. Better than ending up in one of them — what they call 'em — research labs. Poor wee sods. For racing dogs it's the same. Wouldn't wish it on my worst enemy. See, you think I'm kidding? Ask Reggie here.*

Both I and the first whip snapped our eyes onto the huntsman.

Afraid so, he said. *They may be man's best friend and all, but they're still animals and working ones at that. No different from cattle or any other livestock. When their usefulness is spent, it's out with the old and in with the new.*

I looked from one to the other, but they ignored me, and continued to sip their whisky in silence. It never occurred to them to be discreet. Apart from commands they underestimated my ability to comprehend human speech. But I was a keen listener, and Sir Robert's conversations ranged across a wide spectrum of subjects. Even so, this latest piece of information shocked me to my core. I felt dizzy and sick. I tried to stand, but my hind legs gave way and my balance all but deserted me. It was the first whip who noticed.

Major, all right, boy? Steady there.

He stretched out a hand to pat me, but I was already heading for the door. When I reached it I whined and scratched at its ancient oakwood panelling until the first whip rose to let me out. As soon as he opened it I bolted with the speed of a greyhound into the cold night air.

THE GORILLA

Inevitably, Crood tired of me and sold me to Fairground, but not before he suspected I had learned to sign. For my part I was careful to offer him no proof, though I caught him frequently lurking nearby whenever the twins came to clean my cage. Even so he was quick to tell Fairground Master that he possessed an ape of singular intelligence. *A regular Einstein*, he called me.

Fairground Master did not believe him and asked Crood for a demonstration. Crood called for the twins, and when they began to sign I turned my back. Fairground Master mocked Crood and told him that he would only pay him half of what he was asking. This made Crood angry, but by then he was fed up with me, and so he agreed. When the man left, Crood looked at me for a very long time. Grabbing a rusty barrel filled with rubbish, he emptied it onto the ground in front of my cage and used it as stool. He sat, saying nothing and drinking from his bottle until it was drained and his eyes were as clouded and lifeless as a stagnant pool. I watched him, careful not to stare, all the while afraid he would change his mind and refuse to sell me. Finally, he stood and stumbled off. As I watched him go I thought, *At last, I am safe*. But I was wrong.

Early the next morning four burly trainers entered my cage, grabbed me by my arms and legs, tied me to a post and watched while Crood lashed me with his whip. Afterwards, the twins told me the whip had been made from the hide of a kangaroo.

***

Fairground was not much better than Circus except that we no longer travelled from place to place, and none of us were forced to perform. Once again I was the only gorilla. In fact, I was the only ape – apart from the humans. Many days and nights passed, a moon or two or three came and went, and it was not long before my new owner tired of me. Though he had paid Crood only half of what he had asked, to feed and house one as uncooperative as me was not the bargain he had hoped for. When visitors came to stare at me I turned my back on them. Most of them quickly moved away, but a few lingered hoping I would entertain them with grunts and grimaces, chest beating and displays, or at the very least the chance of a face-to-face with a real wild-born gorilla. But when their children came to gawk, well, that was a different matter. Though I was only a juvenile I would charge forward, canines bared, fist alternately pounding my chest and rattling my bars so violently that their startled parents feared I might reach out, grab one of their precious offspring and wring its brittle little neck. I was tempted, to be sure, and they would sweep up their howling brats and run.

Fairground Master was furious, and he complained to anyone who would listen that he had been tricked. With an ape in turns as morose and aggressive as I, he would not make a penny. And so he enquired here and there over many weeks and months until a man in a long white robe wearing a check scarf on his head came to observe me. This man was called Prince, and Fairground Master bowed and babbled whenever he approached. Prince explained that I was to be a gift to his friend, a human he called President, to whom he owed a favour. I quickly understood that this man in the white robe and check scarf was an alpha male, and that whatever he decided was all that mattered.

So it was that I was taken to Zoo.

***

The trip to Zoo lasted several weeks. Fairground Master had me loaded into a crate and taken to a terminal where a cargo ship awaited me. It was a hulking, battered behemoth manned by a filthy crew who looked nearly as unhappy as I, and when I saw it I thought I was surely doomed. From the dock I was hauled aboard the ship by a huge crane and immediately ferried below deck where I was shunted from my crate into a cage.

The hold of the ship was dark and the air was dank and fetid, made worse by my vomiting which continued throughout the journey. I could not help it. I was not used to the ship's constant rocking and swaying, or the smell of saltwater, diesel and oil that surrounded me like an invisible fog. Apart from a small and surly young man who pushed rotten fruit through the bars of my cage and filled my bottle with stale water, I had no contact with any living creature.

I feared I might remain in that hold for the rest of my life when finally we arrived at a port. It was a noisy, bustling place filled with thin, muscular humans who never stopped moving. They reminded me of ants, each carrying a load on his back and scurrying away only to return and pick up another. I was lowered onto the bed of a small truck from where I watched as we drove through a town and onto a long, winding road. We passed through many towns and villages, all of them filled with half-built structures that punctured the sky with jagged edges.

A moon passed away before we reached the edge of a desert. Ahead of us lay a long straight road that extended across a barren land to the horizon. I watched as we travelled a landscape so bleak and devoid of life I thought any creature fool enough to enter it deserved to perish.

At Circus there was a human who could eat fire. Each lungful of air I inhaled in this desert reminded me of him, for every breath was like swallowing flames. Soon the metal bars that surrounded me and upon which I stood became so hot I was unable to touch them, forcing me to hop from one foot to the other. No amount of howling or crying had the least effect upon my drivers. If anything, it caused them much amusement. All day I danced in the back of the truck, unshielded from the sun, while through the bars of my cage I searched the wavering landscape for any sign of water – a river, a lake, a well – but I could neither see nor smell any hope of quenching my thirst.

At dusk a wind blew suddenly and violently, turning the sky the colour of desert dunes. My drivers closed their windows, pulled their scarves over their noses and mouths, and waited. Exposed to the storm's fury I curled into a ball, my eyes and mouth firmly shut, my head tucked between my legs. Even so I thought I might suffocate, and it was days before I was able to clear the sand from my nose and ears.

It was dark when the storm ended and the drivers began digging out the wheels of their truck. Once they were free we carried on. They took turns driving through the night, but our progress was slow.

At midday on the second day we came to an oasis. At first I could not believe my eyes. I saw trees growing on the banks of a winding river, houses built with reeds and mud, and humans everywhere chatting and trading and going about their lives. We stopped and parked in the shade of a palm tree, and the two humans to whom I was entrusted climbed from the truck and went straight to a café. They sat, and soon other humans brought them food and drink, and they ate and drank until they could hardly move. When they returned we drove to the banks of the river where they filled a small barrel with water and placed it on top of my cage. In the side of it they stuck a rubber hose not unlike the one that had cost me my thumb, but much shorter and thinner, and the other end they offered to me. I was careful not to grab it, but once I had hold of it I sucked greedily, and when I could drink no more I held it over my head and let the cool water run down my face onto my back and chest. Then I sat and waited, hoping they would bring me something to eat, but instead they crawled under the truck and slept. Because of the trees I had shade, and, in spite of my hunger, soon I, too, fell asleep.

It might have been five minutes or five hours before I was awakened by the sound of the truck's engine. We carried on. The landscape, as featureless as it had seemed at first, began to change. Whenever we passed through another oasis, a village, a town, we stopped to take on water. As soon as we did the humans gathered to stare at me. My drivers always parked their truck in the shade, but I soon realised it was for their benefit – not mine. Even so it took some time for the metal bars of my cage to cool so that the first impression I made upon the assembled crowds was that of a dancing ape. Most had never seen a gorilla, of this I was certain. Several did their best to provoke me while others watched, and I, in turn, did my best to ignore them. This was not difficult. Hunger and exhaustion had rendered me incapable of anything but apathy.

Only once did I make eye contact. In one village a young human, a female, stood apart from the crowd. She watched me for a long time, making no attempt to approach or call out to me. With her was a boy, by the look of him a juvenile like myself. A brother? A cousin? A son? He was too familiar with her to be a casual acquaintance. Turning to him she spoke, and a moment later he pushed his way through the crowd and climbed onto the truck's rear tyre. Reaching over he touched the bars of my cage. Then he jumped down, said something to the young woman and left. When he returned, he carried with him a bunch of bananas, a worn but colourful carpet, and a length of rope. Together with the woman he approached my drivers and immediately the woman began to shout at them. They looked from the woman to the boy, and then to me, all the while arguing, but she would not back down. By now the crowd had begun to take her side, and the boy climbed once more onto the rear of the truck and draped the carpet over my cage. Three men from the crowd climbed up to assist him, and together they secured it with rope, providing me with shade from the sun while allowing such air as there was to pass through my bars. Then the boy pushed the bananas into my cage and stepped down. I never knew what caused him and the young woman to take pity on me, nor will I ever forget them.

By the time we neared Zoo I was famished and spent. I sat on my haunches, barely able to turn my head. Through the holes in my carpet I saw tents and houses made of bricks and reeds give way to buildings of concrete, stone and marble. Sand was replaced by asphalt, and birds fell silent before horns that blared constantly. I felt I had entered a labyrinth so vast and unfamiliar that I would never escape. When we came to a bridge I smelled water and I hoisted myself up. Underneath it flowed a river, and though I cannot swim I would happily have thrown myself in. As we neared our final destination I reminded myself that Zoo would be just another prison little different from Circus or Fairground, and I was not disappointed. It was nearly identical to them in every essential aspect but one.

It was at Zoo that I met Karim and Dr Sadiq.

The Elephant

In the shade of the willow I lowered myself onto my belly, struggling to keep my breathing shallow and noiseless. Above me the branches were alive with the calls of hornbills jostling for space, and on the riverbank I could see a pair of graceful blue cranes wading in and out of the water, their long pointed beaks poised to stab at passing fish, but in my chest my heart was racing. I felt panic – a sensation I'd never known and couldn't even name. I wanted my mother and I whispered out to her time and again, but it was the old bull elephant who answered.

Beneath me, barely discernible vibrations grew rapidly stronger. I'd learned from my mother that these vibrations told of the approach of other elephants, and until that morning I'd never felt any cause for alarm. Soon I could hear the plodding of four enormous feet, one falling heavier than the others and slightly out of sync. I rose quickly, but the old bull warned me with a low rumble to remain where I was. Above me the hornbills ceased their squabbling, and the cranes on the riverbank stretched their necks and held their heads high as if expecting at any moment the arrival of a long-awaited guest.

Just short of a stand of bush willow the old bull halted. He stood sniffing the air, and when he was satisfied he signalled for me to approach. I broke cover and trotted over to him. He wasted no time on caresses, but turned and began leading me north away from the river towards the cover of the hills. I knew that if I didn't keep up my thoughts would overwhelm me, my legs would collapse beneath me, and I would be lost for ever in this land I'd once considered as safe as my mother's shadow. I grabbed hold of his tail and followed him north along the river to the hills that sat upon the horizon like a caravan of dozing camels.

***

Once outside our protected area the numbers of poachers scouring the landscape in search of trophies and profits were too many to count. We hid in the clumps of bushes that dotted the savannah and waited for darkness. At night the savannah came under attack from prowling carnivores in search of a meal, and the poachers feared these hunters they could not see. But for the old bull and me, it was better to risk an encounter with lions than poachers armed with rifles.

At dusk we left our hide and headed for the open plains. I held onto the old bull's tail as we plodded steadily forward. As night surrounded us a sound like approaching thunder grew steadily louder until, without warning, the bull stopped and, kneeling onto his two front legs, lowered himself to the ground. I knew better than to ask why and lowered myself into the shelter of his enormous frame. Before long the thunder sounded directly overhead chased by a beam of light that neither cracked nor flashed but swept over the land like a lost moonbeam. Then it was gone as quickly as it had come.

We rose and plodded on in silence. The spongy soles of our feet muted the sound of our passing as we trudged across the dusty plain. Now and again the old bull raised his trunk to taste the air. Occasionally he caught a whiff of other elephants, but he avoided them so as to lessen our chances of detection – it was much easier to spot a herd from the air than two solitary figures – but we could not avoid the many elephant remains. All had had their tusks hacked from their skulls. Once we stumbled upon an entire family butchered and left to rot. Sights like this left me sickened and weak, and served as a cruel reminder of my own slain mother.

By the morning of the third day we'd skirted the mountains and could just make out the deep dense hues of the jungle that stretched along the length of the horizon. It was dark before we reached it and the old bull guided us in. Hidden by the dense canopy I grazed until I was full. When I'd finished the old bull used his trunk and tusk to clear an area where we might rest. By then dawn was breaking and a troop of black-and-white colobus monkeys woke and gathered to watch us. I'd never seen such odd-looking creatures, and I watched as they moved effortlessly from tree to tree. A few of them began to tease me, throwing fruit at my head. In an effort to frighten them off, I lifted my trunk and trumpeted as loudly as my small frame allowed.

At the noise, the old bull jerked up his head and glowered with alarm. Instantly, I fell silent. As the monkeys scattered overhead he stretched his ears to catch any sounds, while his trunk searched the air for scents of an enemy's presence. I watched him, ashamed, but at the same time excited and eager to learn. In imitation I raised my trunk and spread my ears, and for several minutes we stood together, comrades-in-arms. Finally, he relaxed and signalled for me to lie down and rest. I lowered my front legs first, then my hind legs, and lastly my head, but when I closed my eyes sleep would not come. The old bull stripped a branch from a nearby tree, and as he chewed he told me of a memory from his childhood; a tale of lush vegetation at the edge of which spread a vast body of water stretching all the way to the sun's cradle, and as I listened I wondered if the unfamiliar smell that blew in from the east might not be coming from the place of which he spoke. For reasons he could not name he said he had an irresistible urge to revisit it. It was to be his last wish.

A spear, hot and poisonous, pierced his belly. A second later a shot rang out, dropping him with a thud that sounded as two separate sounds – one that killed and one that died as quietly as a sigh. I struggled to my feet as men bounded into the clearing and threw a net over me. Screaming and wailing I struggled so that I might stretch out my trunk and wake the old bull, but what I tasted was not sleep but blood. Soon the ground was steeped in it, and the reality of what was happening began to dawn on me. Several of the men grabbed hold of me, pushing and shoving in an attempt to topple me onto my side, while the others raised their machetes and slashed away at the old bull's skull. I heard a girl cry out. She shouted for them to stop, but they took no notice. Then their leader spoke. He ordered them to put up their machetes and instructed the girl to lead me into the forest and wait there until they were finished.

The men removed the net and tied a rope around my neck, and while she pulled the men pushed me from behind until I was forced from the clearing. When I resisted, one of them beat my flanks, but again the girl shouted at him to stop. She held my rope tightly, and resting her hand on my head, stroked me and whispered into my ear until finally she was able to lead me away. As we wound our way through the trees the men behind us resumed hacking at the old bull's head.

THE SOW

It didn't take Boss and his boys long to restore order. Once the shed doors had been closed and the panicked sows herded toward the farrowing shed, all attention was focused on Ina. I could hear her breathing. It was shallow and rapid. The air made her dizzy, made all of us dizzy, and I watched her steady herself against the bars of her stall. As Boss reached forward and swung open her gate she turned her head to look at me, and right away I could te .... tell something was not right. Sure enough, she launched herself upon Boss with all the fury of a creature whose every instinct has been thwarted.

For several seconds no one moved. Then the blows hailed down on her backbone, her rump, her head. Gordo aimed at her legs, her chest, her snout, while Hank attacked her flanks. Only her stomach was spared so as not to kill the litter buried within her. And all the while Billy stood stiff and silent as a shadow with Boss's electric prod locked in his hands.

Boss screamed under Ina's fury. Oh, he screamed like a stuck pig. That's what he'd say himself. *Like a stuck pig.* She bit, stomped, lunged, and finally she threw herself and the whole of her weight upon him, pinning him to the floor. More squeals as another panic erupted and sows thrashed against the bars of their stalls, and those that were loose ran every which way hoping to escape the blows that rained down on Ina and would certainly find them next. Hank and Gordo continued to beat her while Billy, barely able to breathe, watched. It lasted less than thirty seconds. A blow to Ina's head knocked her unconscious. Then Hank and Gordo bent forward and tried with all their strength to shift her off Boss, but they couldn't budge her.

It was then that one of them remembered Billy and shouted at him to come forward, and the three of them grabbed hold of her and pulled and lifted with all their might until they were able to shift her enough for Boss to slide free. Lying on his side, Boss gulped and choked until he was red in the face. Finally, he raised himself onto his elbow and spoke.

Bring me a knife.

Hank and Gordo traded a look, and then Gordo moved to a wall of the shed where tools hung from rusty hooks. When he returned he had a butcher's blade in his hand.

Give it here, said Boss.

On the floor Ina began to stir. Hank raised his iron prod but Boss waved him off.

Leave her, he said.

Boss looked at Billy and then at his own prod still clutched in Billy's hand. He sat up, and when he struggled to stand Hank offered his hand, but Boss wouldn't have it and brushed him off. Instead, he waved to Billy.

Put that damn thing down and help me up.

Billy let the prod drop to the floor and, stepping forward, raised Boss to his feet. As soon as Boss was upright he held out the knife.

Take it, he commanded.

Billy didn't respond, so Boss grabbed his arm and slapped the blade's handle into his palm.

Cut her open, said Boss.

Billy stared. He stared like he hadn't heard him, because he could see that Ina was still very much alive. She'd come round and her eyes were open and he found himself looking straight into them, and what he saw there told him she knew exactly what she'd done. But when she shifted her gaze to the knife in his hand, her eyes filled with a despair so profound I thought the boy would cry.

Oh jeezus, sneered Boss, *gimme that. Might as well ask a little girl to do a man's job as ask a sniveling crybaby like you.*

Boss snatched back his blade and knelt down beside Ina and slit open her belly from side to side. Billy backed away, and then he vomited. Bent over and vomited just like that, but the others paid him no attention. They were busy helping Boss pull the last of Ina's piglets free of her womb.

Get this litter to a nurse sow, Boss grunted. Then he turned his attention to Billy. *And get this useless sonuvabitch outta here before I do something I'll regret.*

Then he handed his knife to Gordo and headed for the door. After that Hank and Gordo set upon Ina's piglets. They grabbed them by the hind legs, two in each hand, and headed for the farrowing shed to find nurse sows for Ina's litter. And that's when Hank noticed Billy as if he was surprised to see him still there.

Don't stand gaping like the town idiot, said Hank. *Help us move 'em.*

We could hear Gordo snigger.

You coming or what? said Hank.

I'm coming, said Billy. *Just gimme a minute.*

Chica is gonna puke again, said Gordo.

I'm not gonna puke, said Billy.

Wouldn't bet on it, replied Hank. And then they made for the farrowing shed.

I watched Billy as he looked one last time into Ina's eyes. The light behind them was fading fast. Nearby, the rest of her litter huddled together for warmth. It was then that Billy bent down to grab what looked to be the runt and a sibling who boasted a dark red splotch on the end of her nose. With a nod to Ina he turned and walked to the end of the shed where he wrapped the squealing runts in his jacket.

Before leaving he looked briefly at those of us still locked in our stalls and shook his head. Then he opened the shed doors, not bothering to close them behind him, and walked into the rising dawn and the place called outside.

THE ORCA

I'm swimming. Around me the sea is warm. By my side swims my mother, and we are surrounded by my sisters and brothers, my cousins and aunts and uncles. Behind us there's a terrific noise, and suddenly the adults among us pick up speed. There's an urgency in their movements and in the waters that surround us, and soon I recognise it as fear. We're heading north now. The females with young split from the main pod and veer west. The remaining adults break to the east. Behind us the noise grows dimmer, and we can feel our mothers' fear begin to abate. But we don't slow. Not yet.

I push this memory from my mind. I've learned that darkness does not dispel darkness, and as if to prove the point there's no light in the saltwater burial chamber where I spend nearly two-thirds of my day. My resting quarters, my off-duty paradise, is a twenty-by-thirty-foot tank. No light. No sound. No nothing but silence and solitude. You can imagine the effect this has on me. What to do? What to do to break the monotony? Sharon says an idle brain is the devil's workshop, and how oh-so-very-right she is.

I repeat this over and over – *idle brain devil's workshop idle brain devil's workshop* – until I'm lulled into a kind of trance. The steel walls of my tank are as smooth and featureless as a void. I can't even rub my teeth on them. But I can bang my head. I can bang my head until all I feel is a dull ache. Tomorrow I'll gnaw the steel gates of the holding tank as I wait to perform. I've been doing this for years and several of my teeth are worn to the gums. Now and again Sharon washes them with an antiseptic solution, rubs them with a salve, and shoots me full of antibiotics to prevent infection. When she finishes she looks at me with affection and concern.

I gaze back with equal affection and think about biting her head off.

The Foxhound

As soon as Sir Robert became aware I'd gone missing he raised the alarm. Naturally, he thought I'd been stolen. Word was sent out to all the neighbours. A search was organised and a handsome reward offered. I was caught the following day and returned to his estate.

In the days and weeks that followed I was unable to eat and became increasingly listless. The kennelman called the vet, but after examining me she declared that there was nothing wrong with me. *A bit depressed perhaps,* she said. Sir Robert decided a good hunt would restore my spirits, but I refused to participate. Unlike before, the thought of catching a fox no longer appealed to me. Instead, I was overwhelmed with a deep and all-consuming apathy.

Sir Robert was patient at first. It was one thing to refuse the hunt. There were plenty of other hounds all too keen to take my place. But when word got round about my condition, my fate was sealed. Request for my stud services disappeared overnight and along with it, his patience. Who, after all, wanted the whelps of a melancholic foxhound who refused to hunt?

To be fair Sir Robert tried everything to revive my interest *and* my mood, but no amount of cajoling or threats or exercise or medication made the least impression. I was moved from his private quarters to the kennels, and just as the kennelman had predicted, other arrangements were soon made for me.

One afternoon about teatime two men arrived. The kennelman fetched me from the kennels and loaded me into their van. To his credit he could hardly bring himself to look at me as the doors were shut and locked, and I was driven to my new home. I shook all the way there, and I didn't stop shaking when I was unloaded, taken into a building that smelled of disinfectant and despair, and unceremoniously placed in a cage.

***

The next morning when I opened my eyes I saw a man dressed in a white coat staring at the floor and swearing under his breath. He'd knocked over a glass beaker, and it was the sound of it shattering against the floor that roused me. Still swearing, he left the room in search of a dustpan and brush.

I looked around the room. There were rows of cages housing rabbits, cats, mice, monkeys and guinea pigs. Others held dogs: beagles, pit bulls, labradors, and an assortment of what were obviously mutts, most likely strays. I guessed that, like me, the pure-breds among them had been abandoned by their owners or stolen and then sold off for a fraction of their worth. Why else would they be there? Only later did I learn that some, like the beagle pups, were specially bred for a single purpose – life in a laboratory.

Directly across the aisle from me was a cage holding a single monkey. He hadn't been there when I arrived, or perhaps I hadn't noticed him. Now, as I studied him, he appeared neither frightened nor anxious nor curious, but merely resigned. I tried to make eye contact but he looked right through me. When finally he focused his gaze upon me I had the impression that he'd only just noticed me.

So you're awake, he said.

A silence followed. I suspected he'd arrived while I was asleep, and in the next instant he confirmed my suspicion.

I was brought here early this morning. Early bird catches the worm.

He spoke in a sing-song voice that was shrill and prone to cackling. It reminded me of a deranged old hag Sir Robert had once employed as housekeeper. She was thin with a slight hump and smelled of mothballs, curds and gin. Sir Robert said she reminded him of the witches in fairy tales his nanny used to read to him as a child. She didn't last long in his service.

So, rumour has it that you're quite the sportsman, continued the monkey. His deliberate use of the word 'sportsman' was not lost on me.

Yes, I said, without an ounce of pride, wondering how he knew this. *I suppose I was.*

But quacky lackey are not your prey, ducky, said the vicar to the viscount, *so pray leave them alone, dear sir, for they harm you not.*

I said nothing, but stared at him with a good deal of confusion and no small amount of shame.

Foxtrot is your preferred dance, dare I say? What? Heh heh, old chap? Still, all good fun must come to an end, he said, but this time there was a hint of sympathy in his voice.

Where are you from? I asked. I was convinced he was completely mad and I wanted only to change the subject.

The land of many temples, he replied, *but please, sahib, to offer me no Shirley. Ever hear of it?*

I hadn't. My silence confirmed this, and immediately the monkey began to sing.

It's a long way to Tipperareeeee, a long, long way from here. To the temple, the sweetest temple, where my family lived for yeeeeears.

I looked at him for some time. As far as I knew there were no temples in Tipperary and even fewer monkeys, but I decided to humour him.

Do you miss it? I asked.

As soon as the words were out of my mouth I realised it was a very stupid question, and I half-expected him to sneer or, at the very least, to turn his back on me. But he did neither. His face remained resigned as though any other expression was far too much effort.

Very warm and many plenty to eat, he said.

And you were free, I added.

Beshak, jawohl, mais oui, he replied. *And why not? Free as the breeze, free to think. Therefore, I am.*

Again, I was sorry to have stated the obvious, but my brain was so rattled with fear and anxiety that I couldn't manage anything else. It was all I could do to be coherent, because the truth was, I felt panic. Panic and despair. I had no idea what was in store for me, but I sensed it wouldn't be good.

Where are we? I enquired at last.

Ah, very good question. The nude arrivals unit, he said, and proceeded to cackle at his own joke.

What happens here? I asked.

The question was so naive and so unanticipated that it caused a shift in the monkey's seemingly imperturbable expression. Emotions skittered across his face in rapid succession: surprise, disbelief, consternation, and finally pity. It was this last that frightened me most.

He hasn't a clue, has he? Dumb as a door, are we, old chap?

My name is Major, I said, *and I'm not the least bit dumb.*

Ah, a military man. I should have known, he replied, and he began to cackle again so loudly that I was forced to cover my ears.

And you'd do well to mind your manners, I added.

A swell, are we? Very well. A swellegant elegant party we'll be.

I lowered my head onto my paws. In truth, I had no idea what he was talking about. I had the impression he sensed this and was making fun of me.

A blab blab blab. A yadda yadda lab. Research, they call it. Tell Grandpa what that is, my child, and he will give you a treat, said the monkey.

I ignored him. I was growing tired of his gibberish.

Well, said the monkey, *no matter. You'll find out soon enough.*

He set about picking his toes with such deliberate concentration that I thought it best to leave him to it. With some difficulty I determined to wait a bit before asking him again.

But as he'd warned, I needn't have bothered, for I did indeed find out soon enough.

THE GORILLA

Every day after school a boy called Karim took a set of keys from his pocket, unlocked the janitor's cupboard where his cleaning cart was stored, and headed along the path to Zoo's Primate Unit – a grand name for what were a series of barren enclosures in which we were caged, 'we' being the apes, his biological cousins – the bonobos, orang-utans, chimpanzees and gorillas that, together with humans, comprise the family *Hominidae*. It was Karim's job to keep our enclosures clean. When news of this leaked to his classmates Karim became known as the shit-sweeper. He took no notice. Apart from his IT classes the time spent at Zoo comprised by far the best part of his day, because it was here that he met me.

Karim had been at his job six months before we became friends. In that time he came to regard me as suspicious and sullen. Little wonder. I barely suffered him a glance. When he approached my enclosure I ignored him. When he persisted I bared my teeth and roared. Any ordinary human would have backed off immediately, but Karim considered my behaviour as perfectly normal. This intrigued me, and by the beginning of our fifth month together my hostility towards him began to wane, and I allowed the lanky juvenile to go about his work undisturbed. Watching him, I soon noticed that he never spoke. Nor did he react when his back was turned and I rattled the bars of my enclosure, or hooted, or made any sound at all. It was only when the boy faced me that I could, if I wished, get his attention. It was the sudden realisation that he might, like the Roma twins, be deaf, that caused me to observe him more closely.

Near the end of the sixth month I decided to make my move. I waited for Karim to come ambling down the path to our enclosures. Mine was the first in a long row, and as he drew near he turned left down a path to a door giving entry into my enclosure's rear section. Once inside it he crossed a small corridor to another door and, pressing a button, raised a gate through which I could pass into a kind of holding cage. When I was safely sequestered he closed the gate and entered the main enclosure. I watched as he removed bucket and shovel from his cart and began to scoop scraps of food and piles of waste from the floor. I waited until he was facing me through the bars that separated us before raising both my hands, palms facing outwards. When I had his attention I began to sign.

Who are you?

Karim was so shocked that at first he did not respond. I waited patiently. When he remained silent I feared he might be illiterate as well as deaf, so I signed again.

Tell me, who are you? If you cannot speak, then sign.

He remained silent and looked about him as if at any moment a mysterious being might appear and reveal the secret behind my bizarre behaviour, but no one appeared and no explanation was forthcoming. Still, a signing gorilla was, as far as he was concerned, preposterous, and so he continued to stare at me in silence when the door behind him opened. I quickly put a finger to my lips before retreating to the far corner of my holding cage. The hand placed upon his shoulder startled him, and turning, he found himself face to face with Dr Sadiq, Zoo's head vet. Immediately, she began to sign.

Forgive me. I didn't mean to frighten you. I hope our silverback is not making trouble for you.

Karim forced a smile and shook his head.

Good, signed the vet. *He can be tricky, especially if he doesn't like you.*

Again Karim smiled and nodded.

Have you had a chance to chat?

As she signed this she studied Karim with an intensity that made him squirm before turning her eyes upon me.

His previous owner told us that he's a fluent signer, but so far young Einstein has disappointed us.

Then she looked back at Karim so that he could read her lips before repeating herself.

His previous owner said he's a fluent signer, but so far he hasn't signed a word.

The boy stole a glance at me, but I remained impassive.

I know you can sign, she said to him, *and lip-read. Can you speak?*

Karim hesitated. When he answered his speech was laboured, but the tone of his voice was soothing and gentle.

Yes, ma'am, if I have to.

Excellent, she signed. *Well, I'm late for a meeting. Be careful. He can snap you in half like a twig if he chooses to.*

She looked at me. I ignored her. Then she left.

For several seconds Karim stood gazing at my bars as if scratched into their surface he might read the answers to the hundred questions careering inside his skull. Then he studied my enclosure, scanning the ceiling, walls and corners. I knew he was looking for the magic eyes that humans call cameras. I also knew that his search would yield no results. Finally, he turned back to me and, raising his hands, began to sign.

Why don't you show Dr Sadiq that you can sign?

I stood and walked forward. I regarded the boy for a long moment before raising my hands. As I did Karim noticed for the first time the butchered thumb on my left hand. Odd what humans miss.

Because I have not yet decided whether to trust her.

Why not? signed Karim.

She is new.

So are you. Relatively new, I mean, he signed.

He had a point, even though my arrival at Zoo had preceded the good doctor's by several months.

Why are there no cameras? he signed.

Dr Sadiq had them removed.

Why?

She got bored with me, I expect.

She doesn't seem bored, he signed. *She seems just the opposite of bored.*

The boy was not stupid. I sat on the floor of my holding cage and, raising my right hand, motioned him forward.

Sit down.

When he was seated, I continued.

First you will tell me about yourself. Then I will tell you about myself. After that, we will decide if we wish to be friends.

Karim regarded me. Once again he stood and scanned the ceiling of my enclosure, then the holding cage and each of its four corners before returning his gaze to me.

As you have already discovered and I have confirmed, there are no cameras.

Karim nodded.

So, shall we begin?

Karim returned to the spot I had previously indicated and, seating himself, began to sign.

Tell me why you're called Einstein, he said.

It is the name given to me by a human called Crood.

Do you know who Einstein was?

No, I said. It had not occurred to me that humans would give any creature a name that already belonged to another.

Well, said Karim, *he was one of the cleverest people that ever lived.*

I could tell by his expression that this was meant to impress me, but experience has taught me that human intelligence is in the mind of the beholder.

I guess Crood must have thought you were fairly clever, he continued. *After all, it's not every day one meets a signing gorilla.*

86

I did not respond. As far as I knew Crood thought about very little apart from money and the bottle of clear liquid that dangled like a glass seedpod from the end of his arm.

Or maybe he was just being ironic, Karim offered.

He said this with a smile, but I did not know the meaning of the word 'ironic' so I remained silent and waited for him to finish. When he said nothing, I spoke.

Now you, I signed. *Tell me about you.*

It was then that I heard the faintest vibration, and a moment later Karim reached into his pocket and removed a thin flat object about the size of his hand. He looked at it, and, much to my astonishment, held it to his mouth and began to speak. I have seen many humans speak into one of these objects they call phones, but none of them were deaf.

When he finished he looked again at the thing in his hand and began tapping it with his thumbs. He would tap it, then look and wait, then tap it again. He did this several times, each time repeating the same actions – look, then tap. Once or twice he smiled, and when he was finished he tapped it briefly before replacing it in his pocket. Then he rose.

I have to go, he signed.

Wait, I said. *Are you not deaf?*

You know I am, he replied.

And returning broom and bucket to his cart, he moved towards the door.

***

I did not see Karim again for another three weeks. While he was away Dr Sadiq came to visit me. She was tall for a female human and had thick, curly brown hair. Male humans were inevitably drawn to her, and I could tell that many of them wanted to mate with her. I did not think she was any more or less desirable than any other human, but she was not threatening either, so I tolerated her.

One day she surprised me. She began to sign. She asked me if there was anything I did not like about my enclosure. I looked at her for a long time before rising and grabbing the bars that surrounded me on all sides. I shook them as hard as I could. Then I jumped up and down on the bare concrete floor. Then I turned my back to her. She remained still for several minutes. When she left I felt confused. I was also angry. Angry with myself. I had not meant to let on that I understood her.

After that she came to visit me every day Karim was away, but I refused to look at her again. I thought that if I proved uncooperative enough, eventually she would tire of me and I would be released and allowed to return home. In retrospect, I realise this was both naive and foolish. But that was then, and then was a very different time.

Then there was still hope.

THE ELEPHANT

Before he was killed the old bull had recalled for me his memories of the sea, but I was unable to imagine the beauty of it until it was spread before me; a savannah of watery emeralds and opals that stretched to the mouth of the cove and then beyond where it melded into the horizon.

You want to ask me something. Let me guess. You want to ask what a young elephant like myself knows of emeralds and opals, and the answer is simple: more than I ever wanted to. But first, I'll tell you this.

I stood with the girl on the edge of the sand. A breeze blew in from the sea promising relief from the heat and water to quench my thirst. I'd smelled it long before I could see it. Looking up and down the shore, I thought of my mother and listened and sniffed for any hint of danger before stepping onto the white sands that bordered the bay. I headed straight for the water, but when I tasted it for the first time I was surprised. It was so beautiful to look at I was sure it'd be as sweet on the tongue as it was on the eyes. I dipped my trunk to drink but immediately spat it out. This wasn't easy because I was thirsty. It was when I lifted my head that I noticed a great shape lying partially submerged in the shallows. It was black and white against the clear green and blue waters of the bay. I waited and watched. When it didn't move I plodded forward for a closer look.

Behind it another vastly larger shape rose and turned and disappeared and then rose again, all the while exhaling vapour like a sigh from the top of its head. It was soon clear to me that the smaller of the two was a calf, and his companion most probably his mother. When she saw me she unleashed a series of cries that sounded like clicks punctuated by a gusting wind. They warned her calf of my approach, and as I drew closer the poor creature began to wheeze. I knew immediately that he was having trouble breathing, and that he was very frightened.

I waded further into the shallows and walked his length from head to tail and back again until I was facing him. I couldn't bear the thought of another death, so I lowered my head and pushed as hard as I could. The girl followed me into the water and together we pushed with all our might, but the whale calf didn't budge. Again and again we tried, and all the while I spoke to him, assuring him that we meant him no harm. Finally, the girl looked at me, shook her head and waded from the water, but I wasn't ready to give up. I continued to push, repositioning myself along the calf's length. The effort nearly defeated me, and I could feel his panic rising with each failed attempt. His breathing was growing increasingly laboured, and with so much of his body exposed to the sun his temperature was rising fast.

I dipped my trunk into the sea, filled it and sprayed him with water hoping to cool him. Then I resumed pushing. While I pushed his mother called to him, and he answered in raspy clicks and low groans. Finally, against all odds, I felt the dead weight of his body begin to shift. Both of us could sense his mother's excitement in the vibrations of the water that surrounded us, and then, quite suddenly, he was floating and able to slap his tail flukes and fins until he was once again weightless and free.

As soon as he could swim his mother guided him into the middle of the bay. They remained there for some time, long enough for the calf to nurse and rest. I watched them, but the effort of freeing the whale calf had left me weak and dizzy. The sun was hot on my back, and though I couldn't drink from the sea I was still able to cool myself in its waters. I waded deeper, careful not to venture too far, keeping my ears and nose alert to danger. I stayed like that until I couldn't bear it any longer. My head was pounding. I felt confused while all around me the world began to spin. I had to find fresh water. As I turned towards the shore my balance deserted me. I fell back into the shallows and called for my mother. She would know where to find water.

THE SOW

An hour passed before Boss discovered that two of Ina's brood were missing. It's a wonder his two hench-men, Gordo and Hank, hadn't noticed sooner. Or maybe they had and didn't say anything for fear of being blamed. No matter. Once Boss found out he blamed them anyway for be .... for being stupid and negligent, and he threatened to withhold their pay. Whatever he meant by that it upset them greatly. When he was out of earshot they complained and swore to each other that they'd quit as soon as their shift was done, but they didn't, because, in the end, none of it mattered. Not to them and not to us. Noth-ing ever mattered to us. Not the barren floor we lay on. Not our condemned litters sucking pitifully at our teats. Not the squalid shed that confined us. Another day in hell was, well, just another day in hell.

After Ina's death Boss started talking to himself. My sisters and I half-listened, taking it in turns to warn the others of anything that might affect our miserable existence. Soon I noticed that one word was repeated constantly and that word was 'Billy'. Billy this and Billy that, and every time Boss said it he grew madder and madder until he spit out the word like a bad taste. And so I began to listen real hard whenever Billy was mentioned. As Boss's rants became more heated, bits and pieces came together until the picture of a man obsessed and bent on revenge began to form.

One morning Boss appeared and called Hank and Gordo, and they joined him at the front of the shed where they spoke for a long time. Boss grew angrier and angrier and Hank and Gordo egged him on. It was hard to make out what they were saying, but now and again I would catch a word or two. None of it made any sense, but I could tell the boy Billy was in danger. I asked my sister sows to listen out and tell me anything they could hear of the conversation and cursing that drifted like a bad smell over our stalls, but they mocked me. Some even got angry, accusing me of betrayal and asking me, *Why do you care? What's the boy ever done for us? He's a human and nothing but suffering can come from him.*

But I did care. Yes, I cared becau .... because he was different from the others, and if I could've warned him I would have. Yes. Yes, I would have.

***

There's talk of thinning us out. Another way of saying away with the old and in with the new. Word's gone round, and all of us are on edge. I've had two healthy litters, and as long as Boss doesn't notice that I'm having trouble breathing I should be all right. But then we all have trouble breathing. If this is the criteria for who goes and who stays he'll have to start from scratch.

An animal welfare inspector came into our shed today. Right away she put us at ease. There was something about her. As if she understood what we were thinking and feeling the moment she laid eyes on us. I heard Boss say to Hank that Billy's grandma had likely made a complaint, and that was why she'd come round. As she poked about, he and Hank walked down the rows while Boss pointed out those among us that had outlived our usefulness. When he came to me he stopped and stood for a moment as if calculating in his mind how many more litters I might produce. I'm carrying my third, and if I'm lucky I'll be allowed to carry one more. Lucky. Imagine that. Am I blessed or cursed? You tell me.

When the inspector was done she stood by the shed doors and waited for Boss to join her. He was eager to see her go and made his way over as quickly as he could. But instead of leaving she started talking, and whatever she was telling him made him mad as hell, and he fussed and fumed until I thought he might pick her up and carry her out. It was hard to hear what she was saying. She spoke softly, refusing to engage with Boss's rants, and when she was done she looked at us as if to say, *Don't you worry, this won't be the last of it.* And then she left.

As soon as she was gone Boss shouted out to Hank, and when he came over Boss let loose again. Something about crazy goddam animal whisperers and how every nut in the country seemed to be out to get him and how she'd told him that keeping pigs in sow stalls was like asking a human to spend its life strapped in an airplane seat and how he'd never heard such nonsense and he'd like to strap *her* into an airplane seat.

I thought Boss was going to hit Hank out of sheer frustration, but suddenly he fell silent and got the strangest look on his face, and all he said was, *Damn. Damn that Beckham boy and his goddam grandma. They wanna mess with me? Let 'em. I'll show 'em who's boss around here.*

And then he left.

Sometimes I think about the two pig . . . . lets that the boy stole. If you want the truth, I often think about them. I wonder how they are, where they're living. Are they kept in a shed? Are they alone or with other pigs? Who feeds them? Who cleans up after them and keeps them warm? I want to know the answers to all these questions and more besides. If I had the answers I could stop wondering. Stop worrying. For now I have to believe as long as they're with Billy they'll be all right. Can't be worse off than here.

I can smell rain in the air. Will it rain today? What does it feel like? The rain, I mean. I think I'd like the rain. Yes, I think I'd like it just fine.

THE ORCA

Memories. These come at night. In the confines of my luxurious quarters there's nothing else to do but torment myself with recollections of my former life, some good, some bad. Tonight, for the umpteenth time, I'm being chased. The adults of my pod execute a diversion while those with young seek an inlet, a bay, a cove in which to hide. My mother breaks away from the others. I follow her. I don't question why. Through a narrow channel tucked between two promontories we enter a shallow bay. I head toward the white sandy shore while behind me my mother swims back and forth guarding the entrance. In my excitement I swim too close to the shallows, and before I know it I'm beached. I cry out. Immediately my mother comes to my side, but there's no room for her to maneuver herself between me and the shore. Both of us are becoming increasingly distressed when, suddenly, she turns and swims back to the narrow channel through which we entered. I call out. I'm afraid. I don't want her to leave me, but she ignores me.

I'm growing hot in the shallows. The sun is fierce on my head and back. But what's this? A creature approaches. An extraordinary-looking thing. It's clearly distressed. Thirsty, it dips a long extension protruding from its face into the water, takes a drink and quickly spits it out. Next to it stands another creature, and while I watch I wonder how long it'll be before they notice me and what will happen when they do.

Back to the present. Tomorrow is a busy day. I have three shows. Sharon and I have been practicing in the show pool all afternoon. She's very pleased with my progress. I'm glad. I want to please her. Poor dear is so conscientious. Of all the trainers she's by far the best: the kindest, the most consistent, the most professional, the most experienced.

And the most deluded.

What goes on in her mind? I often ask myself this. I also wonder if she asks herself what goes on in mine. And if she does, what does she make of it? Does she pity me? Does she suspect that all is not what it seems? I like to think that one day she'll set me free, but her bosses will never allow this. We're happy here, they tell the crowds. We teach them so much about our brethren in the wild. Hah! Do slaves teach their masters about freedom? I suppose in a way we do. And what is the lesson our masters learn?

Why, don't be a slave, of course.

***

Today is collection day. I've sired several calves. Part of what they call the breeding program. For research, they insist. But the truth is legal restrictions now hamper the capture of wild orcas, while the need for more victims to replenish our shows grows ever greater. So, what to do, what to do? Nothing so simple as a frolic with the ladies. Hardly room for it anyway. No, it's a repurposed cow's vagina filled with warm water for me.

Whoopee! I can hardly wait.

It's painful to think of the little elephant calf. Even now. So I don't. Or rather I try not to. Sometimes I can't help it. Yes, he rescued me. No doubt about it. Am I grateful? I was at the time. Hah! How does the song go? *If he could see me now, la dee dah la dee dah.*

So he rescued me at his own peril. You know what they say? No good deed shall go unpunished. As soon as I was freed I swam to my mother and began to suckle. We remained like that in the middle of the bay for some time, and when I surfaced to breathe I could see the elephant calf sitting in the shallows and the girl watching him from the edge of the forest.

Then I saw a man come up behind the girl and put his hand on her shoulder and clasp his other hand

over her mouth. My mother saw them too, and immediately she began to slap her tail against the water in
an effort to warn the little calf, but it only frightened
him, and he left the shallows and began to run along
the shore. From the cover of the jungle other men
appeared carrying a net, and soon they were chasing
the little elephant across the sands to the far end of
the cove where there was no escape. In desperation
I joined my mother, slapping my tail. I cried out and
whistled and some of the men came to the water's
edge to have a closer look, and I could tell by the
way they hesitated that they'd never seen a creature
like me. But soon their boss called out and they left
us to trap the elephant calf in their net.

In some ways he was luckier than me. He was led
away before he could witness what happened next.
Maybe he believes at least one of us escaped. I hope
so. Hey, what you don't know can't hurt you, right?
Sharon told me this. Turns out she was wrong.

Very, very wrong.

THE FOXHOUND

How are you today, old chap?

Unable to turn his head, the monkey stared straight ahead. He was completely constrained, his head, neck, wrists and ankles shackled with metal clamps. A few weeks after our arrival we were made to share a cage. This arrangement was the brainchild of one particular whitecoat, the mere sight of whom filled us with terror. In normal circumstances it would never have been done, our natural instinct to be wary of one another being far too strong. But our instincts soon gave way to curiosity and a shared sense of companionship, and once we were comfortable the real fun began. It consisted of witnessing the various procedures the other was subjected to, and afterwards, their effects. By putting us together I suppose our tormentor wished to see whether we might comfort one another, and indeed we did. But on this particular day we were once again separated, the monkey installed in a cage opposite me.

Still here, I answered. *And you?*

Yes. Still here, he said. *And your paws?*

Could be worse.

This was a lie. The pads of my feet were so raw I could barely stand. Early that morning I'd been forced to run on a treadmill that delivered electric shocks. As long as I kept running I could avoid the shocks, but as soon as I stopped they continued uninterrupted. Eventually, exhaustion got the better of me, and I gave up trying to avoid the shocks. *Learned helplessness,* I heard our whitecoat say to a colleague. And so began another day in hell.

Having completed the day's protocols, we were being held in a small room adjacent to the labs before being returned to the animal housing unit. I looked up and down the rows of cages standing opposite. Some were empty, others held animals in various states of shock and suffering. There was a rabbit whose eyes had been doused in hairspray, and now they were so red and swollen that she could barely see. Next to her was a cat who'd been fed insecticide for a month. Remarkably, she was still among us, but barely. There was a mouse with an ear growing out of its back, and another with a tumour so large it threatened to devour her. And so it went down the row, each animal condemned to its own private hell.

Tell us a story, I said.

I've no more to tell, dear chap. You've heard them all, replied the monkey.

I raised my head. This was uncharacteristic for at heart he was an optimist.

Describe to me the place where you lived, I said.

Alas, he sighed, *it was the most beautiful temple in all of Tipperary.*

There are no temples in Tipperary, I said. *Of course, if you were really from there you'd know this.*

I suppose we've been, have we?

I instantly regretted my remark.

What colour was it? I asked.

The temple? It was the colour of festivals and celebrations, of love and joy, of gaiety and frivolity and eternal optimism.

And freedom, I said. I couldn't help myself.

And freedom most of all, he replied.

And what did you eat? I asked.

We ate moon dust and mangoes and crimson flowers that blossom once every ten years and diamond dewdrops that fall from the eyes of velvet dawns into cups of rose-coloured gold, he replied.

Sounds bloody awful, I said.

Ah, Major, but you have never tasted the delicacies I describe.

He was right, of course.

Perhaps one day I shall, I said.

Perhaps, replied the monkey, *perhaps. But it is not in your nature to eat that which the imagination has prepared. Therefore, I fear you must do without.*

My nature, my nature, I said. *My nature, so I was told, was to be Sir Robert's best friend. Look where it got me.*

He didn't answer right away, and I was quick to realise this line of conversation was doing little to lighten our mood.

What is it, Major? he asked. *You sound worse today than usual.*

I looked at the monkey, but it was more than I could bear. The top of his skull had been removed, and from his brain protruded a series of wires held in place by a crown of metal bands that encircled his skull like a vice. I could hardly remember what he looked like without his weird and fantastical headdress.

I have a bad feeling, I replied.

I didn't like to admit it. I knew the monkey was making a heroic effort to keep us both from lapsing into terminal despair, but the feeling I had was so powerful I could no longer pretend. For months we'd been subjected to experiments as our tormentors poked and probed, injected and isolated us, force-fed or deprived us one at a time. Yet our reactions were always the same: abject terror and indescribable suffering. After months of enduring such unimaginable acts of madness, the only thing that caused us genuine surprise was the fact that we hadn't gone mad ourselves.

***

One afternoon an unfamiliar whitecoat entered our dorm. Scientists they called themselves. Or researchers. Or technicians. But to us they were simply torturers in white coats. I had seen this one once or twice before, but only briefly, and always in the company of the whitecoat in charge of our experiments. On this occasion she came alone, and it only added to my feeling of dread, for anything that deviated from the normal routine, as obscene as the normal routine was, always preceded something worse.

She approached our cages and stood silently for some moments, letting her gaze rest upon me before turning her attention to the monkey who had, singlehandedly, sustained my will to live. When at last she spoke my worst premonition was confirmed.

I think you've reached the end of your useful time here, my friend, she said.

The monkey made no sound, nor did he give anything away as he returned her stare. But for me there was to be no such benign acceptance. My response was immediate and unrestrained. I began to howl, my cries so anguished that the whitecoat felt compelled to respond.

Don't worry, Major, we'll find you another companion, she said, and reaching out she inserted her hand between the bars of my cage to stroke my head.

I would have none of it. Before she could withdraw it I had it between my jaws.

Now it was the whitecoat who howled, and her cries brought another whitecoat running from the adjoining lab. I recognised this other one immediately and so did the monkey, for he was none other than the one who'd directed all of our experiments. Normally, I would have retreated to a corner of my cage at the mere scent of him, shaking and whimpering uncontrollably. But I had the other whitecoat's hand clamped in my jaws, and I refused to let go. It was bleeding profusely, and the taste of her blood caused a familiar and unwelcome surge of excitement to course through me.

It took a direct blow to my head from our own familiar torturer before I released her hand. A first-aid kit was fetched and from it a roll of gauze bandages quickly unfurled. The wounded hand was bound in an attempt to staunch the bleeding, but she was still in pain, and she glared at me with a fury that I could almost taste.

You want to go with him then, eh? Is that what you want? I'll throw you in the oven myself, she said.

In response I growled. A low, angry sound that rumbled up through my body and spilt from my throat. At the same time I drew my lips up and back, exposing all of my teeth. I wanted to leave her in no doubt as to what I thought of her. At that moment the monkey spoke.

Be still, my friend. If you go with me there will be no one to bear witness to what has happened to us here. Bide your time and hope that someone, somehow, rescues you. Stranger things have happened to strangers in the night.

And then, without warning, he began to chant a Hindi lullaby. It was one he often sang to me when I had trouble sleeping which was nearly always. This threw me, and instantly my attention was diverted back to my friend, my only friend, whose name, I realised to my astonishment, I didn't know.

You've never told me your name, I said.

You've never asked me, Major, he replied.

I marvelled at my oversight. In all the months we'd spent together it had never occurred to me. One would have thought I'd been brought up on the streets for all my manners were worth.

Mac, of course, he offered, sensing my embarrassment. *A fitting name for a rhesus macaque, wouldn't you say, old chap?*

And he began to cackle so loudly that the wounded whitecoat looked up from her hand and shook her head.

That one's gone completely round the bend. Should probably have gassed him weeks ago, she said.

Shortly after they departed, the disposal team arrived and took Mac away. We didn't say goodbye. Neither of us could bear to.

What's that? Miss him? Not a day goes by that I don't.

The Gorilla

The first thing I noticed about Karim when he returned was that he had grown taller and slimmer. When I asked him where he had been he told me he was made to study many hours and days in preparation for something called exams, though as far as I was concerned this was no explanation at all. I continued to pester him and was soon able to glean that, for the most part, exams involved answering questions on subjects about which one knew very little.

He also told me that while he was gone a female human called Judge granted two chimpanzees a writ of *habeas corpus*. I had no idea what this meant. He said it meant they had legal person status, and when I asked him to explain this he said that the chimpanzees could not be imprisoned without a very good reason. So I asked if I, too, could have a writ of *habeas corpus*. He did not answer me. I expect he did not know the answer. The next day he told me Judge had changed her mind.

I missed him while he was gone. This surprised me, and I watched him closely as he prepared to clean my enclosure. He seemed preoccupied, and I thought it must be something to do with his exams. Perhaps he had not answered enough questions. Or maybe he had answered too many. I was of the firm belief that the less humans knew about one, even one of their own, the better. I waited for him to say something, but he remained silent. So I began.

Have you told Dr Sadiq that we sign?

He leaned his broom against his cart and raised his hands.

No, he replied.

Why not? I said. I was unsure whether to believe him.

Because I know you don't trust her.

Do you? I signed.

Yes, he said. *She's clever and she's trying her best. Already things have improved.*

He was right. Things had improved, but I had no wish to pursue this.

Shall I tell you how I learned to sign? I asked.

He shrugged. I took this as a yes and continued.

Two young Roma taught me. They look exactly alike. Twins, I think you call them.

He remained silent, but I persisted. It was clear he knew many things the young Roma did not, and I wanted him to teach me.

Tell me more about these exams, I signed.

There's nothing more to tell. They're boring, he replied.

Like being stuck in this enclosure is boring? I asked.

He had no answer to this, and so he looked away, but I continued.

If they are boring, why do them? I signed.

Because I have to.

I thought about this.

Do they lock you up so that you cannot escape?

He laughed.

Not exactly, but sort of.

I have never understood this expression 'sort of'. Humans use it a lot. They use it when they are unsure or confused. I hear it so often I think many of them must be unsure or confused much of the time.

Just then his phone began to vibrate. He reached into his pocket, and when he looked at it he smiled and began to tap it with his fingers. Then he laughed, and when he was finished he returned it to his pocket.

There are many things I want you to teach me, I signed. *You can begin by telling me about the thing you hold in your hand.*

You mean my phone?

Can you see the person with whom you are speaking? I asked.

Sometimes, if I choose to.

This is another thing humans do all the time. They talk to another human who is not present. While they do this they hold their phones against their ears. Then they speak. Or press buttons. Sometimes they do both. Karim's phone was blue like the heavens when the last of the sun's light has faded but it is not yet night. I have thought about this many times, about this thing humans hold.

Show me, I said.

What do you mean?

Show me the person with whom you were speaking.

Why? he said.

I am curious, I replied.

He's just a friend, said Karim.

Does he have a name?

Of course, he replied. *Everyone has a name.*

Tell me. What is his name?

He's called Ali, said Karim. Then he looked away. Pretending to check the contents of his cart he did a cursory inventory: mop, bucket, detergent, shovel, broom.

Go on, I said.

There's nothing more to tell. I like him, is all.

Do you love him?

Karim jerked his head up so suddenly that it startled me.

I never said I love him, he signed. *Why do you ask me that?*

I could see he was upset, but now that I had his attention I would not let it go.

When a gorilla loves another it is because we share a bond, I began. *For this bond to exist there must be complete trust, for our very survival depends on it. Do not humans feel the same way when they love another human?*

Karim hesitated as if our conversation was taking an unlikely and dangerous turn, and one he wished to avoid.

It's different with humans, he replied. *It's more complicated.*

Explain.

He hesitated before raising his hands, and I could see that he was searching for words.

Humans are supposed to love members of the opposite sex. This is so our species can continue. When we love humans of the same sex, this is bad.

Why?

Because it's unnatural, he said.

Unnatural for whom?

Everybody, I guess.

Perhaps you should explain what love means to humans.

He looked at me for a long while as if trying to make up his mind, but I am patient. And so I watched and waited until at last, he spoke.

It means to care very much about someone, he said.

So when you care very much you share a bond. This bond is possible because you do not feel threatened or challenged. You feel safe. You trust this other human completely. Is this correct?

Yes, he said. *But sometimes it's more.*

I'm listening, I said.

It's a feeling that you would rather be with this person more than any other. And when it's very strong it makes you feel that you would sacrifice anything for them. Maybe even your own life.

I was beginning to understand.

But surely many humans care for members of the same sex in this way? Mothers for their daughters, fathers for their sons, friends for their companions.

Karim thought about this.

Yes, he replied. *I suppose they do in one sense. But not in the other.*

What is the other?

It was a simple question, yet Karim seemed at a loss to answer. He began to fidget and again he looked around as if someone might be watching, someone unseen and threatening.

Sexual, replied Karim.

I see, I said. *So what is the problem?*

He was becoming increasingly agitated, but I would not let it go.

Those of us that love a human of the same sex in a sexual way as well as all the other ways, well, it frightens those that don't. It frightens us when one of us is different, he said.

I thought about this. The same was true of gorillas. But it was usually because of a physical or psychological weakness that threatened the welfare or, most importantly, the survival of the group. As far as I could tell this love Karim had for Ali was threatening no one. So I asked him.

Does your love for Ali threaten human survival?

What do you mean? he said.

Well, as you pointed out, two males cannot reproduce.

Hardly, he laughed. *There are far too many of us as it is.*

This was difficult to dispute, so I continued.

I think if you love another human and that human loves you in return, this cannot be a bad thing.

Karim looked at me. He wanted to agree, but I could see that he was afraid.

Humans are very strange creatures, I signed.

Yes, we are, agreed Karim.

Then he opened the gate of my holding cage and waited for me to enter it before taking out his keys and unlocking the heavy gate of my enclosure.

Pushing his cart ahead of him, he stepped inside. Neither of us spoke, but I could see the tears welling up in his eyes. When he was finished cleaning he packed up his cart, released me back into my enclosure and left.

Part 2

THE POACHER

I did not always do this. This inhuman thing.

Once I had a small farm. I will tell you that the place where I lived is now arid. Dry. Very dry. But before, when there was rain, we had livestock, and I planted maize and millet with my family. Then we had crops to eat and our animals grazed. But when the rain stopped famine came and we lost our animals. With no animals and no crops we had nothing left to sell and nothing to eat. This was very hard for me because I have responsibility for my family.

So God sent the drought and then the famine, and this was bad enough. But who sent the rebels? I think it was the Devil who sent them. And so they came. First it was the rebels, then the army. Who sent the army? The government. Sometimes I think the government and the rebels are one and the same, for I cannot tell you which of them is worse. Both of them steal and kill and demand money to go away. But in the end it was the rebels that murdered my wife and son.

I fled with my daughter. We ran with nothing – nothing – and went to a refugee camp. A filthy, crowded place filled with half-families. All had missing children, mothers, fathers, brothers, sisters, aunties, uncles, grandmothers, grandfathers. Half-families. I looked around me and I knew that I could not stay there for ever. And I could not leave and feed my daughter with dust and prayers.

It was then a man came to me in the camp. He ran into our tent early one morning and handed to me a long, heavy bundle wrapped in a bloody sheet.

Hold this for me, he said. *Hide it and I will come back. And I will give you monies for you and your daughter.*

Then he left. He did not even tell his names.

As soon as my daughter went out to fetch water I unwrapped the bloody sheet to look what was inside. What I saw was bad. Very bad. There were two elephant tusks. If I am caught I know I will go to prison, and I was very angry with the man who gave them to me to hide. But he was gone, and I had no choice.

So I hid them under my bed, and in the evening when he returned I said to him, *Are you crazy? Do you want me to go to prison? Who will look after my daughter?*

He smiled and answered to me, *If you listen I will make all your money problems go away, and you and your daughter can leave this place for ever.*

And so I listened because I had no choice. No choice.

We left late that same evening. There was no moon and it was very dark. We walked in a line like blind men, and I told my daughter, *Stay close.*

Along the way the man boasted to me of his family. But when we came to his village there were half a dozen empty houses with mud walls and grass roofs and in one was an old woman who lived alone. She was hunched and her head dropped from her shoulders onto her chest where it swung back and forth like a hyena. When she saw the man she did not smile or greet him like a son or grandson. So right away I had suspicions. Then she looked at my daughter and her eyes grew small and she raised her head and opened her mouth so that I could see the few teeth that remained. And she leaned forward and I thought, *Yes, like a hyena you will sniff my daughter before you decide if you will eat her. But if you think to kill her and make medicine from her bones you will find that this man who is not your son cannot protect you from me.*

The man looked to my face and said something to her in a language I did not understand. Then she stepped to one side and we entered.

Are you hungry? he asked.

I nodded, so he spoke to the old woman and she left us and went to the kitchen. I sent my daughter to help her because the man wished to speak to me in private. Alone. And he explained to me what I must do. He was younger than me, but like me he looked older. He had a strong smile – very white teeth and very straight – but mean eyes he thought to hide with his shiny white smile. He was also much heavier than me which told me he had plenty to eat.

At this moment my daughter came to ask if we were ready because the meal was cooked. She is small for her age and very thin. Too thin. I turned to the man, and this is when I saw how he looked at her – same as Old Woman – a look that spoke his mind before he could silence it.

And I said to him, *If you ever lay one hand on my daughter I will kill you.*

He knew that I am not afraid of him even though he is younger and heavier than me, because he could see this in my eyes and in my voice.

You have my word, he said. *No one will touch your daughter. She will be safe here.*

After we ate he took me into Old Woman's bedroom. Under her bed were hidden several spears and a gun. He told me first I must learn how to use a spear. I know how to use a spear, but I said nothing. He said he must know that I am a brave man and will not bleat like a goat when face to face with an elephant. If I can kill an elephant with a spear, then he will teach me how to use an AK-47. I know this gun because I have seen it many times on soldiers and on rebels, even rebels as young as six, eight, ten years old. It makes them strut like proud young roosters.

There were many of them in the camp, these baby soldiers, the lucky ones who escaped from rebels and government and neighbours. During the day they boasted among themselves. But at night when they lay down on their mats to sleep they cried and made bedwet and dreamt of their murdered families and of the families they had murdered.

Like I told to you in the beginning, when there is nothing I must go out and find monies. But this is more easy said than done. This is why I started to hunt elephant. I had to risk it. I had no choice. No choice. I had to risk it.

THE POACHER'S DAUGHTER

When the rebels attacked our village my father grabbed me from my bed and ran. Mother grabbed my baby brother. The rebels caught my mother and my brother. They raped and killed my mother and then they killed my brother. If they had caught me they would have killed me as well and cut off my head and limbs and sold them to a *mganga* – a witch doctor. Just one of my arms is worth two kilos of ivory, and it is much easier to kill me than to track and kill an elephant.

I was with my father and his men the day they captured the little elephant calf and killed the elephant bull. And later, while they butchered the bull I released the calf. Right away the others blamed me. I am blamed for everything, good and bad, but this time they were right. Now I realise my decision was a bad decision. Not because it was wrong, but because the little elephant calf could not survive on its own.

At first my father did not want to take me on the hunt. *It is too dangerous,* he said.

But it is more dangerous to leave me alone, and that morning Old Woman was sick and could not watch me.

Take me with you, I said, *and I will cook.*

Before my mother was killed I always helped her with cooking. Now my father and I are alone I do all the cooking, washing, cleaning, and going to market to buy what we need, but only when there is monies. I also go to school. When there is monies, and when my father is not working and can walk with me and meet me when I am finished. I cannot go alone. Not because I am too young or do not know the way, but because, just like for Little Calf, it is not safe for one like me.

I remember very well the sound the bull elephant made when the spear found his flesh. His scream was like my mother's scream the night my father and I ran from the rebels into the fields and from the fields to the forest. But before the old bull could run or charge, my father shot him with one bullet in his head, and he dropped like a baobab tree, shaking the earth like God threw him down from heaven. Then I heard a long quiet sound a baby makes when sleeping so that the mother must lean down and feel her baby's breath on her cheek to know her precious one is not dead. But it is the silent sound I remember most. I never heard such silence in my head, which is strange, because Little Calf was not quiet when the old bull was killed. He screamed and called out, and I am sure he said, *Get up! Get up!* But the old elephant could not hear him, and Little Calf did not understand this, and he sniffed and prodded and cried and begged to him to get up, but nothing would make the old bull rise again. And nothing will bring back my mother and brother to me.

My father's men threw a net over Little Calf and pushed him onto his side. They tied his legs with rope. And all while this was happening Little Calf screamed and cried. I knew very well his fear and his grief. I could feel it and taste it, and I shouted for them to stop, but they ignored me. I shouted until my father told his men to leave Little Calf be. And when they backed away I knelt next to him, and very gently I stroked his head and whispered to him that I would not hurt him. Then I told my father that they must not butcher the old elephant in front of the calf, and I saw my father's eyes grow dark, and I knew in that moment he was regretting taking me with him. But I did not back down. I am as strong in my soul as he, and he knows this. And so he told his men to take the net from Little Calf and the rope from his legs and put the rope around his neck so that I could lead him away while they butchered the old bull.

Now the men looked to me with angry eyes. They knew what they were doing is forbidden, and if they are caught they will be arrested or even killed, and their eyes said to me, *Your time will last only while your father is alive to protect you.* But I knew this already, and so I ignored their looks.

Little Calf was in shock and did not want to leave the old elephant. I pulled on the rope, and my father's men pushed from behind until we were many metres into the jungle. Then they left us, and I wrapped the rope around a tree and stood with Little Calf and stroked his head, his ears, his trunk, but still he cried and cried.

The sea was not far away. I could smell it, and I was certain Little Calf smelled it too. I took the rope from the tree, and this time when I led him away he followed. When we got there he pulled me straight into the water. Right away he put his trunk in to drink, but very quickly he spat it out because it was salty and he could not drink it. Only fishes can drink water from the sea, and so he stuck his trunk in the air, and that was when he and I noticed something in the thin water, something big, and right behind it something bigger.

I knew these creatures were killer whales because I have seen pictures of them and read stories of other whales in my Bible. And I thought that God had sent

Satan to swallow me like the whale swallowed Jonah because we killed an elephant. But then I saw that the smaller whale was stranded and I thought maybe it was not Satan but God who brought us there to save it, and if we did this thing then God would forgive my father and me. So I took the rope from around Little Calf's neck, and right away he went further into the water. I followed, and together we tried many times to push the smaller whale from the thin water where it was stuck and into the deep water where its mother was calling and waiting. We tried and tried until I could see that it would not move.

It was early, but the sun was very hot, and I was wanting shade. I wandered back to the edge of the jungle where it meets the sand, and I sat, my back against a mangrove tree. While I watched Little Calf I thought about his mother. What happened to her? Why was Little Calf with the bull elephant and not with her? All this I was thinking when suddenly the smaller whale was free and able to swim to meet its mother. I felt so happy to see that Little Calf had freed it that I jumped up thinking to sing a prayer – the first prayer I had wanted to sing since the rebels came to my village – when my father put his hand on my shoulder and his other hand over my mouth and whispered to my ear, *Be quiet. Do not make a sound.*

MY COUSIN ZHEN

Every day my cousin Zhen and I wake up before dawn, eat our breakfast of rice and salted vegetables and walk across the small yard to an open-sided shed where Zhen's family keeps a half-dozen captive moon bears. It's late spring, and as always Zhen and I get up early to clean the bears' shed and help Zhen's father milk their precious bile. Zhen is used to it. She was born on her family's farm, but I live with my parents in a small town nearby and come only to help during harvest time.

We begin by washing the concrete floor underneath the bears' cages, hosing the blood and urine into a canal that feeds into a pool and shovelling the dung and discarded food into a small pit. Sometimes the pit floods. Other times, when the weather is dry, it evaporates leaving a putrid sludge. In winter it freezes, and the rest of the year it stinks. When the pit fills, Zhen's family use the sludge it contains to fertilise their rice paddy and vegetable garden. I don't know how they live with it — the smell, I mean — but I suppose one can get used to anything. Once the shed is cleaned Zhen's father joins us and the milking begins.

Collecting bear bile is not a pleasant task. Zhen's family use what's called a 'free drip' method. An open passage is created from the bear's gall bladder through to its abdomen. Then a metal tube is fed through the wound and scar tissue to reach the bile stored in the bear's gall bladder. Often the wound becomes infected. Other times it begins to heal and so the tube must be reinserted. It's said to be the most humane method. It doesn't look humane, but until this day I'd never really thought about it. We've used bear bile in our traditional medicines for over a thousand years to treat everything from sore throats to epilepsy. Just one kilogram of pure wild bile can fetch nearly half the price of gold. But this morning our trip to the bears' shed changes all of our lives.

Against a cement wall opposite the shed lies a female bear. Near her head blood pools thick and sticky. Even from a distance of many metres we can see that she's dead; her eyes are open, her ribs and belly are still. Zhen approaches first and crouches over her. Reaching out a hand, she touches the fur on the bear's forehead. It's stiff and matted with blood. I put my hand on Zhen's shoulder and point to the wall. A bloodstain as clear as a stencil marks the spot where the bear has crashed into the concrete, smashing her skull. We stay crouched like that for many minutes. Neither of us speaks.

Finally, Zhen stands and crosses to the shed. Inside are a half-dozen wire crush cages, and inside each, but one, is a bear. The word 'crush cage' tells you all you need to know. They're hardly bigger than the bears themselves, and once inside the bears cannot stand or sit or stretch. I follow Zhen as she walks along the row of cages – two of the bears are licking cracked paws, another chews her own tongue – until she spots a little furry black figure. Its paws dangle through the metal bars and its tongue hangs from its mouth. She recognises it right away. She examined it the day before and told me it wouldn't make bile for another two years. While she examined him his mother became so upset by her cub's cries that the other bears and cubs soon joined in until the shed echoed with their screams. Somehow in the night its mother broke free of her cage and must have tried to rescue her cub, and when she couldn't ... ?

As Zhen stands staring at the dead cub I go to inspect the cage that held its mother. The lock is so badly rusted she was able to break it, open her door and escape. I walk back to rejoin Zhen, and I can see that the questions forming in my mind are the same questions forming in Zhen's. Did the bear kill her cub? And once she was free, why didn't she simply run away? Was she confused? Disoriented? Or was her death intentional?

We remain in the shed for some time while Zhen strokes the dead cub. Then she withdraws her hand and crosses the small yard to her parents' house. I follow, and as she enters the kitchen I wait by the door. For several seconds Zhen watches her mother sweep the concrete floor. At the table her father is finishing his breakfast. She doesn't want to tell them what's happened.

Since her father started bile farming their finances have improved so that they no longer struggle just to survive. Zhen knows this, and knows that the loss of even one animal will make her father lose his temper and take it out on his surviving bears. It's not that he's a cruel man. He's practical. His bears either produce enough bile or they don't. And when they don't Zhen's mother nags him, and when she nags him he becomes bad-tempered, and when he becomes bad-tempered some or all of the bears suffer even more.

After a moment Zhen's mother looks up from her sweeping. Her hands are stiff and her knuckles are swollen, and because of this she has trouble holding a broom.

What is it? Tell me, she says.

And Zhen replies, *One of the bears escaped in the night. She's dead, Māmā, and so is her cub.*

For a moment neither of her parents says a word. Her father looks at his wife and she looks back at her husband, and then they both look at Zhen.

You're joking, he says.

It's no joke, Bàba, Zhen says. *She tried to free her cub and then she must have tried to run away, but instead she ran into a wall, smashing her head.*

Zhen's mother leans on her broom, and while her father stares her mother says, *Are you crazy? Why do you say such crazy things?*

And Zhen answers, *If you don't believe me go and see for yourself.*

I can tell that Zhen's answer makes her mother angry. She looks to Zhen's father, but before he has a chance to respond Zhen turns and walks from the house.

BILLY

I knew I hadn't seen the last of Boss the morning I left his farm, climbed into my pickup, and slipped away in the pre-dawn light. I'd wrapped the slaughtered sow's offspring in my jacket and laid 'em on the seat beside me where they grunted and squirmed like a coupla swaddled infants. Wasn't long before Boss discovered they were missing, and by all accounts he let loose in a fury so violent even his two henchmen, Gordo and Hank, cowered in the face of it. Not even Mrs Boss could calm him down enough to prevent him from climbing into her old Chevy and heading straight to our house.

I live with my parents, my sister, and my paternal grandma. The old lady's been with us for as long as I can remember, and for as long as I can remember it seems to me she's been old. But she's as alert as a fox waiting to pounce. On the whole it's worked out fine. I reckon my mother is as fond of her as it's possible for a daughter-in-law to be, and apart from the odd squabble their relationship is pretty harmonious. Grandma takes care never to come between my mom and dad, and she's way too smart to ever take sides. As far as I'm concerned she's one of the wisest people I've ever known – maybe ever likely to know – even though by her own admission she was never schooled beyond the tenth grade.

I sat parked up in our yard for a good half-hour before I entered our kitchen through the screen door, being as careful as I could not to let it slam behind me. I was glad Grandma was the one I bumped into. She was sitting at the kitchen table, still in her bathrobe, sipping her first cup of coffee – no milk, no sugar. She was always the first up on a Saturday so I wasn't exactly surprised to see her, though a part of me was kinda hoping maybe she'd be sleeping in. Woulda given me a little extra time to collect my thoughts.

Back awful early yet? she said.

I could hear my mom starting to stir upstairs. Soon she'd wake my little sister and then the peace and quiet of the morning'd be shattered for good. I laid my jacket on the kitchen table and opened it for Grandma to have a look-see.

My lord, those two are practically still attached. Where'd you get 'em?

Stole 'em, I said.

Good heavens, boy, why on earth wouldya do that?

There it was, like an accusation demanding a response. I pulled up a chair, the two piglets squealing and wriggling on the table, and me stroking 'em and hoping they'd quieten down so as not to wake my sister.

Because their mother was slaughtered as she was about to farrow, I said.

Grandma sat up in her chair, lifted her napkin from her lap and wiped her mouth. The way she did it, so determined like, made me think maybe she was trying to wipe away my confession.

Good Lord, Billy. Who would do such a thing?

Boss, I said, and right on cue there was a knock at the screen door and the man himself was filling the door frame, forcing the rising sun to retreat to the window over the sink.

'Scuse me, he said. *I've come to see the boy.*

He mighta charged right in without so much as a word if not for the old lady, but he knew better and stayed where he was.

What for? she said.

She wasn't about to be trifled with regardless of what I'd done. With Grandma, nothing in this whole world is thicker than blood. Not even blood.

There's a matter to be settled, and that matter is squirming right there on your kitchen table, said Boss.

There was a moment's silence, the kinda silence so filled with tension it sounds like a hundred jet engines taking off inside your head. But Grandma never turned her eyes from Boss's gaze, though if looks could kill she'd be stone dead.

If you're intending to speak to my grandson go right ahead, but see that you keep it civil.

I'd prefer to speak to him outside. On my own. Ma'am.

He spat the word 'ma'am' like it was a profanity.

You're welcome to speak with him like I said, but you'll do it right here in my kitchen where I happen to be sitting and where I intend to stay sitting. You got a problem with that, you best be on your way.

Boss hesitated. He seemed to be pondering his options, but the truth was he'd figured Grandma for a tough old bird from the moment he laid eyes on her. Reaching out, he opened the screen door and stepped inside.

I'm not going to ask you to take a seat, she said. *I have a feeling you won't be staying long.*

This took Boss aback, but he recovered quick enough. Then he pointed to the piglets.

Those there belong to me. Your grandson stole 'em from my farm this morning.

So he said. He also told me their mother met with an untimely demise.

That's not the issue, said Boss. *The issue's what's right and what's wrong.*

Then we're talking about the same thing, said Grandma. She was sitting slightly forward and ramrod straight. *Why don't you tell me exactly what happened.*

Of all the things he was expecting he hadn't come prepared to explain himself or his actions. Grandma could see she'd hit a nerve.

I'm all ears, she said.

Boss was not a man used to being at a loss for words. Finding himself momentarily silenced, he looked like a kid caught in a lie.

I'm prepared to accept payment and call it quits, he said. *I dare say the boy was upset, being clearly unaccustomed to the line of work for which he was engaged.*

I dare say. And what line of work might that be now?

Farrowing. Farrowing and clipping and docking. Boy's got no stomach for it. Should never have hired him.

How much? said Grandma.

A hundred and twenty should cover it. Then he paused before adding, *That's sixty each.*

Grandma looked up sharp-like, but then she smiled.

I'll give you thirty each. Seeing as you're so good at numbers, you'll know that makes sixty for the pair of 'em. Keep the boy's wages. Billy, quick hurry and fetch my purse. It's upstairs on my dresser.

I looked at Boss and could see that he was about to explode. So I got up, grabbed the piglets and disappeared upstairs. I put 'em in my bedroom, closed the door, and then stood on the landing so I could hear what they were saying.

I trust this'll be the end of it, said Grandma. *If not, I'm sure we'll all be anxious to hear my grandson's side of the story.*

I awready told you what happened, Boss said. *The boy stole 'em, plain and simple.*

So you said. By the way, I heard there was some sort of investigation going on. Unusual cruelty. Over your farm way. Never heard what the outcome was. Maybe they aren't done investigating.

I waited for Boss to say something, and when he didn't I grabbed Grandma's purse and came back downstairs. Soon as I handed it to her she pulled out her wallet and began to count.

Looks like I only got forty. Will that do?

She looked up, sweet as summer hay, and laid the money on the breakfast table. When Boss hesitated, she continued.

About the investigation. Don't believe I caught your answer.

By this time Boss had had enough. Even he could tell when he was licked, and so he snatched the money from the table and left. Soon as the screen door slammed behind him, Grandma looked at me.

Now you sit and tell me exactly what happened.

And I did. The whole sequence of events leading right up to the theft of the sow's piglets. When I was finished she leaned back in her chair and, pursing her lips like she does sometimes, released a thin stream of air somewhere between a whistle and a sigh.

Shame you only grabbed the two, she said.

MRS BOSS

Boss is known to everybody in our farming community. Guess you could say his reputation precedes him. If you're dumb enough to ask, folks'll tell you he's a brutal man who has little time for people and even less for his livestock. They'll also tell you he beats his sows. Rumor has it he beats me as well. I oughta know. It was me started the rumor. I've never filed a complaint, but these days I don't try to hide the bruises neither. Truth is they kinda remind me of tattoos – least that's what I tell myself. But the black eyes, that's something else altogether. The black eyes I hide with sunglasses, even in the dead of winter. It's not that I give a damn what people say. I just don't want him arrested. Not yet, anyways.

Boss has been a hog farmer all his life, and his father before him, and before that his grandfather. Goes all the way back to his great-great-grandfather who was a pig farmer back in the old country. Ask Boss and he'll tell you that for as long as he can remember he's been surrounded by the smell of pigs: pig shit, pig piss, pig slop, pig fear, pig blood. He hates what he does but he knows nothing else, and because he hates what he does he hates his pigs. Course he blames them for his unhappiness. I hate his pigs too, and because of it I've come to hate him. It's a vicious cycle, and try as we might, we can't break it. So he beats his pigs. And he beats me.

He didn't always hate what he did. He told me once that he remembered a time in his childhood when his father's and uncle's and grandparents' hog farm was a family affair. In those days the pigs lived outdoors, and his dad and his uncle and his grandpa knew every pig by name. When it came time to take 'em to market they didn't send 'em miles away but had 'em slaughtered at the local abattoir. The family supervised the whole process from piglet to pork chop, and their farm and the pork it produced was considered the finest in the county.

Then came the war. His uncle was still single and childless and restless as hell. He joined the army as a way of escaping the family farm. Least that's what I think. Boss says he was just looking for a bit of adventure and had every intention of coming back. Bottom line was that his mom and dad, grandpa and grandma were left to run the farm on their own. Then one late spring afternoon two army officers and a minister came to the door and asked to speak to his grandma and grandpa. Afterwards his grandpa never spoke again, and his grandma got the Alzheimer's. So much for intentions.

So from then on it was down to Boss and Boss's mom and dad to look after the farm. Then his mom got pregnant, and 'fore you know it Boss had a little brother. Boss's brother, like their uncle before him, wanted nothing to do with the family business, and soon as he was grown he upped and moved to California thinking he was gonna be a movie star or some such. Ended up selling pot and crystal meth and going to jail. Eventually, it fell to Boss to take over or sell the family's hog business, but the truth is selling was never an option. Never even occurred to him. Boss was born a pig farmer and he'll die a pig farmer, and beyond that he's never given it another thought.

It was around the same time he started to expand that he met me. Back then I owned the town's only diner. My family were also farmers. Small farmers. Wheat and corn mostly. My father was killed in a mishap with a combine leaving my mother, myself and my three younger sisters to fend for ourselves. Mother sold the farm. She didn't want the responsibility, and I can't say I blamed her. With the money she bought a small house on the outskirts of town and a run-down diner on Main Street opposite the gas station. We all set on the place and cleaned it up as best we could, but Mother fell ill and died of the cancer just before we was due to open. My three younger sisters moved away as soon as they could. That left me. I stayed on living in the clapboard house Mother had bought. I liked it well enough. Then I hired a cook, opened the diner, and carried on as owner and sole waitress.

Business was good. Good enough anyway. Customers liked me. I was never no beauty, I know this. But I had something. Even when I was a kid people would say I was ugly in a striking sorta way. Come right out and say it like I was deaf. Now I'm just plain ugly. But back then, when I was young, I had something that made men and boys look at me and want to do things that went way beyond a twirl or two round the dance floor at the high school prom. Ain't my honker, that's for sure. And ain't my front teeth. Kids at school used to tease me saying I had a nose like a parrot and teeth that stuck out proud as an awning on a summer's day. Still do. But back then any boy willing to let his gaze linger a bit longer soon noticed what else was on offer.

My first boyfriend wrote me a poem once. In it he said I had blue-grey eyes the color of Colorado spruce, glossy hair that fell down my back like a black satin waterfall, and a figure that could stop a stampede. Say I'm bragging if you like, but those were his words, not mine. By the time I was a junior in high school grown men were starting to stare, and I could tell when I looked at 'em and smiled they'd feel like they were the most desirable studs in the world. I was sexy, plain and simple, and Boss saw this the first time he stepped into the diner and laid eyes on me in my pink starched uniform and white toile apron. I'm also left-handed. He told me later he deduced this from the pencil stuck behind my left ear. Deduced. Imagine that. When I came to take his order first thing he said to me was, *You're left-handed, aintcha?* And right away I smiled in spite of myself.

So I took his order, brought his food and he ate it. He tried not to stare at me and pretended instead that he was staring at his hands, or out the window at the cars and pickups passing by. When he asked for the check I told him, *It's on the house.*

He came back every day for the next two weeks. I never once brought him a check, but before he got up to leave he'd calculate the cost of his meal – plus tip – and leave it in cash on the table next to his plate. By the end of the second week he asked me to marry him. I said, *Sure, but I ain't on the house.*

We were married two weeks later. Right afterwards I sold my house, and a month later I sold the diner to the town's first fast food chain. Yep. Got married and sold two properties in the space of six weeks.

Turned out to be the three worst decisions I ever made.

THE WHITECOAT

After I'd wrapped my colleague's hand I escorted her to the lab's infirmary. She was still fuming about the hound that bit her. I tried to calm her and pointed out that, at the very least, we could now surmise with some certainty that the hound and his mate, the monkey, had developed a genuine camaraderie, perhaps even empathy. What's more I felt certain that the hound knew exactly what was in store for his friend, and this realisation is what motivated his extraordinary behaviour. How he knew I couldn't say. Still can't. But I'm absolutely convinced. My colleague, however, was still smarting from her wound, though whether it was the pain of the bite which, admittedly, was quite deep, or her own miscalculation that caused her the most suffering, I can't say. At any rate, at that moment she appeared deeply uninterested in my conclusions.

I'd been at the lab for about a year and was determined to make a name for myself. Broadly speaking my aim was to induce psychoneurosis and psychopathy into my animal subjects in an effort to gain insights into their causes in humans, and with this knowledge to devise better treatments and cures. To this end I conducted experiments using a variety of techniques: learned helplessness, deprivation, long-term isolation, hunger, fear, forced addiction, and so on.

Ethical concerns? Not really. When I look back I find it hard to believe, but at the time I sincerely believed the things I was doing were necessary in order to do my work. And believe me, I was not alone. I guess you could say our collective denial was not only necessary but essential. Without it the ability to remain emotionally and morally aloof would have been impossible. But on the particular day in question – the day the foxhound attacked my colleague – I was quite unprepared for what happened next.

After wrapping my colleague's wound I escorted her to the infirmary before returning to the lab. By then the monkey had been removed and the hound was howling. Actually, it was more like a cry – a cry born of profound grief and despair – as if the world was coming to an end. In a sense I guess his world *had* come to an end, for the two had rarely been separated. This was largely down to me. You see, another aspect of my experiments involved creating bonds between individuals and then testing the various effects of one individual's suffering upon the other. The purpose was to examine the potential for empathy, not only between individuals, but between individuals of two entirely different species: one a non-human primate, in this case a monkey, and the other a non-primate mammal, in this case a foxhound. Ultimately, I hoped to gain insights into human empathy and our potential to create bonds of friendship and empathy with, for example, alien life forms.

Anyway, as I approached the hound's cage he stopped howling and looked me straight in the eye. It's hard for me even now to describe his look except to say that he succeeded absolutely in conveying to me the depths of his despair. It was ironic, because it was the very thing I'd hoped to observe. And here it was, so nakedly conveyed, so overwhelming in its intensity, a profound plea to communicate, to understand how I or anyone could inflict such suffering on him and his friend. At the same time it was an admission that such understanding was entirely beyond his capabilities, because the thing that caused his despair was, quite literally, inhuman. Or you could say that it was – *is* – entirely human. Quintessentially human. Our extreme propensity for cruelty defines us. Who was it that said a beast can never be so cruel as a man? So artfully cruel, I would add. Other species demonstrate a range of emotions and behaviours: cooperation, affection, empathy, love, jealousy, deceit, and yes, violence. But none, as far as I know, can imagine or sustain the cruelty of which we humans are capable.

So there we were, and we held each other's gaze until he looked away. It could have been a minute or an eternity. I really don't know. When I left work that evening I couldn't get the day's events out of my mind, and by the time I went to bed I decided that I must find him a home.

The next morning I followed my usual routine. Quick shower and shave, cup of tea, scroll through the morning headlines – then off to work. As I drove through the countryside I thought of Major – that was the hound's name – and the chance at another life that I would shortly provide him. When I arrived I parked my car, entered the building, made my way to my office, checked my messages, and headed to the animal housing unit. I went straight to Major's cage. It was empty. I couldn't recall any protocols having been set for him that day, so I went in search of our supervisor. It was then I happened to pass my colleague in the hall, her hand still bandaged from the wound she'd sustained the day before.

Morning, I said. *Any idea where they've taken Major?*

To the chambers, she said. *Had him taken there myself just a few minutes a …*

I didn't wait for her to finish but ran down the corridor, down the emergency stairwell to the basement

151

and through the swing doors leading to the euthanasia unit, or the gas chambers as they were commonly referred to. So-called because CO_2, or carbon dioxide, is the most widely used method for killing rodents, and rodents comprise the vast majority of test subjects. With larger specimens, such as dogs, euthanasia is normally, but not always, performed by lethal injection, and, as luck would have it, I arrived just as an attendant was trying to calm him while his colleague prepared the injection.

As soon as Major saw me he began to yelp. The oddest thing is he looked genuinely pleased to see me, though why I cannot imagine. In the past he'd often fouled himself at the mere sight of me. I can only surmise that he understood why I'd arrived at that particular moment. Not merely to spare him death, but to rescue him permanently from the hell he'd endured for nearly a year. I think if he'd thought I was there just to prevent his death he would have willingly impaled himself on the syringe.

The administering vet told me I would have to get permission to have him spared as the head of our unit had already approved it. I assured him I'd return in five minutes with whatever was required, and he in turn assured me he would wait. In the time it took me to find my boss and acquire the necessary signature, my colleague returned to the gas chambers with the intention of coercing the vet into administering the injection. She made much of her wound, saying that the hound had become too dangerous, and assured the vet that she would take full responsibility for any repercussions. She'd guessed my intention from my reaction in the hall and, unbeknown to me, had made her way back to the chambers, waited until I went to find our head of unit – as she knew I must – and in my absence thought to persuade the vet to continue with the procedure.

I suppose every human being can point to an event that fundamentally changes their world view. By this I mean the entirety of the way in which he or she perceives life and everything that comprises it. For me Major's aborted execution was that event, because that's what it very nearly was – an execution – and the basest sort of execution at that. One based on personal revenge.

When I returned to the chambers Major was lying on the table, inert as a stone, and beside him stood my colleague. In order to calm him the vet had administered a sedative, and now he stood hovering over him, hypodermic in hand, about to administer the lethal injection. As I entered my colleague turned, looked at me without expression and left. I wish now I'd stopped her and given her a piece of my mind. Instead, I picked up Major and made my way from the gas chambers to my office. I instructed my assistant to collect my car keys and my personal belongings and follow me to my car. With Major in my arms I left the building, laid him on the seat of my car and drove home. I never went back.

What became of my research? In all honesty it had little if any impact. I suppose one could say that it had some theoretical value, but as far as results which have since been clinically applied to humans, fairly marginal. Like the monkey I am a primate, but I am not a monkey, and he was not a man. And though dogs may be man's best friend, they are not humans and we are not dogs.

So in answer to your question, I think it's more than fair to ask what was the point, after all, of so much suffering?

And the answer is none. Absolutely none.

MY COUSIN ZHEN

Each morning Zhen and I walk the short distance from our lodgings to the factory in the town where we work. For the next ten hours she sews eyes onto toy pandas and I pack them into boxes ready for shipping. When we finish our shift we leave the factory, cross the courtyard past the endless rows of bicycles, and begin the walk home.

Six months ago we each lived at home with our parents. Now Zhen and I live near the factory in a converted warehouse where we rent one of many dozens of cramped rooms let by an unscrupulous landlord. Each floor in the warehouse has one communal toilet, one bath, and one kitchen meant for twenty workers. There are forty of us on our floor, and access to each is a question of first come, first served. Our landlord cares little for our safety even though he makes regular inspections and is quick to discover stowaways. It makes no difference to him how many are stuffed into a room as long as we pay.

Our room is like a box with barely enough space for one. There's a small bed, so each night Zhen and

I switch: one in the bed, one on the floor. We've fashioned a spare mattress from a rug and the few clothes and blankets we own between us, and we use our dirty laundry for pillows. There's no heating, so we scavenge cardboard and newspaper to use as insulation against the cold that seeps up from the concrete floor.

When Zhen left home I arranged the job for her at the factory where I work with my parents. We lost our own small farm some years before, confiscated by local officials to make way for a chemical plant. In the end it was never built. Corruption made construction costs swell, and we were left without our farm, our home, or the promised jobs. After that we migrated to the nearest town, and my parents used their meagre savings to buy employment at the town's only factory. I went to the local school, and as soon as I graduated I joined them.

At first my parents were against Zhen coming to work with us. Following 'the incident' they feared her capable of any mischief. *If we lose our jobs because of Zhen,* they said, *we'll starve.* But Zhen and her parents are family, and her parents, like mine, are getting old. Without Zhen's help they would struggle, and my parents and I would lose an important source of vegetables and rice. When I reminded them of this they agreed, but they weren't happy, and they rumbled like an approaching storm.

Where will she live? my mother asked.

With us, I answered.

My parents looked at each other. I knew right away what they were thinking.

Tell her to keep her head down and her mouth shut, warned my father.

I'll wring her neck myself if she makes trouble, added my mother. *My poor sister. What did she do to deserve her?*

In the end Zhen left us and moved into the warehouse. She could tell that my parents didn't want her, and after a month or so I joined her. They protested, but I couldn't bear the thought of her being on her own.

The incident my parents spoke of happened shortly after my visit. For several weeks after the bear and her cub died, Zhen went about her duties on her parents' farm as if nothing had happened. She never mentioned the bear and her cub. But later her mother told me a sea change had come over her. Suddenly she was interested in every aspect of bile production, and all the things she'd taken for granted she now questioned. She wanted to know about the bears' behaviour and habits in the forest: what they ate, whether they were solitary or social, how many cubs each sow bore in an average litter. She asked her father exactly how he determined bile quality and what steps he took to ensure it remained high. She challenged his methods for collecting it and for reducing infection. But when she asked about the bears' pain he became suspicious and looked at her as if he didn't understand the question. When she suggested making their cages larger so that they could stand and move about, he told her, *You pay, I'll make.* She made charts of each bear's level of muscle atrophy and stress and tacked them to the wall of the shed. Finally, she told her father that she no longer wanted him to milk the bears in front of their cubs. This was the last straw, and he complained to his wife that their daughter was going mad.

During this period a new buyer came. He buys bile from many small farmers throughout the region, always paying a fair price and sometimes a bit more to ensure that his suppliers remain loyal. Zhen met him only once. Though they never spoke he nodded politely when she served him tea. After that he always sent a local agent to collect the bile.

One day she overheard her father telling the agent about the dead sow and her cub and how his daughter had been acting strangely ever since. Afterwards, Zhen told me the agent watched her as one might watch a familiar pet about whom one harbours sudden doubts. When he left, Zhen asked her father if everything was all right, but instead of answering he turned away and shook his head as if the very question itself was a sign of her increasingly bizarre behaviour.

Months later a fearful racket woke Zhen's parents. It was late at night and there was an autumn chill in the air. I remember because I was there. It was Zhen's birthday and she'd asked me to come. When I heard the ruckus I got up from our bed, threw on a coat, and stumbled outside. A moment later her father appeared. By the light of the setting moon we could just make out the last dark shapes lumbering across the rice paddies towards the forest. Then Zhen appeared from the darkness, her shadow like a spirit on the ground before us.

Don't worry, Bàba, she said. *With your rice paddy and vegetable garden you won't starve. I'll find a job, one that pays well, and you and Māmā will be able to buy whatever you need.*

It was then that her father realised the shapes fleeing into the forest were his past, present and future. He ran, howling like a scorned demon, as if his fury alone would summon the bears back. When his wife came into the yard she followed the sound of her husband's cries and, turning to her daughter, looked beyond her to the open-sided shed. Silhouettes of empty cages, like sculptures cast from darkness, triggered the sound of her own despair. Even the fleeing bears were startled by her screams, and they turned and changed direction before vanishing into the forest.

Zhen's sorrow at the memory of her mother's tears and her father's rage still hasn't passed. For three days her mother wept as Zhen prepared to leave, and for three days her father remained silent. Not one sound passed from his lips. He couldn't bring himself even to look at her, and sat with his head turned to the wall. When she said goodbye he refused to look up, and when she left she did not ask his forgiveness.

***

As I come into the room Zhen raises her head from her stool to look out of the factory window. It's a view she knows well and one that never changes. From her stool she can see a red-brick wall crowned with razor wire. In front of it dozens of battered bicycles stand slotted into metal stands. None of them is hers – or mine.

I watch her as her gaze moves from the window to the toy pandas dropped haphazardly at her feet. Their blue-and-white plastic eyes stare vacantly back, and it seems to me that the irony of her situation is not lost on them. From a pile on the table next to her she grabs another and begins to sew on its eyes. There are twenty-five other young girls on stools working near her, each with her head bent to her task, and I'm sure Zhen wonders what they did to land themselves among the endless cartons filled with toy bears.

I call out to her. The other girls look up briefly before returning to their task. In my right hand I hold a letter, and when I wave it Zhen rises and crosses the planked wooden floor, a half-sighted panda clutched in her hands. As she approaches I back into the corridor, signalling to her to follow. When we're out of earshot I hand her the letter.

Open it, I say.

She looks at the envelope and then at me.

Go on, I say.

She takes the letter and hands me the toy bear. It doesn't take her long to read it, and as I watch her disbelief spreads like spilt tea across her face.

Well?

They've offered me a job, she says.

Who? Who's offered you a job?

The bear sanctuary. The one I told you about. I wrote to them months ago, and they've ... they've offered me a job. They say they'll pay me. They also want me to take classes at the university.

I grab the letter from her hand and begin to read.

This is ... it's incredible. When do they want you to start?

As soon as possible.

Then go and tell the boss you're quitting.

Now?

Now.

And I throw my arms around her and hug her for all I'm worth.

THE POACHER'S DAUGHTER

I want very much to warn Little Calf, but my father's hand on my shoulder is firm, and I know that if I shout out he will be angry. I do not wish to make my father angry. He is always worrying for me and it is not fair to cause him more worry. At the same time I feel very sad for Little Calf, because he suffers much pain when my father kills the old bull. And then I realise that the pain of Little Calf and the pain I feel for my mother and baby brother are the same pain, and this makes me even sadder.

Still, I watch and say nothing as my father's men hurry across the sand towards Little Calf. At first he does not see them, but soon he smells them and when he does he spins and runs along the sand to the far end of the cove. He is very thirsty and very tired and my father's men have no trouble to throw the net over him. Soon he is on his knees and crying so loudly I am sure his cries will kill him. When they return to where we are standing, my father lets Little Calf drink from his gourd until it is empty, and also from another belonging to one of his men. He knows

Little Calf will not make it to the nearest watering hole without it. Then we head back into the forest.

While we walk I ask my father what he will do now with Little Calf and he tells me what I already know. I want to keep Little Calf but I know without asking this is not possible. Little Calf will need milk every day. More milk in one day than we can afford in three months. Even with poaching monies my father cannot pay for Little Calf's milk. He will sell him to the same man that first gave him the tusks to hide that made my father a poacher. I ask what this man will do with Little Calf.

He will sell him, he says.

And I ask, *Who will buy him?*

But this time he doesn't answer because I am sure he does not know. Or he does not wish to know. I don't let myself think that he doesn't care, because I'm afraid how this will make me think of him.

So I say to him, *Father, we must take Little Calf to the elephant refuge.*

Now he is angry and tries to calm his voice, but his words mock him.

I will kill Little Calf and eat him myself before I take him there, he says, *because without monies he is our only food. Or do you want us to starve?*

I have no answer. I say only that I hate the man that gave my father the tusks and made him to become a poacher. I say he is an evil man, a cruel man, and I am sure he would sell me if he could. And my father says he will never do that because he gave his word, and my father will kill him if he harms me. But I am not so sure. I am not so sure his word and my father's threat are enough.

All this time we are talking, my father's men are listening. They are listening to my questions, but mostly they are listening to my father's answers. Some of them talk, but quietly, like children who are afraid their parents will hear them. The others say nothing, but they look at me, and then at my father, and I can see they are thinking whether he will change his mind, and what they will do if he does.

My father knows they are listening, and part of me hopes his answers are for them, and when we are alone he will tell me different answers, answers I want to hear. But I know in my heart I am wrong, because he is no longer the man who tells me stories that make me laugh, or stories that make me forget my fears. That man died with my mother and baby brother.

In the end my father sells Little Calf to Tusk Man, Tusk Man sells him to his *sonko* – his boss – and this *sonko* sells Little Calf to a very rich man who lives far away. My father tells me this rich man has many animals, and Little Calf will be well looked after.

Tell me about this rich man, I say. *Where does he live? How can you be so sure he will take care of him?*

This time my father looks away. He doesn't know and he doesn't try to make me believe his lies. He says to me that he is finished with lies.

I want to believe him, but in my heart I cry every night.

THE POACHER

Man with tusks, boss man of me, is very pleased when he sees my tusks because they are bigger than any I bring before. His eyes light up like little round suns with black seed centres, and his shiny smile is wide as a crocodile's. But when he sees Little Calf his mouth shuts and in its place comes a dead stare like rebel gives when his mind is thinking only of killing.

He says to me, *Why did you bring this calf to me? Are you crazy?*

But I ignore him and say, *You will get many monies for him, but if you don't want him it makes no problem for me. I will sell him to another tusk man who will pay plenty monies for him, and I will take my tusks to him as well.*

He does not like this and right away he looks to my daughter. But I pretend not to notice so that his threat falls away like rain off a buffalo's back.

Then he says to me, *I know of a man who will buy him.*

And I answer, *If I give you to sell you must give me half the monies.*

I watch him carefully because I am playing a dangerous game and I am afraid, but I do not show this. I look at him with the same dead eyes he looks to me, and I do not pull my eyes away until he nods.

I know bringing Little Calf to Tusk Man is stupid, but my daughter will not allow me to leave him in the jungle to die and I cannot feed him. And if I take him to the elephant refuge they will pay no monies and ask many questions. My men are not happy, but they say nothing. They are thinking whatever happens it is my problem, not theirs. They are right, because they know I will never betray them.

Next day my daughter cries and cries when Tusk Man takes Little Calf away. We put him in the back of a truck with plenty of milk and water for the journey, and cover the truck with a large sheet made from canvas, and Tusk Man takes two of my men to sit in the truck with Little Calf. They leave very early, before the sun rises, and I think to let my daughter sleep so not to upset her. But she stays all night with Little Calf, so there is no hiding what happens from her. When they are gone my daughter does not look to me but goes inside without any words, and I wonder how long she will be silent to me.

Tusk Man pays to me monies he promised from the sale of Little Calf, and with these monies I am able to pay my daughter's school. Not long later police raid my house. I do not think it is Tusk Man who betrayed me. He knows I know too much. My daughter thinks it is Old Woman, but Old Woman would not squash a fly without permission from Tusk Man. So who? I do not know. Maybe I will never know. Maybe it is just bad luck.

I am remembering all this while I am sitting in prison waiting for my trial. It is a filthy place, and I am covered with lice. There are a few like me here – poachers – but mostly it is murderers and thieves and rapists. All the time I must keep my eyes open for danger because no one is safe here. I have difficulty to say who is more dangerous – criminal or guard. Like rebel and army, only God can tell the difference.

My daughter does not visit me. I forbid it. This is the hardest for me to bear. Before I come here I say to her, *You must stay away. It is too dangerous. Too dangerous. When prisoners and guards see you, right away they will think bad things, and there is nothing I can do to protect you.*

She is very afraid and she asks me, *Who will look after me?*

And I answer her, *Tusk Man.*

When she hears this she laughs and says, *Tusk Man will kill me and cut me up himself.*

I explain to her that I will tell everything about Tusk Man to police if he touches her so much as one finger, and I will tell to police everything I know if others touch her so much as one finger, and Tusk Man knows this because I have told the same to him.

And then I tell her what Tusk Man promises to me for my silence. He says, *You have my word. She will live with Old Woman. She will go to school and have all that she needs until you return.*

And my daughter answers me, *How will you know?*

And I say, *I have made arrangements with your teachers. They will send to me a message if you do not come to school every day.*

She thinks about this. I see she wants to believe me, but she has many doubts. I turn away. My fear for her is so great I am afraid unless I cannot hide it from my face.

Many weeks later I am in the prison yard when I hear a big commotion. One man has a knife and he sticks it in another man's chest and this man falls to the ground. Quickly they are surrounded so that I cannot see who is it that falls. Soon guards come with clubs and beat the others away. They lift the bleeding man, and it is only then that I see it is Tusk Man. I shake like a dog who is leaving the river, because right away I think who will protect my daughter now that he is dead.

For many days after I beg guards to send her a message, but they ignore me. Finally, a priest comes. I tell him my problem, and he promises to me that he will go to my daughter's school and seek her and speak with her. I don't have many faith in priests. They claim power from God, but I have never seen them use this power when it is needed. If not when rebels and army raid villages and kill children and women and take young boys to be soldiers, then when?

But this priest does return and he says to me, *I have seen your daughter. She is safe. But she does not want to stay with Old Woman.*

And I say to the priest, *She has no one else. My wife is dead.*

He looks at me and I can read in his eyes that he is thinking what to do and whether he will help me.

Our sisters run a charity, he says. *A home for children whose parents cannot keep them. They have two places. I will arrange for your daughter one place.*

And I thank him before I even take time and properly think on it, because, like I say to you before, I have no choice. No choice.

My Cousin Zhen

A year after Zhen left I quit my job at the factory and went to work with her at the bear sanctuary. Now I help her to organise everything the bears need to live comfortable, happy lives, while Zhen helps them to recover. While she works she talks to the bears, studying and recording their every movement. They're so used to her that she can observe them for hours at a time. Even those that have been subjected to the worst abuse feel safe in her company.

There's one bear in particular she's especially fond of. A young sow, very playful and very intelligent. But she's also very mischievous, and for this reason Zhen has named her Tiáopí. She is always the first to master the games and tasks Zhen devises to prove her theory that bears, like humans, can think and feel. Every morning Tiáopí waits for Zhen to appear. She's as cunning as a thief and very affectionate, but only with Zhen.

One week a group of bile farmers arrived for a seminar. Zhen gives regular talks for everyone involved in bile farming, from the farmers who collect it to the shopkeepers who sell it. Among the group that day was a man of medium height. He was lean and slightly stooped, like one who spends his days hunched over a desk, but there was nothing of an old man about him. When I saw him I had the impression that he rarely smiled. He wasn't a farmer like the others, of this I was certain. His hands were too smooth and his nails too clean. He wore a plain white cotton shirt, long-sleeved, unbuttoned at the neck and rolled up at the wrist, and his trousers were of an old-fashioned cut, pleated and cuffed. I guessed he didn't like to go shopping, because even his shoes were old-fashioned – sturdy – designed for comfort rather than style. Even so they were neat and polished. He looked like a man who'd worked hard to build a business and had no interest in spending his money on frivolous things like clothes. His only extravagance was a gold watch, not a flashy affair like so many wear now to show off their success, but tasteful and discreet. I reckon it once belonged to his father or grandfather.

He remained silent during Zhen's lecture. I remember this. He sat in the front row in a seat directly opposite the lectern, but didn't ask a single question. When we stopped for lunch he sat alone in the cafeteria. The others recognised him. Some bowed, calling him Uncle. While they ate Zhen moved from table to table speaking with the farmers, eager for their thoughts. But when she approached this man known as Uncle, he rose, cleared the debris from his lunch tray, returned his tray to the counter, and left without a word or a nod to anyone.

After lunch Zhen took the group on a tour of the sanctuary. Again the man stood near the front. He ignored Zhen as she moved from one enclosure to the next, but whenever the bears approached he watched them with the eyes of a predator. I was with them that day, and I saw Tiáopí hurry forward as soon as she saw Zhen. As Zhen turned to greet her, Tiáopí stood, sniffed the air, and immediately ran back to the cover of her den. Zhen was busy explaining the tasks she and her professor devised to test the bears' intelligence and didn't notice what happened. But I did. Before she ran away Tiáopí looked directly at Uncle, and he returned her gaze with a look that said, *We share nothing, you and I. You provide something I need. That is all.*

Later, Zhen and I spoke, and it was then she told me that Uncle is the same man who used to buy bear bile from her father and to whom she once served tea. When I asked why he ignored her she shrugged and smiled, but I could see that she was worried.

Since that day a month has passed, and I dream about it every night. In the happier versions Tiáopí morphs into a kind of ursine superhero who breaks free of her enclosure, vanquishes Uncle and his army of bile-farming soldiers and, with Zhen and me, establishes a kingdom in which all animals are sacred. Other nights, when I cry myself to sleep, my dreams have less happy outcomes.

I didn't realise it at the time, but thinking back I see that Zhen *had* noticed Tiáopí's reaction to Uncle, and, like me, read his thoughts. Before I left work that evening to catch the bus home, Zhen took my hand and said, *Never give up. Never.* I didn't think much about it at the time, only that it was strange. Why did she think I would give up?

My mother says I mustn't blame myself for what happened next. No one could have predicted it. I know she's right, but still it's hard not to feel that, if only I'd done this or that, things might have turned out differently.

THE JOURNALIST

Dressed in a white cotton shirt and pleated trousers, a man makes his way through the shoal of shoppers, tourists and vendors with the steady determination of a fish swimming upstream. He never hurries or dawdles, but keeps his gaze fixed on a point in the distance that only he can see, catching no one's eye or elbow as he slips through the shifting tide of bodies to his destination. Soon a small group of street children sitting on a kerb call out to him, shouting, *Uncle! Uncle!* and rush as one across the street to greet him, dodging and bounding through the traffic as gingerly as antelopes. Without breaking stride he reaches into his pocket using the hand that bears the watch upon its wrist, and withdrawing it holds out his palm. The children pluck from the proffered sweets with beak-like fingers as quickly and expertly as birds from a feeder. It's his rule that each child takes only one, and the children know this and know the consequences if they violate it.

It's to teach you to share, he tells them, *and to learn trust. You must be able to depend on each other, to look out for each other. If one of you cheats by taking more than the rest, then the group's bond will be broken. Once this happens there is no longer trust. It will be every child for himself. This is no way to achieve success,* he reminds them again, *for it will never last. Only if you can be trusted will your colleagues and customers remain constant.*

As soon as the children receive their sweets they fan out around him to form a wedge through the last few metres of grime-ridden pavement towards an ancient apothecary. They part at the entrance, allowing Uncle to reach out and grab the heavy polished brass handle cast in the shape of a dragon's head. He opens the carved mahogany door around the edges of which curl the dragon's body, and steps into the shop. Once clear of the threshold the door closes behind him, slowly, and with the soft creak and sigh of an old man sinking into his favourite chair.

In the shop is a centre aisle on either side of which stands a row of mahogany-and-glass display cabinets, each one topped with a polished zinc counter. Behind one, teak shelves lined with hundreds of ancient jars, each boasting what look like the ghoulish contents of a witch's pantry, climb the wall; behind the other, row upon row of teak drawers ascend from floor to ceiling, their contents calligraphically inscribed on yellowing rice-paper labels. An odour heady with decay, dehydration, brine and formaldehyde blends with the patina of antique wood as reassuring and familiar as a pair of old leather shoes. Together they provide an airlock against the sweat, grease and fumes of the street.

Behind the left counter as you enter stands a young woman in a physician's white coat, and directly opposite her behind the right counter stands her clone. When Uncle enters they bow in tandem and watch as he makes his way to the quaint register at the back of the shop. Taking a key from his pocket he unlocks it, removes the cash, and carefully counts it, keeping some and returning the rest to the correct slots according to their denominations. This is the cue the young women are waiting for, and immediately one leaves her post, crosses the floor to the door and removes a sign that reads *CLOSED*. No sooner does she return to her counter than the first customer appears.

I observe all of this from the building opposite: a three-storey colonial hotel that sits abandoned, the casualty of a spat between the developer, the city's preservation society and the local planning authority. Today marks one month since I arranged with the managing company to rent a room on the first floor, and since then my assistant and I have taken it in turns to sit for ten hours a day on a rickety stool behind a grimy window, or near the window of what was once the lobby, watching the apothecary opposite.

Uncle's routine seldom varies. He arrives every morning and departs every evening, as punctual and reliable as an atomic clock. He rarely goes out for lunch, sending instead one of his urchins to fetch him something to eat from one of the dozen vendors that line the street. He has a steady flow of customers, each hoping for a cure produced from one of the hundreds of jars and drawers whose contents promise bitter and unsavoury remedies divined from thousand-year-old recipes. Bear bile is just one of Uncle's specialities, and he's said to have some of the purest money can buy. There are other more rarefied items, if one knows how to ask, and now and again someone appears who is more than willing to pay for a variety of unctions and formulas derived from forbidden ingredients. It's these customers that interest me.

I'm a freelance journalist working on a story about the illegal trade in rare and endangered flora and fauna – to the uninitiated, plants and animals. Some say it's a losing battle, but I say it's one that has to be fought. If you ask people whether they think elephants and pangolins, or rhinos and rainforest, should be rendered extinct or demolished, most will look at you as if you've sprouted horns. Others will express little interest one way or the other. But now and again someone will look at you in a way that causes you to glance over your shoulder and hope that your escape will be quick and merciful.

It's rumoured that Uncle is the head of an international smuggling cartel, and that he can provide whatever one desires no matter how threatened or rare: elephant ivory, rhino horn, pangolin scales, shark fins, Bengal tiger and snow-leopard pelts, teeth, claws, bones and penises. All these and more are merely his stock-in-trade along with a variety of exotic plants, birds, reptiles and pets, all destined to be abandoned as soon as their owners grow tired of them. Uncle trades in all of them, but his bread and butter is bear bile and virtually every part of a bear one could wish for, in particular the paws which are considered a gastronomic delicacy – the more rancid the better.

I notice that when a customer comes in search of exotic items the urchins jump from their kerbside perches and race to position themselves at each end of the street. In this way they're able to see who enters from either side. Only one is left to stand guard at the shop's entrance, and as soon as he gets the nod from his companions he reaches behind and knocks twice on the door. In this way Uncle is warned that a special customer is arriving, and it's safe to receive them and to conduct his business.

Yesterday, as I was sitting my watch, Uncle went out for lunch. I knew he'd be gone for precisely one hour. On those rare occasions when he ventured out it was always one hour from the time he left until he returned, and I had no reason to think that yesterday would be any different. As he turned the corner I picked up my newspaper and reread the lead article breaking the news of an attack at the university's famous bear sanctuary – an article I'd written – and I knew that the details, though not yet released, would be brutal.

I let the newspaper drop to the floor and sat staring out of the window for the remainder of the hour until I noticed Uncle returning from his lunch. Upon his approach one of the urchins jumped up from the kerb and thrust the same paper I'd been reading into his hands. Glancing at it he stopped, and as he read the headline a smile as indiscernible as the breath of a butterfly passed across his face. In the next instant it was gone as he grabbed the handle to his shop and entered.

For a long while I sat on my stool and thought about it. What was it that bothered me apart from the fact that his was a reaction one doesn't normally expect when presented with news of a violent attack? But it wasn't just that. It was something else, and it wasn't until early evening when he locked the carved mahogany door of his colonial-era apothecary that it hit me.

It was the first time I'd seen him smile.

BILLY

In the beginning I was bottle-feeding those two piglets as much as four to six times a day, and that's not all. In order to keep 'em warm at night they were sleeping with me, but truth be told, it was mostly to keep 'em from crying. At first my mother complained. But then Grandma spoke to her and after that she just shook her head and said, *Well, awright, but they're not staying in the house forever, so get that straight. And no way am I cleaning up after 'em. So get that straight, too, hear me now?*

I asked my little sister if she wanted to name 'em and right away she comes out with Piggy and Porky like she'd been thinking about it her whole life. I let it be for a day. Then I told her if she wanted to be a writer when she grew up she had to come up with something more original than Piggy and Porky. So she thought about it some more and came up with Bristles and Diana. I get Bristles. But Diana? Who names a pig Diana? She said there was a princess or some such called Diana, which is even more ridiculous. My advice? Don't ask your little sister to name your pets.

Anyway, when I'm home Bristles and Diana follow me everywhere I go. Luckily, it's summer vacation and school doesn't start up again 'til September. But I still have to go to work. So I pay my little sister fifty cents a day to look after 'em while I work at the local supermarket in the meat department. I think it's the combination of my job and Boss's pig farm that got me thinking about the way our meat is produced, and not just our meat, but all our food. And the more I learn the more I realise that the way we're raising our food and the way most people are eating is crazy. Cruelty aside, most of us are eating shit, at least the folks I know.

We're lucky. My grandma, mom and dad love to cook, so we eat pretty well. But none of us have ever really thought about where our meat comes from. So when I started making a fuss about where it's raised and how it's raised my mom got pretty annoyed. And as far as eating pork is concerned, soon as I had those two orphaned runts to look after, well, that was that. I might as well've tried eating my own foot. You can imagine how all this went down.

One night during supper I said, *You know, maybe we just oughta eat less meat.*

You woulda thought I farted at the table the way it went quiet and everyone looked at me. Finally, my sister broke the silence.

Where does meat come from? she said.

Turns out she didn't really break the silence. If anything, she extended it. My mom looked at my dad, and my dad looked at Grandma, and then everyone looked at me as if the whole damn thing was my fault, and in a way I guess it was.

My little sister is ten years younger than me. She's what you might call an accident. My mom had a difficult birth with me and the doctors told her she'd never have another kid. I've since learned that doctors are wrong as often as not.

Anyway, we were all of us just sitting there like deaf mutes. So she asked again, *Where does meat come from?*

And I said, *From animals. It comes from animals.*

What kinda animals? she said.

All kinds, I said.

What kinds? she said again.

Mostly cows and chickens and sheep and goats and lambs.

And pigs? she said.

Yep. And pigs, too, I said, because at that point there was no point in lying.

Do they grow it? she said.

Whaddaya mean?

Like vegetables, she said.

Now everyone was staring at me as if I was about to tell 'em the winning lottery numbers. Only difference was, they weren't quite sure they wanted to know.

Kinda, I said, but I knew what was coming next. Everyone did.

How? she said.

I looked at my grandma and she barely nodded, but I saw it and I thought, *Okay, here goes.* And I started talking like the clock was ticking.

Animals are *meat. We kill 'em and then we butcher 'em and then we send 'em to the supermarket where they get packaged up and laid out in the meat section nice and tidy like. And we go and choose which animal we want to eat and we buy it, bring it home and cook it.*

For a moment my little sister didn't move and her expression didn't change. It was like she was trying to process everything I'd said. Didn't take her long, though. Next thing she jumped up from the table and bolted upstairs, and we heard my door slam shut and lock.

My mom gave me a look that said *I'd like to butcher you* before heading upstairs. I heard her calling through my door, but my sister just kept shouting, *Go away! Go away!* and after a couple of minutes my mom called down and I left the table and went up.

When I got upstairs I stood at my door and said to my sister, *Come on, lemme in. I just wanna talk.*

By then she was wailing and in between sobs she said, *No, I won't let you kill 'em, I won't let you kill 'em.*

I knew she was referring to Bristles and Diana because I could hear 'em grunting. They were obviously upset, too, what with all the mayhem going on. I told my mom to go away, and I talked to my little sister through the door for about ten minutes, promising her that nobody was going to lay a hand on Bristles or Diana.

How do I know? she said. *How do I know you won't butcher 'em and eat 'em? What about their mommy and daddy? Did you eat them too? Is that why they live with us?*

Nobody's gonna eat 'em because they're our pets, I said. *Nobody eats their pets.*

She continued wailing, and then she said, *How would Mommy and Daddy feel if somebody ate me? Or if somebody ate them? Then there'd be nobody to look after us.*

Well, I didn't have an answer for that, at least not one that made any sense to me or to her. Not at that moment.

Personally, I've got no problem with people eating meat. We're omnivores, and we've been doing it since

Adam and Eve got kicked outta Eden. And to eat meat we gotta kill animals. But what I can't understand is why we gotta torture 'em first.

Anyway, the long and the short of it is that me and my little sister are now vegetarians. As for my parents and Grandma, well, they're trying. Good news is they don't eat nearly as much meat as they used to, and when they do they're a lot more careful about what they buy and where it comes from.

For all kindsa reasons, says Grandma, *that can't be a bad thing.*

And I reckon she's right.

It's been a month since I quit Boss's pig farm and that sow was slaughtered, and every day since then I've thought about her. I just can't get the images outta my mind. That look she gave me before she died, I knew exactly what she was thinking. Hell, you only had to walk into that shed one time to know what all those sows were thinking. It was pure hell, plain and simple. You don't gotta be a genius to know that any creature in its right mind would want outta there no matter what it took.

The whole experience made me think long and hard about being human. It was like a revelation. After that I thought about all the times I've spent lying on my back and staring up at the night sky – weather permitting – wondering if there's intelligent life somewhere out there in the universe. And what for? Hell, we don't gotta spend all that money sending people into outer space, building great telescopes and peering all over the galaxy looking for little green men. We only gotta open our eyes and look around us. There's intelligent life everywhere. *Hiding in plain sight,* as Grandma likes to say.

Anyways, if we're so smart and animals are so dumb, how come is it that we're the ones have made such a mess of everything?

UNCLE

I know I'm being watched.

I own many of the buildings on the road where my shop is located, so naturally I'm aware that a young reporter has rented a room in the hotel opposite. First floor, to be precise. It makes little difference to me. I have nothing to hide. The police have interviewed me and released me. Why? Because I am innocent. I also have a very successful and well-respected business, one that's been in my family for generations. But please, take me and my personal affairs out of the equation, because the fact is that this young reporter is entirely misguided. Does she honestly believe that her attempts to incriminate me will put an end to an entire tradition, a culture as old and respected as our own? I think not.

Even so, the pressure is mounting. Activists and campaigners, even government officials, are making noise about the environment, endangered species, animal cruelty and the like. Utter nonsense. What do I care for a bear? I have no feelings one way or the other. It's enough that I have a gang of street urchins to look after. If it were not for me they'd be stealing and begging and worse. I employ them. I teach them. And one day, if they're clever, they'll go into business for themselves.

And what of the others, many others, who depend on me? What do I tell them? That I will close my business and they and their families must find other work or starve? Do I seem a cruel man to you? Because of me they are able to feed their families and send their children to school. Is this a bad thing?

As to the other matter you mentioned, exotic viruses and such. All right, I'll admit they're a worry, but only because some people are ignorant and careless. Should the many suffer because of the few? Should we ban cars because a handful of idiots insist on driving drunk? Of course not. We punish the offenders so that those among us who act responsibly may continue to provide services and carry on with our lives.

Forgive me, repeat that, please.

Yes, it's true. My work, like yours, entails a certain amount of travelling. I would prefer to remain where I am, but sometimes it's unavoidable. One must be vigilant or run the risk of employees and competitors mistakenly sensing an opportunity that doesn't exist. It's all about motivation and discipline. With regard to the former, let's just say that I reward those individuals necessary to ensure the smooth running of my business. It's the most effective means, and one that's as old and timeless as civilisation itself.

Believe me, there are many, too many to count, who agree with me and who are happy to do business with me. They trust me. They know I'm a man of my word. Of course, I pay well. Extremely well. And they don't forget this. What they do and how they do it is not my concern. They supply a product. I buy it. And I can tell you that business has never been better. Now many of my countrymen are rich, and more of them than ever are able to buy what they want, and what they want are the very things that before only a select few could afford. Why? They want to feel special. They want to feel important. They want to impress their families and friends. And why not? Is this not what we all strive for?

Still, I'll admit that this reporter is a nuisance. It would be unfortunate for her as well as for me if she were to persist in her so-called investigation. I'm not an unreasonable man, but I cannot speak for others. Without being specific, let's just say that she's walking on thin ice. In any business there are unscrupulous actors. My business is no exception. I prefer to use charm and persuasion to solve my problems, such as they are, but others will tell you a different story. They'll tell you that the one thing most crucial to their success is the very thing most people lack the courage to employ. Ruthlessness. A good business-man, like a good leader, must be ruthless if he – or she – wishes to succeed. Perhaps, as you suggest, I will give her an interview. Yes, to set the record straight. After all, I have nothing to hide.

Now, if you will permit me, I will ask *you* a question. Who among your fellows wields the power? Who decides what is and what is not? Or, to put it more bluntly, who eats whom? Do the meek devour the strong? I think not. No, my esteemed friend, I think not. Therefore, if you don't want to be eaten you must be strong. You must prevail. The survival of the fittest. To turn the other cheek is the surest way to perish. If one wants to live and live well, one must be ruthless. Nature demands it. All of us must choose, and I have made my choice.

Have you?

MRS BOSS

I decided early on that I didn't want children despite coming from a Catholic family, and Boss didn't argue. He said raising pigs was enough of a headache, and if we didn't breed the help we needed we'd hire it. By the time we got married he was already starting to expand. His herd of two hundred pigs increased by three hundred, and with the money I made selling the diner he was looking to add another five hundred by the end of that year.

When Billy came to work for Boss we had a thousand pigs and two full-time hired hands, and Boss was thinking about adding another three hundred sows by the end of the year. Didn't matter to him one iota that I wanted more pigs like I wanted a third eye smack in the center of my forehead. But this wasn't all that had changed in the years since we got married.

As the farm grew so did the stench emanating from our manure pits. How else you gonna hold tons of slurry produced by a thousand animals crammed together in a confined space? The more pigs the more pits, and it wasn't long before I developed eczema and chronic bronchitis. Was clear as day to me what was causing it. There was a cloud of fumes hanging over our farm like a sorcerer's curse. I took to staying indoors with the windows and doors shut, venturing out only to go into town to fetch my shopping, and occasionally to have my hair done or catch a movie at the local cineplex. I don't have many friends and what few I had stopped coming because of the stench. Even my sisters and their husbands and kids refused to visit. So naturally, I became depressed and argumentative and took to drinking in the late afternoons before dinner. By the time Boss rolled in from his rounds I was barely coherent. Yeah, he was tired of my 'drunken harangues' as he called 'em. So what. Think I gave a damn? But he slapped me around. Soon enough the slaps turned to punches, and punches to beatings, and before long what they like to call over at the women's shelter the 'cycle of abuse' was well established. I didn't mind people seeing the bruises. Like I already said, they didn't bother me. Mighta been some sorta defense mechanism. Hell, I don't know. But the black eyes were something else. Yeah, I wore sunglasses when I went to town. Didn't fool nobody, but what the hell.

One evening shortly after the trouble with Billy, Boss rose from his chair in front of the TV and made his way to the verandah. I was sitting in a rocker, smoking a cigarette and reading a magazine I'd borrowed that afternoon from the beauty parlor. I always returned 'em, case you're thinking I'm a thief or a shoplifter or some such. I remember it was one of those rare summer evenings a breeze was blowing just strong enough to carry the stench downwind from the house. When he opened the screen door I looked up, and right away I could see he was in a foul mood. He ignored me, walked straight to the railing and looked up at the harvest moon. Bright as a Christmas bauble, it was. I'll never forget.

Feel that? he said.

Yeah, I feel it.

Gonna be a thunderstorm later, he said.

Uh-huh.

Then he looked over at me and at the bottle and pack of cigarettes resting on the porch next to my rocker. Both were near empty. I knew this, but I pretended to ignore him just the same. Then he looked again at the sky.

I don't like it, he said. *Something's not right.*

It was true. The sky was as clear as a polished diamond, but there was something in the air — like a bad dream that hangs about long after you've woken up.

Thunderstorm coming, like you said. It'll pass. Anyways, nothing you can do about it. It'll be what it is.

195

He grunted. I'm sure he'd like to have hit me, but he couldn't be bothered.

It's that damn boy that's bothering me, he said. *Useless as tits on a boar. Thieving sonuvabitch stole two piglets from me.*

Which boy you referring to? I said.

The Beckham boy.

Now I knew it was the Beckham boy he was moaning about sure as I know my own name, because ever since he made off with two of Boss's piglets it was all I'd been hearing about. But if I've learned anything, it's that pointing out the obvious doesn't change a thing, and sure as hell isn't appreciated.

Wouldn't surprise me if he was snooping for one of those damned animal rights outfits, he said.

I doubt it.

He didn't answer right away. Just leaned over the railing and spat into the dirt.

I'll get that little sonuvabitch if it's the last thing I do, he said. Then he turned and went back inside.

I waited until I heard him settle into his chair. I didn't want to follow him in, so I lit another cigarette and sat staring into the bright darkness. The moon was so big and its light so strong it was enough to make the sun jealous, and I thought if I was in charge of an army and set that night to launch a surprise attack, I wouldn't think twice about canceling it. I don't know if it was having this crazy thought or what, but something made me smile. More likely it was thinking about Boss beating on the Beckham boy instead of beating on me. That shock you?

Well, it shouldn't. I reckon you'd feel the same if you was me.

MĀMĀ

When daughter arrives at university she feels like a small stone in a bowl of pearls. How do I know this? She writes to me. I don't tell Bàba. I'm afraid he will find her letters and throw them away and tell me not to write or speak to her. So I keep quiet.

She tells me everyone at the university looks very smart, very well dressed. Students are not shy to speak out in class, but daughter is very shy. Says nothing for a long time. Does not even ask questions. People think she's dumb and cannot speak. She's not dumb. Not stupid either. She gets A marks every time.

I say to her, *Why not tell other students you are clever, maybe cleverer than they?*

But daughter is not worried. She listens and listens hard to everything her professor says. When she goes home at night she reads and reads. Then sleeps four hours. Then reads more. She does this every day. University pays everything for daughter, and daughter sends the money she makes at the bear sanctuary to Bàba and me. Bàba knows this but says nothing.

One day her professor comes to her and asks, *What do you do for fun?*

Daughter answers, *I study at university and work at the bear sanctuary.*

She tells me this. He laughs, but then he invites her to his lab. They talk and he asks her many questions. When she tells him she comes from family's bear bile farm he looks at her very hard. She worries and thinks maybe he will ask her to leave, but instead he shows her everything, everything about his work. Then she tells him all she has learned on parents' farm. He listens and says she is very clever.

When he tells her this it makes her happy. She works even harder. Soon he asks if she wants to work with him. She says yes. Now she is professor's assistant.

So I ask her, *Tell me, what is your professor's work?*

She says his main work is research. He says the best way to make people stop torturing bears is to make artificial bile. Daughter tells him she thinks this is a very good idea. I think it's not possible, and even if possible it's not the same thing. I tell this to daughter, but daughter tells me she and her professor will make the same thing, but better.

When daughter comes home we talk. She explains to me that change is very hard for people and she understands this. She also tells me many animals are threatened by humans. Too many to name. Even fish in the sea and birds in the trees. Professor says maybe one day the sea and land and air will be empty of all wildlife, and we will have animals only in zoos. I think about this, but it's hard to imagine a world with no animals in the forests, mountains, skies or seas.

Then I remember how I never imagined daughter would go to university. Or I imagined, but I thought it was not possible. And so I think maybe this is the way of humans. We cannot imagine many things until they happen. Or we don't believe they will happen until it's too late. And I wonder if this is the same way animals think.

I tell daughter how I wonder if animals think like humans. And she says to me, *Māmā, animals think and feel many things we don't understand. If we understood then maybe everything would change and we would treat them differently.*

I ask her how we can know this.

I will find out, she says.

She asks her professor, but he tells her it's not possible to understand how animals think.

Everything is possible, she says. *You taught me this.*

This time he looks at her and smiles, and says, *Okay, we'll find out.*

After that her professor comes to the bear sanctuary many times to speak with the director, and afterwards they make a team – professor, director, daughter – and daughter tells me that what they discover will make many people understand bears and all animals better.

Now daughter is in hospital. Why? Why has someone done this to her? I ask Bàba. He's so angry with daughter he never speaks with her again after she sets bears free. But even he does not understand why someone hurts her so bad she must go to hospital.

Now I talk to Bàba. I tell him he must go see her. He cannot stay silent for ever. He listens, but says nothing. No matter. I will not leave him in peace. Angry or not, Zhen is still his daughter.

THE VET

I knew that Einstein could sign, but I wanted him to admit it. To admit it would mean that he trusted me, and it was his trust I needed most of all.

It's true that I took away all the cameras. Even so, when I came to visit him he ignored me. Then I had an idea. I would give him a mirror and see what happened. Most gorillas won't pass the mirror test. They look and they don't recognise themselves, but I was certain Einstein would. So I went to find one, and when I returned I approached his cage and held it up against his bars.

At first he ignored it. No problem, I'm patient. Then he looked, but still no sign that he was interested. So I left and went to find Karim. I gave him the mirror and told him to take it with him the next time he visited Einstein. He did, and very soon Einstein was curious. Karim held it up so that Einstein could see his – Karim's – face in the glass. Then he angled it so that Einstein saw his own face. Then the two of them together. He did this many times. Finally, Einstein held out his hand and Karim passed him the mirror, and when he asked for it back, Einstein refused. When Karim told me this I thought, *Typical man, he only pretends not to be vain.*

Did I say man? Sorry. I meant male. Soon after that I installed a two-way mirror in the rear wall of his enclosure. No one but me knew it was two-way, not even Karim, because I covered the back of it with a piece of plywood on hinges, and I fixed on a lock with only one key – mine – so I was able to observe him whenever I wanted. I watched him for months, gathering evidence that he could sign about many things. Many more than I ever imagined.

One evening after finishing my work I went to visit him. I stood in front of his enclosure listening to the music of Miriam Makeba. Most young people today have never heard of her, but for me, I can't listen to her without wanting to dance. I started to sway, and when I saw that Einstein was watching me, I took out my earbuds and disconnected them from my phone so he could listen.

The song was 'Pata Pata'. When the song ended I played it again. This time he stood and began to dance. It's the only way I can describe it. Then I played it again and danced with him. Next I played 'Ha Po Zamani' and 'The Click Song', and we danced like that for some time. I'd never seen him so free. So abandoned. So ... happy.

After that I put two small speakers in his enclosure and made sure that whenever the zoo was closed he had as many hours of music as he wanted. I chose many different genres and styles. I also played to him the very best of Spanish classical guitar and flamenco, music my mother listened to and played for me as a child. But Einstein's favourite music was African. I think it was the drumbeat. Maybe it reminded him of something very old, something ancient, like the forest where he was born, and so when there was no one around I put it on for him, and we danced until my work or the evening called me away.

It was during one of these sessions that I began to sign. He pretended not to see me and I pretended not to notice. I told him how much I enjoyed our dancing and how I wished some of my friends enjoyed dancing as much as him, but when I asked if there was anything about his enclosure he didn't like, he stopped and looked at me for a long time. Finally, he grabbed his bars and shook them as hard as he could before turning away. Not the reaction I was hoping for. Still, it was the first time he let on to me that he understood sign language. For me it was a huge step, and I felt exhilarated. But not for long.

Three months later our world turned upside down.

Part 3

THE GORILLA

Never say never.

Karim taught me this. He said it whenever he misjudged something. This thing he misjudged might be good or bad, but more often than not it was bad. It was odd to hear him say it the first time because I did not understand its meaning. After the soldiers in black came I found myself thinking that things could not get any worse. As soon as I had the thought I repeated to myself, *Never say never.*

For many weeks Karim and Dr Sadiq bustled about checking on us in a way they had not done before. There was a tension in their movements, and when they approached I felt agitated and afraid. For the first time since Karim and I had become friends I ignored his visits. This upset him greatly, but I did not want his company. I could smell his fear, and fear is something no animal can abide. If one of us is afraid the others must know why. Our survival depends on it. When I asked Karim why he was afraid he signed to me that I must not worry. He and Dr Sadiq had everything under control. I did not believe him because his actions and his scent spoke otherwise.

As for Dr Sadiq, she annoyed me even more than usual. She was nervous, tense and distracted, and when she looked at me she gave the impression that she was seeing me for the first time. This confused me. All those months of playing music and dancing seemed to have been forgotten. She even had what she called my speakers removed – two small boxes that hung from the ceiling of my enclosure and sang whenever she came to dance with me. Finally, she took away the mirror that Karim had given me, and so, in an effort to discourage further visits, I hooted at her and beat my chest whenever she approached.

After several days she gave up and called for Karim, sending him to do this or that, to inspect this or that, to check on my mood or merely to keep me company. Even so I did not relent but continued to ignore him, watching and waiting as he became more and more anxious. Whatever the reason for his fear, it was not apparent. Zoo's other inmates were also aware of the change, and they became, like me, restless and withdrawn. Each new day brought with it more confusion and shorter tempers until a kind of stealthy panic, unnamed and unseen, spread through Zoo like a virus.

Then they came. They wore black uniforms and they waved black flags and they spoke in loud harsh voices. They carried rifles and guns and they pointed them at the sky and fired as if even the heavens made them angry, but mostly they pointed them at other humans and shouted, and if the humans did not obey they were shot. It was not long before Zoo ceased to be a zoo and became instead a place of killing, and we watched as men and women and children were herded in to fall and bleed and twitch until they were still. After dark their friends and families appeared like foraging rats to drag or carry them away. The next day other humans who refused to obey the soldiers in black took their places on the ground and watered it with their blood until they, too, were carried away.

After their arrival Dr Sadiq wore black robes which covered her from head to foot. Were it not for her scent, her gestures, her voice, it would have been impossible to distinguish her from all the other female humans forced to cover themselves so that only their eyes were visible. Of those females who worked at Zoo before the Black Uniforms arrived, only Dr Sadiq and her assistant Sadiya were allowed to remain. I liked Sadiya. She was young and soft-spoken and smelled of mimosa and sweat. I never understood why one young Black Uniform took against her, but he did. So much so that one day he beat her until she was unable to stand. No one came to help her, not even Dr Sadiq.

At first I did not understand this, but then I realised that everyone was very afraid of the Black Uniforms. So afraid that they could not bring themselves even to rescue one of their own. In that moment I knew that if they came for us we were finished. No one would help us, not Karim, not Dr Sadiq, and certainly not Sadiya. Another beating would kill her.

I need not have worried. After the first she never returned.

***

Enclosure is just a fancy word for a cage, signed Karim.

Explain, I responded.

So began our last conversation. He never spoke with me now except at night long after Zoo's remaining staff had gone home and curfew had emptied the city's streets of all life and sound. On these occasions Karim slept on a bed of straw in my holding cage and we talked long into the night. He told me that only the Black Uniforms were allowed out after dark, and anyone else who got caught rarely had a second chance to repeat their mistake.

Humans say enclosure instead of cage because it makes us feel better, he said. *But in the end an animal in an enclosure is no freer than an animal in a cage.*

I thought about this. It was true, but still I pre-ferred my enclosure to any cage I had ever known. There was a tyre I could swing on and a raised platform on which to sleep, all of it provided by Dr Sadiq. But in the end, whether cage or enclosure, it made little difference. The defining characteristic of each was always the same. I was the sole inhab-itant. As if Karim could read my thoughts, he continued.

You must be terribly lonely, he signed.

I have you, I replied.

It's not the same thing. I'm not a gorilla. I'm not even a chimp. If I was a chimp at least we'd be first cousins. Don't repeat this, he added.

I was amused and surprised by this comment. Did he honestly believe that I would suddenly start sign-ing with another human? But he was already staring into the shadows in front of my enclosure to see if anyone was about. He did this even when Zoo was closed and all of the visitors and staff had gone for the day. After nightfall the city around Zoo grew unnaturally quiet, and even on moonless nights the sky seemed darker than usual.

After the Black Uniforms arrived Karim never again spoke of Ali, and I never saw the phone into which he would speak or jab. When I asked him about it he said it had been confiscated.

Another fancy word, he explained.

What does it mean? I asked.

Stolen, he said.

By whom? I asked.

He didn't answer. He was looking into the distance, a thing humans often do when they are not listening to what has been said.

You can't trust anyone these days, he signed.

Not even Ali?

I don't know any Ali.

We both knew this was a lie.

You can trust me, I said.

He looked at me, a look filled with sadness.

And you can trust me, he replied. *You can trust me until the day I die.*

I did not want him to die, yet I had no answer to this. So I grunted.

Those were the last words we shared. The next morning when Karim returned to clean my cage he ignored me. He entered, swept up my shit, left my daily ration of food and departed without so much as a glance. He did not come at all the next morning or the day after or the day after that. For the first time I had an overwhelming urge to break my silence and speak with Dr Sadiq, but then I thought of what

Karim had said to me when the Black Uniforms first arrived. He said that I must never sign to anyone apart from himself, and only then after dark and when we were absolutely certain we were alone.

Some days later when Zoo closed for the day, Dr Sadiq came to check on me. She signed to me that Karim and the boy called Ali had been thrown from the roof of their building. When she finished, it was all I could do to keep from breaking my silence.

The Vet

When the insurgents arrived they wasted no time in taking control of the city's infrastructure and immediately began a system of rationing. Anyone who attempted to cheat or circumvent it was executed, in public, as gruesomely as possible. Everything was calculated to intimidate us, to make us feel helpless and obedient, and with few exceptions their strategy proved to be a resounding success.

My staff and I did what we could to care for the animals. Each day I rose early with the pre-dawn call to prayer. I washed with a cloth in water I'd used the day before, dressed, and made myself invisible beneath a chador and niqab. Only my eyes and hands were exposed, but soon even this would be forbidden. Then I sat on an old chair in the half-light and read while I waited for a knock at the window. When it sounded I rose and opened the door. An insurgent wearing a black uniform and toting a Kalashnikov was always there to escort me, and we would walk in silence to the zoo. I made a point never to look at him and kept my head lowered whenever we faced one another. As I walked he followed a few paces behind me so that I became in my own mind like an animal being herded to pasture. Or to slaughter. One could never be sure. I kept my eyes lowered. Occasionally, I looked up at the buildings, but there was rarely anyone standing at a window or watching from a balcony. On the street people avoided us. They were only too happy for me to be the focus of this one insurgent, because it meant that for another few seconds, or minutes, or perhaps even a day, they might escape his attention.

THE GORILLA

For weeks after learning of Karim's death I was beset by a sadness I had not known since the death of my family at the hands of poachers. From that moment I came to hate the Black Uniforms even more than the humans around me hated them. My hatred became so intense that it consumed my fear. And there was much about them to fear.

From the first they made their presence known with guns and killing and shouting and gestures that bellowed violence and terror. As for the animals, the abuse we suffered was unrelenting. It took many forms, and the more outlandish it became the more it delighted them. They threw rocks at us, beat and jabbed us with sticks, heaved buckets of slop into our cages, urinated in our water, lit fires and left them to blaze so near to us that the smoke threatened to choke us.

One day a Black Uniform arrived with a gun that spat fire. He pointed it at the llama and within an instant the unsuspecting creature was ablaze. She screamed and tried in vain to escape the flames that devoured her, but there was nowhere to go and no water to extinguish her suffering. Sometimes they fired their guns into our cages so that we jumped in terror and tried to flee, but again there was nowhere to go, and more than a few animals were killed.

After each incident Dr Sadiq went to their alpha male and pleaded with him. Sometimes he listened. Mostly he sent her away without a word. Then one day the taunting stopped, but by this time we were growing too weak to care. Our food and water had been diminishing for weeks. Rationing, they called it. Dr Sadiq said it was calculated starvation. She told their alpha male that if it did not stop we would all die, and it was important for the people's morale that Zoo be allowed to reopen as soon as possible. This time he listened, and for several weeks conditions and rations improved, but it was short-lived. Once again deliveries of food and water became as unpredictable as our enemy.

By the end of the third month many of Zoo's staff were gone. They disappeared steadily over several weeks, and at first I thought nothing of it. Many took with them whatever existing supplies and equipment they could find, though Dr Sadiq took great pains to secure it. One day she called before her the few staff that remained. She demanded to know who among them intended to stay and who wished to leave. They looked at one another with guilty glances, but no one spoke. She said they were free to go, and anyone who wanted to go should leave immediately, but if they chose to stay the stealing must stop. No one left that day, and the stealing continued.

In the end there were no buckets, no mops, no shovels, no brooms, and our faeces piled up until the stench was unbearable. Water was also in short supply, and what little remained was stagnant and sour to the taste. When the last of it ran out a few of us took to drinking our own urine, but not for long. We soon discovered that it only made us feel worse.

***

By the time summer arrived we were slouched in our enclosures barely able to move. Only the flies continued to swarm, oblivious to the sun, dust and stench that rendered the rest of us as inanimate as wood. I lay on the filth-encrusted cement under my platform hoping to avoid the worst of the sun's heat. The air was so heavy and foul I struggled to breathe, the only sound that of thousands of frenzied flies. Each day our food and water, as scarce as it was, arrived later and later. We came to expect this. Even so, I half-listened for the movement of human footsteps, the bumpy wheels of a broken trolley, the swearing of the few disgruntled staff that remained. But there was nothing but buzzing. Buzzing interrupted only by the silence and the heat.

Then I heard her. Her gait had changed since the Black Uniforms arrived. Once it was confident and determined. Now it sagged, sending an uneven rhythm along the path that led to my enclosure. Still, I recognised it immediately. Though I had not seen her for several days, lethargy and lack of food and water dampened my curiosity, so that I did not even raise my head when she approached to stand at my bars. She remained silent, but I felt her presence and knew she was looking at me. Eventually, I opened one eye and turned my head in her direction. To my shock I could see her. By this I mean I could see her face, her hair, her body. The long black robe that once covered her like a shroud was gone, and she was as thin and grey and beaten-looking as an old donkey.

I raised myself onto my side. For a long time we gazed at one another. Then she began to sign. It was broad daylight and I was alarmed by her actions. Karim had warned me many times that if the Black Uniforms discovered I could sign they would carve me into bits. Such heresy would never be allowed. I asked him to explain the word heresy.

When a majority of people believe one thing, but one or some among them believe something different, this different belief is called heresy, he said, *and the persons who believe this heresy are called heretics, and sometimes heretics are beaten and killed because they refuse to stop believing this different thing.*

This all sounded very complicated.

Give me an example, I said.

Well, many people believe that apes and humans are unrelated, and to say that we're cousins is heresy.

But you said yourself that we are cousins. Does this make you a heretic?

Yes, he said. *I suppose it does.*

Is that all? I signed.

Humans have souls.

What are souls? I said.

He thought about this. I could tell he was not sure himself, but he tried to explain.

A soul is the essence of life, and when we die it leaves us.

Where does it go?

That depends, he said.

On what?

On how we behave.

Where does it come from, this soul of yours? I asked.

From Allah.

What is allah?

Who *is Allah,* he signed.

There is no point in asking me, I replied. *I do not know.*

He looked at me, unsure if I was making a joke. I could see this was a matter he took very seriously, and so I remained silent and waited for him to continue.

Allah is all powerful and he creates everything that exists. Sometimes he's called God or Yahweh, but all humans must obey him regardless of what he's called. We must do as he says at all times or we will suffer.

But you are suffering now and you have suffered before, I said. *I have observed that all humans suffer. Does this mean that none of you obey this allahgodyahweh of yours?*

We try, he answered.

Perhaps you should try harder, I said.

As if he could read my thoughts Karim said, *Allah doesn't expect animals to obey him. At least not in the same way.*

Then why do we suffer? I asked.

I don't know, said Karim. *It's a mystery.*

I did not bother to ask what he meant by mystery. I have learned that humans often use this word when they do not know the answer and are unlikely ever to know it. Nor did I tell him that what he was saying made no sense to me. Why would an allahgodyahweh demand the impossible? Why do animals suffer? And if it is this soul that is the essence of life, then all living creatures must have souls – or something very similar.

We never spoke about allahgodyahweh again.

When I looked at Dr Sadiq and she began to sign I remembered Karim's words and thought if anyone saw her – or worse, if I responded – I would be killed and cut into bits, soul or no soul, and so I ignored her. She persisted and I waited, but no one came. At that moment I realised the silence all around us was not silence, but the absence of threat. Where were all the Black Uniforms? I stood, hoisted myself onto my platform and strained to look about. Dr Sadiq called out, and as she did I turned to face her.

The Black Uniforms have left, she signed. *There's no one here but me.*

Still I did not respond. She signed again.

They're not coming back. At least for now.

I thought about this. Why should I believe her? She had not warned us of their arrival. Even Karim had assured us there was nothing to worry about. I was certain he would not have said this unless she had told him to. Then I began to sign, and to this day I cannot explain why.

Was Karim a heretic? Is that why they killed him? I signed.

Dr Sadiq hesitated for the briefest second before raising her hands to reply.

If you ask me, the answer is no, she said. *If you ask the Black Uniforms, they will tell you yes.*

I thought about this.

Was it because of me? I signed.

No.

Because he loved Ali?

Yes.

From the moment I heard of Karim's death I had feared he was murdered because of me. As illogical as it now seems, I was certain that somehow I was at fault. My relief was enormous, though it did not lessen the pain of missing him.

Is this why you stopped dancing? I signed. *Why you took away the music? Because of the Black Uniforms? Because you were afraid they would kill you?*

Yes, she said. *And you. They would have killed you, too.*

If she was telling the truth, then there was more to her than I thought.

Do you have children? I asked.

Not yet, she said, *but one day I hope to very much.*

Will you play music for them and teach them to dance?

Of course, she said.

Good, I replied. *If this makes them heretics at least they will be happy heretics.*

I swung down from my platform and once again lay underneath it in an attempt to hide from the sun's wrath. Then I fell asleep.

The Vet

When I went to see Einstein I had every intention of telling him what was about to happen, but when I faced him I realised it was pointless. He was lying on his side in the shade underneath his platform, the hand with the mangled thumb under his head. I didn't call out to him. I knew he was aware of my presence. Even so, he ignored me.

I waited until he opened one eye and turned his head in my direction. Still he refused to raise himself up, but when I began to sign he stood, swung himself onto his platform and looked about. I knew what he was thinking. He was looking for the insurgents, the 'black uniforms' as he called them. I hooted to get his attention, and when I had it I signed that they were gone, but I saw that he didn't believe me.

Then something happened, something I shall never forget. He began for the first time to sign back. I'm sure if he hadn't been so exhausted, so frightened, he would never have done this.

The first thing he asked me about was Karim. I answered all of his questions as honestly as I could.

He didn't seem surprised by my answers. Not at all. He looked relieved. This confused me at first, but then I understood his relief lay in knowing that Karim's death was not his fault. Once I had assured him of this, he soon lost interest and lowered himself from his platform to the ground where he curled up and fell asleep. Or maybe he was pretending to sleep. I'm not sure.

I stood for a few minutes more, watching and thinking what it was I wanted to tell him. That the sky might soon rain terror? That I couldn't protect him and I couldn't release him because, if I did, where would he go? I had no transport and nowhere to take him, and a gorilla running wild through the streets of the city would hardly go unnoticed. Someone would shoot him, this I knew for certain. At least at the zoo he had some chance of surviving. On the streets he had none.

Of course, we had no way to know for certain if or when the bombs would fall, so I did my best to find out. I remembered a clerk at the post office whose brother had worked with the insurgents as a courier. This had offered the clerk some protection, but now that they were gone and his brother was dead, it would certainly count against him. To be safe I put on my chador, covered my face with a niqab, and made my way as best I could through

225

streets I once knew as well as my own mind, only I no longer seemed to recognise them. Most of the shops were closed and the streets were virtually empty. I had to stop and get my bearings several times. I walked alone, and the men I encountered stared because, unlike me, the women and girls I passed were still escorted. Here and there I saw among them a familiar shape – or a shape that had once been familiar. Often I couldn't be sure. The stress and fear and hunger we'd suffered made us unrecognisable to one another, and when we did see a familiar form, suspicion and a lingering fear of betrayal more often than not made us look away.

Eventually, I found the post office. I entered and went directly to the counter. The clerk standing behind it ate from a small tin that smelled too strongly of the fish it contained. Six months ago he would have thrown it away. When he saw me he put it down, wiped his hands on a rag he took from his pocket and turned to face me. Because we were alone I lowered my niqab, exposing my face. If he was surprised he made no sign. I wasted no time but came right out and asked him what he knew.

Soon, he replied.

But the insurgents have left, I said.

For now.

Will they come back? I asked.

It depends on whether there is anything left to come back to, he said.

But surely everyone knows they've fled, I said. *No one will bomb a city full of civilians knowing the enemy has fled.*

One would hope not, he replied. *But in war nothing is certain.*

About this, at least, he was right.

I thanked him and left. The truth was, any idiot knew it might be soon. Rumours were as rife as food and water were scarce and as persistent as the bed bugs that plagued us nightly. When the insurgents fled the city they left a skeleton rearguard to prevent us from sabotaging their retreat. Some of the more courageous and foolhardy among us did what they could to harass them using Molotov cocktails, booby traps and improvised roadblocks. In response I saw a desperate, trigger-happy group of insurgents empty a small apartment block they suspected of hiding saboteurs. They ordered everyone – men, women and children – to stand in a line with their backs against the building's facade. Parents held their small children in their arms to comfort them while trying in vain to shield the older ones.

Then the insurgents opened fire.

THE GORILLA

It was the big cats who warned us. In the darkness, while the rest of us slept, they fidgeted and paced and snarled and growled, their unease wafting on the air like a foul mist, and soon the rest of us woke. We filled our senses with their fear and to it we added our own until the sound of the approaching hum was drowned by the stomping, trumpeting, cawing, screeching, flapping, roaring, bleating, grunting and howling of our collective panic. How to describe it? It was a symphony of terror.

The first bombs fell to the north. Great metal cylinders that whistled and shrieked as they fell, making a sound at once unfamiliar and full of foreboding. On they came, relentless as locusts, the sound like a hundred trees falling in the forest, and the light from their fires scorched our eyes, and their heat singed our bodies, and in their wake they left a landscape of shattered concrete and carbonised flesh.

Throughout the raid our cries never ceased, and afterwards all was silent. I tried to stand, but I could not. My vision was blurred, and in my mouth I recognised the taste of my own blood. I lay where I was, confused and unaware of the scale of the destruction around me. Slowly, shapes began to take form, sound returned, and I was able to raise myself to a sitting position. As if aware of what awaited us the night lingered, and so for a short time I was spared the full horror of what lay around me. But I could smell and hear enough to know that a catastrophe had befallen us unlike anything we had ever experienced.

I have since seen photos of the bombing of Zoo. As terrible as they are, they cannot convey the sights and sounds and smells that defined the days and weeks that followed. A shard of metal embedded in my jaw caused me much pain. Even so I was among the lucky ones. I survived. Those animals not killed by the bombs and who could not defend themselves from the looters were captured and slaughtered. An ostrich in a cage near to mine was one such victim. She lay on the ground in a puddle of feathers and shredded flesh, too shocked to scream. Even so the looters carried her off to make a meal of what was left, but by then she was too weak to protest. Eventually only the great apes and predators remained. Trapped in our mangled enclosures without food or water, we waited to die.

THE VET

I woke in complete darkness, unable to move. It took me several moments, maybe minutes, to realise that my eyes were open but I couldn't see, that I was alive but I couldn't move. I lay there, too confused at first to panic. I tried to remember what had happened in the moments before I couldn't remember. Then I heard voices. They were as dim as distant memories, but gradually they grew louder until they felt like the precursor to an assault. I became terrified that the insurgents had returned and were searching for me, and that if I made a sound they would find me and execute me. So I lay still, barely breathing, thinking how this took all of my effort, not knowing that I couldn't breathe because I was trapped under a collapsed wall.

More shouting and cursing. I felt a pain in my head and chest. I tried to touch my head, and it was then that I realised my hands were trapped. All of me was trapped. I was buried. Buried alive. *So they haven't even bothered to kill me,* I thought. And then I panicked. I tried to scream, but my throat was dry, and the pain in my chest made my breath retreat into my lungs.

Someone shouted, *I hear her. She's over here.* Others joined in. I thought I recognised the voices of my neighbours. Where was I? I must be in my apartment. My apartment has collapsed. The bombing has started and my building has been destroyed and I am buried beneath it and they are looking for me.

When I woke again I was in hospital. What was left of the hospital. It, too, had been bombed. Soon after I awoke two men and a nurse came to move me. They carried me on a stretcher along a corridor filled with casualties and down a stairwell to a basement which was crammed with countless other wounded. It was like a cross between an abattoir and an attic crammed with all the broken and discarded possessions a family no longer wants but cannot bear to throw away. It was unbearably hot and smelled of dried blood, urine and suffering. I had a sharp pain in my chest and felt like I was suffocating.

The nurse must have noticed because she told me, *You have two fractured ribs and one of your lungs has collapsed. It will take one or two weeks for your lung to heal. Longer for your ribs. You also have a concussion, but you survived.*

I pulled the oxygen mask from my face and told her I had to go to the zoo and see to the animals. I tried to sit up. She pushed me back down onto the stretcher, and I fell immediately to sleep.

The next time I woke I was no longer in the basement. It was morning and I was lying in a courtyard under a covering rigged from torn sheets, plastic and corrugated iron. All around me other women and children lay on makeshift beds, on rugs, trolleys and mats. They chatted and cried and moaned and slept. I still had an oxygen mask, but I noticed that my breathing was easier. I couldn't tell if it was because I was no longer confined in the crowded, windowless basement, or because my lung was healing. I told myself it was the latter and that soon I'd be released.

About midday a nurse passed. I grabbed her arm and pulled the mask from my face.

How long have I been asleep? I asked.

Not long, she told me.

I asked if I still needed the oxygen. She answered that it was up to the doctor. I begged her to summon him and she promised she would. Then she replaced my mask and left. As soon as she was gone I knew she would forget to summon him, and she did.

Next to me was a young girl lying in a hammock. She'd been watching me. At her side, on a plastic crate, sat her mother. I guessed the girl was somewhere between seven and ten years old. I could see that both of her legs were missing, but she never cried or complained. Sometimes she spoke, very quietly, but mostly she slept.

In the afternoon the girl woke, and her mother got up to fetch her some water. That was when she looked at me and said, *Zoo*. I was quite taken aback and racked my memory for any hint of recognition, but we had thousands of children visit the zoo every month before the insurgents arrived, and it was entirely possible she'd attended one of my lectures or noticed me as I did my rounds among the animals. I removed my oxygen mask and asked her which of the zoo's creatures she liked best. She told me the gorilla was her favourite. I said he was mine as well and asked her why she'd chosen him.

Because he has intelligent eyes, she said.

Then she smiled and I smiled back. After that she said that when she grew up she wanted to work with animals.

I'm going to be a vet, she said, *and work at the zoo*.

I told her I was also a vet and how much I loved my work. Again she smiled, a smile that said, *So, just as I thought. I've made the right decision*.

She died that night. Her name was Amal.

***

Looking back it's hard to say which was worse, being kept away from the animals or being with them. I worried about them all the time I was in hospital, but at least

I was not confronted with the reality of what had happened to them during the bombing. This would come. In war there is always what politicians describe as collateral damage. Always. When civilians and animals die we're told it can't be helped. This is the common refrain of war. It can't be helped. As if this makes it all right.

When I was released from hospital I went to stay with a friend who lives near the zoo. She lent me clothes, shared what food she had, and made me feel as welcome as she could. As soon as I arrived I asked to wash myself. Because of my ribs it was difficult for me to move my arms, and so she helped me to undress and bathe. My body was a tapestry of cuts and bruises. She pretended not to notice, but she couldn't help wincing. In order to distract her I asked her if she would accompany me to the zoo. She looked at me as if I'd lost my mind, but she agreed. I couldn't prepare her for what I feared awaited us, so I didn't try. Maybe this was foolish of me. Or selfish. I don't know.

***

The first thing we saw when we arrived were the gates. They'd been blasted from their hinges, bent and twisted like children's straws. Beyond them the mangled remains of the animals' enclosures greeted us like creatures from the underworld straining to rise from the destruction around them. Many had been completely obliterated. Those left intact were so filthy it was hard to distinguish their occupants from the chaos that surrounded them. Many held only carcasses. Those animals that had by some miracle survived were too ill or too shocked to lift their heads.

We wandered about like aliens launched onto a landscape so foreign and repulsive that it was impossible to comprehend the images that confronted us. My friend quickly gave up. She sat on the ground, arms and legs crossed, head bowed, like a toddler who has had enough and refuses to budge. I couldn't blame her. Even though she'd witnessed atrocities inflicted on her fellow humans for months, there's something about seeing animals subjected to such extremes of cruelty that affects us in unexpected ways. It's their innocence, their inability to comprehend the events unfolding around them. In this they are like children. What do we tell them, these innocents who trust and depend on us? How do we explain our actions, actions that are completely and totally avoidable? That we could have chosen to forgo such suffering and slaughter and destruction, but we didn't?

And why? Why didn't you? they ask with their voices and their eyes.

And then our shameful, shameless admission.

We just didn't. That's all there is to it. We just didn't.

THE CAPTAIN

The glue. That was our job description. Our mission? To reinforce the link between the military and a future civilian government. Hell, you could've fooled me. I thought our job was to get the lights on, the water running, reinstate the food distribution networks, set up a functioning justice system, and in our spare time win the hearts and minds of the local population. In our spare time. We didn't have enough spare time to wipe our butts or the paper to do it with. By we I mean my buddies and me assigned to the Civil Affairs Brigade.

My expertise is archeology, so I was in charge of helping the locals restore their cultural heritage. Some dedicated museum staff had done their best to protect their treasures, stashing them away and sandbagging what they couldn't move. But standing up to the insurgents was like trying to swim upstream in a flood. If you were fool enough to try you were beaten, and if that didn't persuade you, you were shot. Even after we arrived things hardly improved. Looting was rampant, and it took time before we realised the extent of what was happening. By the time we did, much of what was left had been stolen and sold on the black market.

One day I was sitting in my office at HQ dealing with some admin crap and shooting the breeze with a private security dude I'd recently met. He and his gung-ho gun-for-hire buddies had stumbled into the bar where me and my pals from Civil Affairs hung out in the evenings after work with some guys from Special Ops. This ex-soldier turned mercenary turned PMC – private military contractor – was built like a wall, and his buddies were the four pillars. As the saying goes, they worked hard and they played hard, and you didn't want to get in their way when they were doing either one.

So like I said, I was sitting at my desk moaning to him about the latest hiccup in communications with the interim director of the National Archeological Museum when he turned his head and hooked his thumb toward the open door on my left. Standing there was a woman. Early thirties, curly brown hair, very very thin. Almost haggard, I'd say, though I could tell that with some meat on her bones, a good wash and some rest she'd be a real looker. Was a real looker. Before the war. Now she looked like the rest of the locals. Worn and dog-tired. She had some scratching and bruising on her face and neck and her arm was in a sling, and when she moved you could tell she was in pain. But she had something else that made you pay attention. I'd call it determination. You could tell right away she was a force to be reckoned with.

So I said, *Come in,* but she was already across the threshold and standing in front of my desk.

She said, *Captain Conran? My name is Dr Sadiq, and I'm the head vet at the city's zoo.*

What can I do for you? I said, and waited for her to continue. Didn't take her long.

I need your help, she said.

And what makes you think I can help you? I replied.

Well, she said, *if you can't then nobody can, because I've been told that you're the man who gets things done.*

My buddy shot me a look and I said, *Who told you that?*

She smiled like she'd been waiting for me to ask this, and I could tell right then that I'd taken the bait.

A mutual friend, she said, and she mentioned the name of a conservationist pal of mine I'd met some years ago on safari.

As soon as I heard his name I thought, *Oh no, here we go,* because I knew what was coming next, and it wasn't like I didn't have enough on my plate. Just then my gun-for-hire buddy got up, and I could tell by the look on his face that he knew what was coming too, and wanted to hightail it out of there before she corralled him as well.

Hey, where're you going? I said.

Without missing a beat he answered, *Only road from here to the zoo is Hell's Highway,* and made to leave.

I didn't want him to go, so I said, *Hang on, buddy. We won't be long.*

Naw, mate, you got this, he said.

Then he winked at the doctor. *Enjoy the ride,* he said, and he left.

I'd heard about the zoo. It wasn't the only place that got hit that wasn't supposed to. In war shit happens. People and places and things get bombed that have no business being bombed, and if anybody asks why, a lot of excuses get bandied about. But in the end the answer is always the same. Shit happens.

So there we were. Alone and looking at one another and waiting to see who was going to make the next move. And it was then she fixed her eyes on me and I noticed them, really noticed them. Like big chocolate puddings, dark and delicious and irresistible, and I had the feeling that if I didn't shift my gaze my will would no longer be my own.

I figured she knew this because she smiled and, trust me, she's got a killer smile, and said, *What does your friend do?*

He's with a private security outfit, I said. *His name is Bowden, but everybody calls him Bowzer.*

What I didn't tell her is that he's got like fourteen dogs. Rescues and strays. He and his wife can't have kids so they adopt dogs. But like I said, I didn't tell her any of this. Not then.

She nodded and said, *Right now I'm free, and I'd like to show you around the zoo myself.*

Now I knew she was determined, but I wasn't expecting this, and while I was looking at her I thought, *Be careful, pal, you've been down this road before.* But she flashed that killer smile again like she'd just read my mind, and, well, that was pretty much that.

I let the staff sergeant know where I was going and told him to organize a vehicle, a driver and an armored escort. By the time we arrived in front of the building a Humvee, driver and two armed soldiers were waiting. They informed us that our escort would be arriving shortly.

Just then a vet technician I was friendly with passed by, and when she asked where I was going I said, *The zoo. Want to join us?*

She looked up at the sky and said, *Nice day for it. Why not?*

So then we were six. As we climbed into the vehicle another Humvee pulled up with my buddy, Bowzer, and his four mates. Rambos to a man. The difference was they knew this was no movie and you only got one chance to get it right. Soon as I saw him he caught my eye and immediately gave me a crooked smile and shook his head as if to say, *One born every minute*. Sucker, he meant, only this time he was referring to himself.

Like I said, I'd heard stories. Vague reports about some kind of zoo. Word was it once held six hundred and fifty animals – give or take. No one knew how many, if any, were left. None of us had ever been there to check it out. With everything else we had on our plates it wasn't exactly a high priority.

On the way over Dr Sadiq gave us some background. What the zoo was like before the insurgents arrived, what kind of animals they had, how many visitors and so on. Basic stats. She didn't describe its current status. Just said, *It's better if you see it for yourself.*

If I've heard this line once during my tours I've heard it a hundred times. Translation: you're not going to believe it, words cannot describe, it's unspeakable, who could do such a thing, etc., etc. In other words, business as usual.

There was only one incident on the way over. I heard a shot. Our radio crackled to life and the word 'Sniper' rang out. Immediately our driver gunned it. I glanced round. Bowzer and his buddies were right behind us, their weapons pointing up and out of their windows, their gunner in his turret firing in the direction of the shot, and as I faced forward a bullet penetrated our roof causing our driver to swerve. When he regained control I looked over at the doc. She was staring straight ahead, cool as ice, and I thought to myself, *What's a sniper or two compared to what she's seen and been through.*

It took us about twenty minutes to get to the zoo and two hours to tour what was left of it. They were, without a doubt, among the worst and, well, I guess I'd say most heartbreaking hours of my life, and ones I hope never to repeat.

So in answer to my initial question, *What can I do for you?* turns out that there was plenty I could do, and the good doc wasted no time in getting me started. At our first meeting I was all set to agree to help her just to be polite. And yeah, I liked her. But the truth is, I was thinking she'd say her piece and I'd make some excuse and she'd go away and then I could buy some time, or better yet, find somebody else to do it, whatever *it* was. Didn't quite turn out that way, no small thanks to my buddy, Bowzer.

And that's how it began. My new mission to save the zoo. Turns out it wasn't my only mission. My God, if you'd told me then what I was in for I would've laughed and said you were crazy as a sack full of ferrets.

THE GORILLA

When Dr Sadiq told me she was bringing them I thought she had gone mad. She looked mad. After the bombing several weeks passed before she appeared again. To be honest I thought she was dead, because if she was not dead I knew she would have come. When finally she did, I understood. She moved slowly, hesitating like one who is lost, and when I asked what had happened she looked at me and bared her teeth in what humans call a smile.

I'm going to bring some soldiers, she signed.

I was too shocked to sign a reply. I thought more soldiers was the very last thing we needed unless it was to finish off the few of us that remained. And in spite of everything, there *were* still a few of us.

There was bear, who padded back and forth in his cage hour after hour, day after day, until the pads on his feet were raw. When I called out to him he ignored me. Maybe he was too far gone to hear me.

There were monkeys released to an uncertain freedom after the bombers shattered their cages and looters ransacked what remained. They took refuge in the trees and on the roofs in and around Zoo, looking for any opportunity to poach a bit of food unearthed by gangs that scavenged unchecked day and night. When they found it they seldom shared, even among their own, and so I learned that we are not so unlike humans in this.

Circling in the skies above them and resting in the naked trees left unclaimed by the monkeys, birds cawed and squawked, all ex-inmates of Zoo, and now that they were free they had nowhere to go.

There was dog and lion. They lived together. Both were starving, and yet lion refused to eat dog, though she could have killed him with one swipe of her claws. They had grown up together, bonded, and they would die together. And Bengal tiger, a rare and beautiful creature. Having survived the bombs he later relieved a soldier of his arm when, in an attempt to taunt him, the fool reached through the bars of his enclosure. While the soldier bled to death his companion shot tiger for his trouble.

Pelican was tied by her leg to an iron post on the edge of a filthy pond too fetid to drink, but she drank because there was nothing else. Her feathers were mottled with dust, and she had no shade and no food. How she escaped the looters' relentless search for a meal I never understood.

Camel's fur was so tangled and matted with faeces and mud that it resembled the coat of an armadillo. We had one of those, too, but she ended up on a spit. Her captors came in the night and prepared their fire on a patch of dirt directly in front of her enclosure. I could smell her as she roasted.

Badger went the same way. When the bombing started he burrowed through the rock-hard dirt of his enclosure and managed to hide himself for a week or two until, driven to desperation by thirst, he came out in search of water. He found it, but when he did it was already beginning to boil.

And lastly, our two cheetahs. Listless as cement they lay in their cage and waited while their tongues swelled and cracked, their muscles withered and their fur, once glossy and sleek, became as dull and patchy as a moth-eaten rug. They were twins, orphaned by a human who had killed their mother, mounted her head on the wall of his study, and made a rug of her hide to give to his wife. Afterwards, cheetah and her sister were found by farmers and sold to Zoo to live out their days in captivity as wondrous examples of their kind.

Now more soldiers were coming, soldiers in sand-coloured uniforms, and in that moment I thought I had been right to refuse Karim. Once, near the end, he had pleaded with me to trust Dr Sadiq, and in a moment of desperation I had. But he was wrong. She could not be trusted. Or perhaps the trauma had been too much for her, and now she and these new soldiers intended to finish us off.

I watched them as they did their rounds: Dr Sadiq, an army captain, a female soldier, and the men that hovered round them bearing weapons, ready to raise them in anger or simply because they were humans and could kill us on a whim. I watched them because I was afraid of what would happen when they came to me, and because I had nothing else to do. Boredom was a factor of our lives, and this did not change. It was our one constant.

As Dr Sadiq approached I tried to read in her eyes her intentions. She did not bare her teeth as she approached, but whether or not she smiled was of no concern. I wanted only to see if she would raise her hands to sign. I dreaded this more than anything.

This is our silverback. He's nearly fully grown now, she said.

Her companions watched me. Sized me up, as you humans say. The mirror that Karim had given me was long gone, so I had no opportunity to see for myself the state I was in. But I could guess, and my guesses were confirmed by the looks on their faces as the female soldier took notes.

Did all of his injuries happen during the bombing? asked the captain.

Just the jaw, replied Dr Sadiq, *but it's healing well. The scars on his back and the mutilated thumb happened before he arrived.*

Could be worse, said the captain.

Yes, said Dr Sadiq. *He could be dead.*

The captain glanced at her.

What's his name?

Einstein.

I watched Dr Sadiq even more closely now.

Interesting choice, he said.

He has intelligent eyes, she replied.

That was all she said before turning away from the captain to look at me, and when she did there was the slightest hint of a wink. I had learned from Karim what this gesture means, and in that moment when the doctor winked my relief was so great that, in spite of myself, I let out a grunt.

Once Karim tried to teach me to wink. In truth, I think he was making fun of me. When I was unable to master it he shook his head and said, *You can sign, but you can't wink.* It was of little interest to me, for at the time I did not intend to reveal to anyone that I was capable of either, and I told him so. When Dr Sadiq winked at me I was relieved, but at the same time I wondered just how much

Karim had told her. I already suspected it was far too much.

Dr Sadiq and her companions lingered for several minutes. If I had had the strength to retreat to the rear of my enclosure, I would have. As it was, I quickly lost interest, being certain that, for the moment at least, my secret was safe. It was only when Dr Sadiq and the others moved off and the captain remained that I began to worry. He watched me as if trying to make up his mind. Then he spoke.

Intelligent eyes, eh, buddy? Yeah, I suppose you do. So tell me, what's going on behind those eyes? Care to share with me?

I remained impassive and silent.

Well, maybe another time. Whaddaya say, buddy?

Had I chosen to answer him I would have said, *Mind your own business and leave me in peace.* But instead I turned away and closed my eyes.

THE VET

A terrible thing happened. Terrible. And it was all my fault. To this day I ask myself how I could have been so stupid, so careless, as if an answer will come that absolves my guilt or lessens my shame. But I know it's futile. For such moments of profound stupidity there's no absolution. They stand in our memory like monuments to our hubris reminding us that we're not gods, but only fools.

A week or so after the captain's initial visit he and I were touring the zoo with our new director. The previous director fled with his family as soon as the insurgents' arrival seemed inevitable. My family also begged me to leave, but I couldn't. I couldn't leave the animals and I couldn't protect them, but I knew I had to try.

I remember the day because there was a light wind. It stirred the dust that covered everything like a fine coating of flour, but we welcomed it. It dispersed the stench and afforded us some relief from the heat. Our new director had no experience of running a zoo, but in our favour he seemed genuinely concerned

249

by the plight of the animals. More importantly, he understood the value of the zoo as a means of boosting the people's spirits. He also knew the captain. They'd met on several occasions, and they talked and laughed easily together. Maybe it was because of this – because I felt relaxed – that I forgot myself.

Among our animals Einstein was invariably the one who commanded the most attention. Was it his human-like qualities? His intensely intelligent eyes? The sheer splendour of his size and physique, though he was hardly in peak form? Or merely his reputation as the angry ape? Whatever it was, when people saw Einstein they lingered as if hoping to enter into conversation with him. Many tried without even realising it. It was remarkable really, because no one who was left knew of his special talent apart from me.

So there we were – the three of us. Our new director asked many questions, all the while keeping his eyes on Einstein. I thought Einstein would ignore us as soon as we approached, but he seemed to take a reciprocal interest in our new director. Of course, this was not lost on our director. It flattered him and piqued his curiosity even more. I tried to answer his questions as best I could. Where and when did we acquire Einstein? How old was he? When would his wounds heal? He only half-listened to my answers as if he was waiting for Einstein to interject at any moment. For his part Einstein sat and watched in silence. He wasn't about to be drawn in.

Then the director turned his attention to the captain. They discussed this and that: funding, practical logistics, supplies, staff. Finally, the director said that his intention was to get the zoo up and running and open to the public as soon as possible. The captain agreed wholeheartedly, glancing at me briefly for confirmation. This was music to my ears, and I could hardly contain my excitement. As they turned to go I remained, explaining that I would join them shortly. I watched as they headed back to our administration building. After the bombing its east- and south-facing walls and a good part of its roof had been patched with corrugated metal sheets making it more like a microwave in summer than an office, but it was all we had.

I don't know what made me do it. I think it was the joy I felt at knowing that our new director was in agreement with the captain and me, and that we would enjoy his full support. I watched as they headed back to our admin building and waited until they were safely out of sight. When I was certain they wouldn't turn back I signed to Einstein, telling him briefly what had transpired. I wanted him to know that at last there was hope, a real chance we would save the zoo and, with luck, improve it considerably over what it had been. He watched me, and when I was finished he raised his hands and began to sign.

How do you know?

The captain is a man of his word, I said.

Do you trust him?

Yes, I trust him, I said.

But he is a soldier.

Yes, I said. *But not all soldiers are alike. Some are good and some are bad, just like everyone else.*

For the first time in months I felt anxiety fall from my shoulders like a discarded chador. I was so caught up in my optimism and so intent on reassuring him that as I signed I failed to notice the look of alarm that appeared on his face. He rushed to the back of his enclosure where he began to jump up and down and hoot and slap his hands on the floor until finally he roared and charged at the spot where I stood. It was so sudden and unexpected a display of aggression that I stumbled and fell backwards, straight into the captain's arms. He gave me a moment to collect myself, all the while looking at me with a mixture of reproval and wonder. Then he spoke.

Well, this complicates things, doesn't it?

I couldn't answer. I looked beyond him to the director who stood a few metres behind him, and I could see by his expression that he, too, had been watching us. Then the captain shifted his gaze to Einstein.

A signing ape. I'll be damned. So this is your secret, eh, buddy?

The Captain

Once that cat was out of the bag there was no way to coax it back in. Within forty-eight hours everybody that mattered knew the zoo had a signing gorilla and one that was, by all appearances, more than a little fluent. If it had been just me that'd witnessed it, well, maybe – I'm not saying definitely – but maybe we could have kept it between us. Now it was out of the question. Doc Sadie – that quickly became her new handle courtesy of Bowzer – knew this even as she pleaded with me to have a word with our new director, and if that didn't work to put the entire pressure of the coalition to bear. But I was quick to point out that the coalition, particularly the army, would be just as interested in a signing ape as our new director, and possibly a great deal more interested.

That same afternoon our director called a meeting. Everybody connected to the zoo that mattered was invited. The gist of it was whether to keep the gorilla or sell him. The director argued that if he sold Einstein he could probably get enough to fund a whole raft of improvements and supplies as well as hire staff, especially if he sold him to a private buyer. On the other hand, if he kept him, Einstein would be the biggest draw of any zoo anywhere, and lend a helluva lot of prestige as well.

The committee swung back and forth, but there was no question as to which side of the fence the doc sat on. She wanted to keep Einstein at all costs, arguing that his presence alone would guarantee funding for the zoo and plenty of it. I had to agree with her on this, but it went deeper than that. For her to betray a trust was the worst thing she could possibly do, and the shame and guilt she felt for revealing Einstein's special talent clouded her judgement. She launched into a tirade about how nobody should know that the gorilla could sign because it was bound to end in tears. But it was too late for that, and even as she pleaded she knew it was hopeless.

After our meeting she couldn't bring herself to visit him. It took all my powers of persuasion to convince her that the only way to make amends was to confront her mistake head-on. This was easier said than done. Several days passed before she approached Einstein again, and when she did he ignored her. This was predictable and she knew it. After that she waited another day or two. In the interim he developed some sort of stomach virus. No surprise there given the conditions he'd been living in. When finally she stood again at the bars of his cage he grabbed a great handful of runny excrement and threw it at her. To her credit she didn't bat an eye, even when it hit her square in the chest and ran down the front of her shirt like puréed spinach. Anybody else would've called it a day, but not the doc. She went back again the next day and every day after that for a week, and each time she visited him he chucked at her whatever came to hand. She soon learned to duck and dive, but she never gave up. Then one day the director called her to his office and told her that he'd agreed to sell Einstein to a private buyer and use the proceeds to fund some new acquisitions. As soon as he had government approval, the deal would be sealed.

The buyer was a billionaire who'd made his fortune by acquiring certain of his country's resources for a song and then selling portions of them off to the highest bidders. In other words, money was no object. I asked the doc what he intended to do with Einstein once he got him. She said he likely planned to house him in his private menagerie so he could show him off to his wife and mistress, friends and guests, and display him like a party trick at his kids' birthdays. The mere thought of it sent her into such a deep depression that for days afterwards she could barely speak. She even joked to me privately that she'd rather see Einstein dead than sold to a state-sanctioned criminal, only I sensed that maybe she wasn't joking. It was this that got me to thinking of ways I might help her – and him.

The obvious solution was to have the army appropriate Einstein. And just as I'd predicted, they were more than a little keen to get their hands on him. They'd taken the whole matter of the signing ape so seriously they'd assigned a special guard to watch him 24/7, headed, no less, by my buddy, Bowzer. Some idiot in Intel even suggested debriefing Einstein about the insurgents in order to find out if he could add anything to what they already knew. One in every bunch, I guess.

One evening me, Bowzer, and some of the guys were sharing a beer and shooting the breeze. Bowzer was spouting off about who'd stolen his team's private stash of toilet paper. All the guys were razzing him about it and jokes were flying when suddenly he went dead quiet. The others were still laughing, but I noticed right away that his mood had changed and he was no longer listening to a word they said. I asked him what was on his mind, and after a moment he looked up and said two words.

United Nations.

Yeah, I said, *what about it?*

I've got an idea.

So I gathered. Want to tell me about it?

You and I are both keen on the fluffy shit, right?

The fluffy shit?

You know, save the animals, save the planet, save the ...

Sure, I said, cutting him off. I was beginning to worry where this was leading. *Why?*

Why? Who better to make a pitch for animals than an animal?

What the hell are you getting at? I said. *And anyway, what does any of it have to do with the UN?*

As I watched him he leaned in and smiled like a small boy about to reveal a naughty secret.

Ambassador, he replied.

It took me a moment to register the word, and when I did I repeated it like an alien trying to learn English.

Ambassador?

Yeah, goodwill ambassador for the IUCN.

The what?

International Union for the Conservation of Nature.

Of course, I said.

Well?

Have you lost your mind? Anyway, as far as I know, the IUCN is not a member of the United Nations.

True, he answered. *But they have observer and con-sultative status which means they have influence. They're connected.*

By now the laughter had died down and the others were starting to listen as he proceeded to tell me his idea in its entirety. When he was finished I sat like a deaf mute waiting for a punchline that never came.

You gotta admit, mate, it's bloody brilliant, he said.

Yeah, if you're certifiably insane, I replied.

I glanced at the others, but they, like me, were speechless as goldfish.

Ah, c'mon, mate, he said, *use your imagination.*

Seriously, I replied, *I think somebody's spiked your drink.*

Look, mate. If chimps can be astronauts, why can't gorillas be goodwill ambassadors?

Finally, one of his buddies chimed in.

That was one chimp, and he was hardly in command of the bloody spacecraft, he said.

That's not the point, said Bowzer.

That's entirely the point, his mate added, but this did nothing to dampen Bowzer's enthusiasm.

Try thinking outside the box, he said. *This gorilla can sign. He has a vocabulary. An extensive vocabulary.*

Doesn't make him bloody Shakespeare now, does it? said another.

Crikey, do I have to spell it out for you sheilas? he said. *He can communicate with animals and humans. He can actually tell us exactly what they think, what they feel, what they're capable of. Think what this means.*

Then he turned to me.

Well, mate? Speak up. Are you gonna ride shotgun with me on this one, or am I going it alone?

THE GORILLA

That was how what came to be known as The Great Ape-escape began. Dr Sadiq and the captain came to see me and to explain.

The plan is simple, they said, *a case of bait-and-switch*.

Simply put, the buyer would think he was getting me, but, in fact, he would be getting nothing more than an empty crate. For this ploy to be successful it was obvious to me that he must not discover he had been duped until it was too late to do anything about it. This was the part that worried me most.

The first thing the buyer will do is examine the crate, and when he does he will discover he has been cheated, I signed.

Dr Sadiq turned to the captain and translated. When she was finished he smiled and said, *One smart cookie, aren't we?*

I had no idea what a cookie was or what it had to do with the subject at hand, but secretly I was beginning to worry that he was losing his grip.

We won't switch them until after he's checked, he said.

Where will you make the switch? I signed.

This time when they looked at each other they hesitated, and immediately I sensed that they were hiding something from me.

At the airport, he said. *We'll make the switch at the airport.*

I watched them, and as I did Dr Sadiq looked away. I waited for several breaths before continuing.

The buyer will want proof that I can sign, I said.

We hope you'll give him a demonstration, she signed. *Is this what you want?*

It would help, she said, *to put his mind at ease.*

What will happen to me afterwards? I signed. *Where will I go?*

Again they exchanged a look. Then the captain answered.

This is where it gets complicated, he said.

I have noticed that when humans have one crazy idea it almost always leads to another, and this was no exception. They did not answer my question. Instead, they bared their teeth in an attempt, I suppose, to put me at ease, but I noticed right away that their smiles were different from others they had used before. They were forced. I was reminded of a chimp I once observed preparing to steal his companion's food. He grinned, showing only his bottom teeth, a signal intended to put his companion at ease. Then he distracted him, and in the split second that his companion's attention was elsewhere, grabbed his food and ran off.

I repeated my question. Again Dr Sadiq translated and the captain answered.

Best leave this to us, he said.

The Vet

I walked the captain back across the zoo's main square to where his Humvee was parked under what had once been the shade of a palm tree. Its trunk was charred and the crown blown clear, reminding me of a spent Roman candle. As we walked neither of us said a word.

In the Humvee's front seat sat a soldier smoking a cigarette. Several other soldiers stood nearby, their rifles slung round their necks, and just beyond them was parked another Humvee, this one with a mounted gun turret. As we approached I could hear a stream of military jargon crackling from a radio. When the captain's driver caught sight of us, he flicked his cigarette onto the stones of the square and started his engine.

We said our goodbyes, and I waited until the captain and his escort were through the gates and travelling down Hell's Highway in a straight line from the zoo to what was then the coalition's headquarters. As I watched I held my breath. Both sides of the four-lane highway were heavily barricaded.

Even so there was an element of Russian roulette to any trip along this road, and I half-expected the captain and his vehicle to evaporate in an IED fireball at any moment. Then I turned and walked back to Einstein.

He watched me as I approached. As soon as I reached the bars of his cage he began to sign. There was no need for caution now. Thanks to me, everyone knew his secret.

I am afraid, he said.

I understand. It's risky.

And you? Are you afraid?

I didn't want to lie to him.

Yes, I said, *a little.*

We watched each other in silence, each of us trying to read the other's mind.

And afterwards? he said. *What then?*

I didn't have an answer, or rather I didn't want to answer. He sensed this and signed again.

Tell me. What then?

I looked at him. I was of two minds whether to tell him or not. I didn't want to get his hopes up or, more likely, frighten him off altogether. As briefly as I could I outlined our plan, or rather, Bowzer's plan. I tried my best to keep it simple and to sound positive, yet even as I was listening to myself I couldn't help but wonder if we'd all gone mad. The idea of a gorilla being a goodwill ambassador for the IUCN was an outrageous notion and one that would be almost impossible to sell, but if it worked it had the potential to be a global game changer. More importantly, it was his best shot at escaping the fate that otherwise awaited him.

When I'd finished he shifted his weight, emitting a slight grunt. If gorillas could roll their eyes I'm sure he would have.

Was this your idea? he signed.

No, I said.

Good, he replied.

I decided to take this as a compliment.

Will it take long? he signed.

An amount of time, yes.

How long?

First, we have to train you, I said. *Afterwards, as long as you like. As long as is necessary.*

And if I refuse?

I looked away. I hated what I was about to tell him, but I had no choice. Bowzer's idea was his best shot at escaping this hell – and worse.

Nobody can force you. But if you don't do as we ask you'll be sold to a rich oligarch who will put you in a cage and parade you as a plaything to amuse his spoiled children and idle wife and fat colleagues until the day you die – or until he tires of you. Whichever comes first.

He looked at me. In all the time we'd spent together I'd never been so brutally frank.

And when I am finished, when I have done what you ask of me, what then?

I hadn't given much thought to this, to what would happen to him once his mission was completed. The realisation left me feeling deeply ashamed.

That's up to you, I said.

I want to go home.

Home?

To the mountains where I was born.

I don't know why this hadn't occurred to me. It was so obvious I had to stop myself from looking surprised.

Of course. This can be arranged.

Then I will do it, he signed.

I telephoned the captain and told him about our conversation. Now it remained to convince the individuals who could make it happen. This would be hard, maybe even impossible, but it was a gamble we had to take.

We owed it to him. *I* owed it to him.

THE CAPTAIN

We set to work immediately, contacting anyone we knew who could help.

First person I found was an old high-school buddy of mine, a sergeant in the engineer corps. I was on my second tour of duty, he on his first. I asked him if he knew where I could get a container big enough to hold and transport a very large primate. He knew better than to ask me why and I didn't tell him, but he had a pretty good idea. Within a day he managed to scrounge a wooden crate and immediately went to work modifying and reinforcing it.

Be careful, he said.

Aren't I always, I answered.

I knew exactly what he was referring to. In our junior year of high school I started up with a senior, a gorgeous gal who happened to be in my sister's class. She also happened to be a cheerleader and the girlfriend of the senior captain of the football team. My pal warned me, but like young men everywhere, when it came to love and lust, I took no notice. Her boyfriend found out I was wooing her and beat the bejeezus out of me. Sure as hell didn't do much for my looks, but didn't dampen my ardour either.

So now I had a crate, but I also needed a truck, hay to use as bedding, tranquilisers, a medical kit, food and water. All this doesn't sound like much, but there was virtually nothing left after the insurgents fled, and what we were able to scrounge was constantly being 'requisitioned' by a seemingly endless stream of looters. There were permits and shipping documents to be arranged. I also needed someone to travel with Einstein, ideally a qualified vet, and immediately Doc Sadie volunteered. I told her it was too dangerous. If she got caught I might not be able to protect her. But she insisted. More than insisted. She demanded, quick to point out that she knew Einstein better than anyone. I couldn't argue with this and I didn't try, mostly because there was nobody else.

Bowzer contacted his mate in conservation. As luck would have it, he put us in touch with the head honcho at the org we needed help from most – a woman who was considered a bit of a renegade in her own right. She was also someone who was known for getting things done even if her methods were a little unorthodox. From our POV she was a perfect fit. When we told her about Einstein and our plan to rescue him, she laughed out loud, calling us crazy cowboys. But she didn't dismiss it – or us. Quite the opposite. She considered our mission a personal challenge and one she was determined would succeed. All music to our ears, but all of this would take time, and time was in short supply. Einstein's buyer wanted to move immediately.

The legalities, or rather illegalities, of what we were suggesting were clear. We were going to kidnap a gorilla that didn't belong to us. Worse, he belonged to the very country we were supposed to be helping, a country that our own government had pledged to support. In short, we were proposing to break all the rules and protocols for which we'd been trained and were expected to uphold. Because of this we had to keep the circle of those in the know as tight as possible. Everyone involved was a potential leak, but we needed help, and we needed to get Einstein out of the country as quickly as possible.

THE GORILLA

When Dr Sadiq left I sat for some time contemplating what she had said. I did not ask for any more details. To be honest I did not want to know, having little hope it would succeed.

I told my fellow creatures of the plan – the few that still remained – and afterwards whenever I caught them observing me they would look away, afraid I might read in their expressions the certainty of my own impending doom.

The next day Dr Sadiq returned with Bowzer and his band of former mercenaries. Ironically, they had been sent to protect me from kidnappers, for once it was out that I could sign and communicate with humans a price was put on my head. As they chatted I thought about the term 'mercenary', and in an attempt to alleviate my boredom I asked Bowzer what it meant. Dr Sadiq translated while he explained that mercenaries are humans who fight and kill for other humans unable or unwilling to fight for themselves.

Humans who are threatened? I signed.

Well, yes, mostly, he said.

Were you also threatened? I signed.

No, he replied, *not directly.*

Were your children threatened?

No.

Were you part of the same troop as the humans who were threatened?

No.

Did you share territory then?

He shook his head.

I do not understand, I said. *Why did you fight for these other humans? Did you receive female humans with whom you could mate?*

He laughed. *Not likely,* he said.

Then why?

Strewth, mate. I got paid, all right?

Paid?

Money, he said. *It's a ... a form of barter made of paper or—*

I know what money is, I signed. *Humans exchange it for something of practical value and in return give something which has no practical value.*

Dr Sadiq laughed. Then she translated.

You've got a point, mate, he said.

I did not ask any more questions, though I found it impossible to understand why any human would risk his life for so little. Maybe humans were more stupid than I thought, a notion I found hard to believe and one that did little to reassure me.

Then Dr Sadiq left us alone. *To have a chat,* she said, *primate to primate.*

I liked Bowzer. He was relaxed and did not make me feel threatened. He had taken the time to learn a bit of sign language, and I could see he was keen to communicate with me, so I humoured him. While we signed his team stood around us.

Bowzer told me how he and his wife rescued dogs, and from this he had come to understand and respect animals in ways he had never done before. He said he was ashamed of the way many humans treated us. I wanted to say to him that he should be ashamed, that all humans should be ashamed, but I did not. I knew that my life in large part rested in his hands, and I had no wish to antagonise him. But it was also true that the better I got to know him the more I liked him. He said that when the time came I must trust him. If I did not, the plan would not succeed. I understood that this was probably true and said I would try. He told me that I must also trust his men. Again, I said I would try, and he nodded.

When will it happen? I signed.

He glanced at his team.

Soon, he said.

THE MERCENARY

Me and my mates stood aside while the zoo's director introduced the buyer to his prize. Mother of God, he was as unsavoury a mongrel as ever I've laid eyes on, and no amount of bling and designer clobber could hide that fact. *Flash as a rat with gold teeth* as my dad would have said.

I watched as he sized Einstein up while Doc Sadie stood by to give a demonstration of his communication skills. Unbeknown to her, my hairy friend and I had had a few private sessions before the buyer showed up in which I'd schooled him in one or two of my favourite gestures. When it came to showtime I suggested Doc ask our celebrity what he made of his new owner. She obliged, and immediately Einstein stretched out his right hand, made a fist, and began to pump it up and down in a universal gesture that speaks for itself. I thought the zoo's director would have a stroke. As it was, me and my mates played dumb as dirt. I snuck a look at the captain, and as soon as our eyes met he shook his head and looked away. Didn't fool anybody, least of all me. The

274

director made a show of pretending it was all a joke and hustled the buyer out of there as fast as he could.

When they'd all left I went over the plan. It was as much for me as it was for Einstein. It's not easy trying to smuggle a whacking great gorilla out of a war zone, and don't let anyone tell you differently. But we had no choice. It was that or watch the poor bugger condemned to kiddie-party hell for the rest of his life. Couldn't stand by and see that happen. And as he was set to be moved the following morning, there was no time to waste. The doc stayed behind to translate.

We'll arrive here tomorrow at zero six hundred, I said. *Me and the lads'll have a truck and escort ready and waiting, and the doc and the captain'll be here to oversee your loading along with the zoo's director and the buyer's vet. Once you're loaded we'll head for the airport. At the airport we'll make the switch. By the time the buyer discovers he's been duped you'll be airborne and on your way, and when you land you'll be in Switzerland.*

He listened carefully. When I was done he lost no time in asking questions. Doc Sadie translated.

What is a jet? he signed.

A big silver metal bird that flies, I said.

What is Switzerland?

Not what. Where. In the mountains. You'll like it.

How do you know?

275

He had me there. But this was no time to quibble.

Because anywhere's better than this stinking hellhole. And you'll have refugee status and diplomatic immunity, which means you'll be safe.

This shut his gob, at least for the time being. He watched as I repeated the plan, and again Doc Sadie translated. It was as much for me as it was for him. Truth is, I was nervous. It's one thing riding shotgun for army brass and corporate and political bigwigs, but smuggling a signing gorilla in order to steal him from a billionaire oligarch with connections at the highest levels of government was another. Not to mention kidnapping him right from under the nose of the coalition. One thing was for certain, the whole thing was an international incident in the making.

And Dr Sadiq? Will she accompany me?

I looked at the doc.

Yes, she signed, *every step of the way.*

He grunted. As he watched me I had the impression he was trying to make up his mind, and when he signed his gestures were slow and deliberate.

And you? he said.

What do you mean?

What will happen to you and the captain?

Don't worry about us, I said. *We'll be fine.*

You will be risking much for me.

I looked at him. Here was a creature who'd been imprisoned and abused by humans his entire life, and yet he was concerned about our fate.

No worries, I said. *When you get to Switzerland you can send us a postcard.*

Doc Sadie stopped signing and looked at me in a way that only a sheila can.

A postcard? she said.

All right then, he can call us, I offered.

She did everything but roll her eyes at me before turning back to the ape. I don't know what she said to him after that, but whatever it was it seemed to satisfy him, and this was all that mattered.

The very last thing I needed was a gorilla with a guilty conscience.

THE GORILLA

Humans have a theory known as Murphy's Law. According to this law if something can go wrong, it will. I asked Bowzer why Murphy would make such a law. Would it not have been better to make one that said if something can go right, it will? But Bowzer just shook his head, smiled, and said, *You got me there, mate. Who said animals are stupid, eh?*

I did not answer, but I can tell you this with certainty: it was not an animal.

As the day of my departure neared, the humans around me grew increasingly anxious, and the more anxious they became the more convinced I was that I was doomed. Even Bowzer appeared sceptical. I knew he was never one to mince his words – or his thoughts – so that when I saw him shake his head and sigh my heart sank. When he saw that I had been watching him, he ambled over to reassure me.

Listen, mate, no worries. You'll see.

He was a lousy liar.

Seriously, mate. It's as sure as mozzies in summer.

He gave me a thumbs-up to confirm the gist of his limited signing vocabulary. In return I gave him the finger, another gesture he had taught me. He laughed and walked away in the swaggering gait peculiar to him and his comrades. They reminded me of the young silverbacks I had seen as an infant, eager to test their strength against each other and, eventually, the alpha male. If one succeeded he would take over the troop and reign as the new leader until it was his turn to be pushed aside.

If.

At this stage I had no desire to be any troop's alpha male. My only concern was to survive. To survive and be free to return to the forest and mountains where I was born. Then I would think about a troop. A family. A mate. In the meantime I could only imagine what would happen to all of us if we were caught.

THE CAPTAIN

A situation report? For any serious incident there's always a situation report – or SITREP as it's called – and in a conflict zone any incident involving an explosion at a military installation or checkpoint is regarded as a serious incident. In this case it was an incident involving PMCs – private military contractors – and though, strictly speaking, no regular army personnel were involved in transporting Einstein to the airport, the incident was considered a political hot potato. A SITREP served two purposes: it fulfilled a military requirement, and it provided an official explanation intended to de-escalate the situation and discourage any further investigation.

The SITREP pertaining to this incident is unclassified. You can request a copy if you wish, but the gist of it is this.

We arrived at the zoo at 06.00. Altogether there were just over a dozen of us: the zoo's director, Doc Sadic, me, Bowzer, his team, my driver, gunner, two armed escorts, a forklift operator and the buyer's vet. The mood among all of us was somber. I was there only as an observer and to say goodbye. Once Einstein had been sold the army had no more responsibility, and it was decided that Bowzer and his team would handle Einstein's transport from the zoo to the airport.

It was obvious Einstein was nervous. He paced back and forth in his enclosure, stopping once to stare at us before mounting a mock charge. After this Doc Sadie asked for a moment alone with him, and we moved away. Then she faced his enclosure and began to sign. Whatever it was she said to him seemed to calm him. After that he entered his crate and the door was shut and secured.

Bowzer and his team had two vehicles: a Humvee and a 2½- ton LMTV – light medium transport vehicle, essentially a truck – for transporting the ape. Both were armed with crew-served weapons systems, in this case 50-caliber machine guns. The doc signaled to the forklift operator to approach, and we watched as Einstein's crate was lowered onto the bed of the truck. At the airport the buyer's vet and a team of handlers would take over loading Einstein onto their private jet, and the vet would then accompany and deliver him to his new home.

The buyer's vet rode in the transport truck with Bowzer, Bowzer's gunner and Einstein. The rest of Bowzer's team – a driver, two teammates and another gunner – rode in the Humvee. I stayed behind along with Doc Sadie. In the end she'd decided not to accompany Einstein to the airport. As far as she was concerned two goodbyes were two too many.

Once Einstein was loaded, Bowzer and his team headed out of the zoo's main gates. The Humvee led the way with Bowzer, the buyer's vet and Einstein close behind. They hadn't driven 50 yards before Bowzer radioed to say that they were heading back. A call had come in from the director's office saying there was a problem with one of the buyer's documents. Both ve-hicles pulled over, the buyer's vet dismounted, climbed into the Humvee and was driven back to the zoo. As he entered the main gate Doc Sadie appeared and accompanied him to the admin building. I radioed Bowzer and told him to sit tight. They wouldn't be long. Ten minutes later the buyer's vet reappeared, passed through the zoo's main gates where he rejoined Bowzer in the cab of the transport truck, and once more they headed down Hell's Highway to the airport.

There were two checkpoints between the zoo and the airport. The first was about halfway between the two, and the second was at the airport's main entrance. As they approached the first checkpoint a soldier stepped from the guardhouse and waved them down. Standard procedure. After a brief chat the Humvee was allowed through. It passed the checkpoint, pulled over, and waited for the truck carrying Einstein to clear.

As it approached the guardhouse – a concrete blockhouse fortified on all sides with sandbags – a soldier stepped up and Bowzer handed him a sheaf of documents. The soldier scanned the documents, did a quick once-around their vehicle, and asked the buyer's vet to step out and accompany him into the guardhouse. Bowzer assumed all of the documents had, by now, been checked and double-checked, and whatever it was wouldn't take long. They were on schedule and, all things being equal, expected to arrive at the airport on time. But all things being equal in a conflict zone doesn't necessarily mean two plus two equals four – ever.

So they waited. After a few minutes Bowzer climbed down from the truck's cab and requested permission to enter the guardhouse. He told his gunner to stretch his legs if he wished, but to hurry it up. By stretching his legs, he meant feel free to relieve himself. The gunner had a mild case of the squits, and when you gotta go, you gotta go. He requested permission to pass through the checkpoint and headed straight for the portable latrines, or 'blue canoes' as they were known, entered one and closed the door.

That's when it happened. The explosion. It rocked the Humvee and knocked over the latrine with

Bowzer's gunner still inside. In the guardhouse Bowzer, the vet, and the soldiers on duty were dazed, but there were no injuries or fatalities. Not so the transport truck. The rear section and Einstein's crate were ripped apart by the explosion, and the vehicle was engulfed in flames.

And that's it. End of situation report.

As for the buyer, his reaction was predictable, but there was nothing he or anyone else could do about it. Whether or not he ever got his money back was none of my business. Like I said, once Einstein was sold he was no longer my responsibility, and as far as I was *officially* concerned that was the end of it.

Part 4

THE GORILLA

Once we boarded the cargo jet bound for Switzerland,
Dr Sadiq gave me a mild sedative. I remained awake
but relaxed, and as we prepared to land I rose and
stretched. As soon as she heard me stir she approached
my crate and began to sign. She asked how I was
feeling, was I afraid and so on. Of course I was afraid.
I had no idea what or who awaited me.

Tell me, I said.

Tell you what?

Tell me how you did it, I answered.

Are you sure you want to know? she said.

Yes.

We blew you up.

But I am here.

She smiled. *Yes you are*, she said.

Explain, I signed.

*What I mean is we made it look like you'd been blown
up. Once you were loaded onto the transport truck and
on your way we radioed the buyer's vet to tell him there
was a mistake on one of his documents and he had to
return to the ʒoo to have it amended. I met him at the*

gate and escorted him into the zoo's offices to sort it out. He handed me his documents. I checked them, corrected the error and handed them back. But before I did, I removed another crucial document.

Meanwhile, Bowzer had pulled over just outside the zoo's entrance, and that's when they made the switch. The truck transporting you was replaced with an identical one loaded with an empty crate, and Bowzer and his gunner climbed aboard it and waited. I walked the buyer's vet back to the gates where we said our goodbyes, and watched as he hoisted himself into the cab next to Bowzer and headed off. Once they were out of sight the truck transporting you reappeared, and you and I were driven straight to the airport. There are two airports. One for civilian traffic, the other for military. They're connected but separate. While you and I headed to the military airport, Bowzer, the buyer's vet and their escort proceeded in convoy to the civilian airport as if nothing had happened.

This does not explain how you blew me up, I said. She sighed as if hoping I had not noticed, and then she continued.

On the way to the airport there are two checkpoints, she said, *and at each one every vehicle is stopped. Unbeknown to the buyer's vet he was missing a document. When he arrived at the first checkpoint and handed over his paperwork the soldier called him into* the guardhouse to question him. *That's when one of Bowzer's men detonated an IED, a kind of bomb they'd placed under the truck.*

Was anyone hurt? I signed.

No.

What will happen to Bowzer and the captain?

They'll be fine.

And the buyer?

He thinks you're dead.

I thought about all that she had told me. It was a lot to take in — even for a gorilla.

You told me the switch would take place at the airport.

Yes, but that would've been too late and too dangerous.

Why did you not tell me this before?

The less you knew the better. I didn't want to frighten you. After what happened at the zoo — the bombing — I was afraid any mention of an explosion would be too much for you.

I still had many questions, but we were about to land. They would have to wait.

Was I wrong not to tell you? she said.

No, I replied.

BILLY

I've decided not to tell Grandma. It'll only upset her. And anyway, I know what she'll say. She'll say don't go. She doesn't trust Boss. Can't blame her. Nobody trust that ol' sonuvabitch. *His reputation precedes him,* as Grandma says. Not a soul in the community, it seems, doesn't know how he beats on his wife, never mind how he treats his livestock. Even the other farmers shake their heads and, believe me, they've got nothing to brag about.

I'm off school for a week. Fall break. So I'll go along tomorrow after work and see what there is to see. Boss claims he's got a coupla runts he wants to get rid of. *Too small to bother with,* he says. Okay by me. Given what's gone before I reckon he figures I'll be happy to take 'em off his hands, and he's right. Not so sure my mom feels the same. In fact, I'm damn sure she doesn't. But they don't cost us much, and what expenses there are I cover, at least for now. I even persuaded our local vet to come along and check 'em out for free. Truth be told it didn't take all that much persuading. He's an old school buddy of my dad's. It sickens him what goes on in animal farming these days, and round here Boss's farm is the worst of the bunch.

I'm not gonna tell my sister neither. She can't keep a secret to save her life. Not this kinda secret. The grin on her face at the prospect of two more piglets to fuss over'll tell Mom sure as hell that something's up even if she does manage to keep her trap shut. Best to leave it and just show up mission accomplished. It's always harder to undo a thing that's been done than to stop it before it happens.

Boss has asked me to come at the end of the day because that's when the farrowing's finished. Suits me just fine. I don't even wanna think about farrowing much less witness it again. And those two thugs he's got working for him? Hell, if I never see 'em again it'll be too soon. But it means I won't be able to pick my sister up from school like I promised.

Naturally, when I told her she wanted to know why, and when I said that I had to work late she gave me that look of hers that says, *You're lying to me*. And she was right. She's got some kinda radar when it comes to telling the truth, and never once has she been wrong. If she had the same unfailing sense about the stock market we'd all be rich as kings.

Anyway, before you know it she was jumping up and down all excited like and barely able to contain herself and squealing, *I know, I know, you're gonna bring back another runt.*

Now I haven't mentioned a thing about Boss or his pigs since I showed up with Bristles and Diana, but she still goes to bed at night thinking every morning's gonna be Christmas all over again. Every little sound, no matter how slight, and she wakes up wide-eyed and eager as a squirrel in spring. Then she wakes my mom saying she can't get back to sleep. Drives my mom crazy. Her teachers, too, because she tends to doze off in class due to sheer exhaustion. So I told her to shut her trap and we'd do something the day after tomorrow – something special – to make up for me not picking her up tomorrow like I promised. She just stood there with a grin on her face as wide as Lake Michigan and dancing in place like she was about to wet herself and whispering, *I get to name 'em, I get to name 'em,* 'til I picked her up and dumped her in her room and closed the door and told her that we weren't likely to do anything the whole time I was off school if she didn't shut up.

All of a sudden there was a dead silence. She went so quiet I was beginning to worry. So I opened the door a crack to see if she was still breathing. She was standing next to her bed with her hands clasped over her mouth.

You awright? I said, and she nodded.

But as soon as I went to close the door she took her hands from her mouth and whispered, *But I get to name 'em, I get to name 'em.*

So I went back in and threw her onto her bed and told her not only am I not picking her up from school again *ever*, but when I finish work tomorrow I'm heading straight over to a friend's. I said, *You'll be asleep by the time I get home, so I won't be seeing you until the day after at the earliest.*

This part, at least, is true. After I swing by Boss's I'm going over to my friend's to hang out for the evening. You woulda thought this would've settled it, but she didn't give up. Oh no.

She said, *Which friend? Which friend?* and I told her to mind her own damn business and left.

THE ELEPHANT

The man who bought me is called Don Tejón. It's
not the name given to him by his mother and father.
It's a nickname his soldiers have given him because,
like the badger, he's a master of escape. He's short
and his legs are bowed so that when he walks he
sways from side to side as if he has trouble keeping
his balance. But when he's angry his movements are
quick, and he's angry often. He has a bad temper and
sometimes he pulls out his gun and fires it at anyone
who happens to be near. Then he laughs. He says he
doesn't intend to shoot them, only to frighten them,
but no one believes him.

Don Tejón has many enemies. Because of this he
lives in a great house surrounded by land that
stretches to the horizon in every direction. Around
the house is a garden with many brightly coloured
flowers. Don Tejón's female likes these flowers, and
she tells the servants to pick them, and when they
do she hides them in the house. Soon afterwards she
tells the gardener he must plant more flowers, and I
think he must tire of this game because it never stops.

Beyond the garden are pastures, and beyond these are thick forests and gloomy jungles, and all day and all night angry-looking men with guns patrol them in search of enemies. Some of Don Tejón's enemies look like the men with guns who search for them; others wear uniforms, but to Don Tejón they're all the same. Enemies.

One day a man came to meet with him. Many men come often to meet with him, but this one was dressed in a suit the colour of corn and on his feet he wore boots made from the skins of snakes. Underneath his jacket his shirt was unbuttoned, and on his chest hung many chains of a bright, shiny yellow metal called gold.

Don Tejón listened carefully while this man in the corn-coloured suit spoke. Now and again he nodded and asked a question, but mostly he was silent. After a time he had me brought from my pasture and introduced me to his visitor. I guessed that he wished to show me off, and so I was able to watch them while they talked. Don Tejón had food and drinks brought. His guest drank but he didn't eat. Don Tejón ate but he didn't drink. As the afternoon wore on his guest became livelier, but I sensed that Don Tejón didn't share his enthusiasm. I could read his eyes, smell his suspicion, sense his body language. Humans, like animals, give away all sorts of clues as to what they're thinking and feeling, and I'd come to know Don Tejón well. It was clear to me that something wasn't right.

Near the end of their meeting the man in the corn-coloured suit took from his pocket a small red pouch and emptied it onto the table. Out tumbled a handful of stones whose colours mingled and sparkled in the sunlight. As I listened I learned the names of these stones: opals and emeralds. When Don Tejón saw them he leaned forward slowly, picked up one or two, inspected them briefly and returned them to the table. The man in the suit waited for him to speak, but Don Tejón remained silent. He looked from one of Don Tejón's bodyguards to another, but none gave any hint of what their boss was thinking. And so he picked up his stones, put them back in the red pouch and returned the pouch to his pocket.

I'm sorry if I've offended you, Don Tejón, he said. *I was told that your wife likes precious stones, especially opals and emeralds.*

Don Tejón waved his hand to indicate that it wasn't important, and their meeting came to an end. They stood and shook hands, and Don Tejón ordered one of his bodyguards to fetch the man's car. When the car arrived Don Tejón opened the door, waited until his guest was comfortably seated, closed the door, pulled a gun from the waistband of his trousers and shot his guest through the head. Later I heard one of his bodyguards call the murdered guest a snitch.

The forest and jungle that surround us are wild and filled with strange creatures, and I watch and listen for them to appear. Some, like the spectacled bear and the Andean condor, visit me during the day. The spectacled bear has a white face with dark circles around his eyes. He reminds me of Don Tejón's female with her pale skin, painted eyes and thick black hair. Others, like the giant anteater with his long tapered nose and bushy tail, and the jaguar wrapped in his orange-and-black spotted coat, visit me at night. None of them have ever seen an elephant, and they spend many hours watching me. Sometimes I call out to them, hoping they'll come closer so I can get a better look, but they're afraid of the men with guns and run away as soon as they see them. I'm afraid, too, but I can't run away.

Don Tejón keeps many animals – hippopotamuses, antelopes, giraffes, panthers, lions, and a bird he calls Oskar who's so big he's unable to fly. They come from all over the world and most of them are new to me, but I'm the only elephant. Every day after his siesta, Don Tejón comes to visit me. He puts his hand in his pocket, fills it with peanuts and calls out to me. When I wander over he strokes my trunk and scratches my ears. I let him because I like the peanuts and I sense that Don Tejón will not hurt me, but I'm lonely, and Don Tejón knows this.

That was how Amigo came to live with me. Amigo is older than me and, like me, he was captured and sold. He's also bigger and has tusks, and he rubs them on the bark of an ancient oak that stands in the centre of our pasture. He likes to tussle with me, but sometimes he forgets his size and I run away, afraid he'll knock me over. But I enjoy his company. He teaches me many things about being an elephant. Not as much as he might because, like me, he was orphaned when he was very young. With no elders to teach us there's much we cannot know.

One evening a hard rain began to fall that lasted many weeks. Amigo grew restless and urine began to stream down his legs in a constant dribble. Then the glands behind his eyes swelled causing him much pain, and a sticky, odorous liquid trickled down each side of his face and into his mouth. As the days wore on he became more and more irritable until the slightest thing sent him into a rage. It was no longer safe to be near him. Don Tejón's bodyguards laughed and joked among themselves saying that what Amigo needed was a companion. A female companion. They failed to notice that what I needed was to be moved to a safe place until his condition, whatever it was, ceased. I did my best to stay out of his way, but his mood only worsened.

Many days later some of Don Tejón's bodyguards approached our pasture. It was late at night, and they stood by our fence, laughing and boasting and sharing a bottle containing a liquid the colour of honey. The more of it they drank, the more they laughed and the louder they talked. One started to sing and the others joined in. When they finished the youngest among them pointed to Amigo and dared his companions to enter our pasture. They refused. He laughed and called them cowards, and hurling himself at our fence he began to scale it.

By then it had started to rain again. Even so, the young man reached the top with little effort, climbing it as quickly as a spider climbs its web. As he lowered himself down the other side he lost his grip and landed on his back. The fall knocked the wind from his lungs, and before he could find the breath to stand Amigo was on him. With his tusk he lifted him as easily as a lioness lifts her cubs and carried him to the ancient oak in the centre of our pasture. I thought he meant to put him down under its wide canopy where the young man would be sheltered from the rain, but instead he swung his head in a great arc and flung him into the trunk. As he slid to the ground Amigo speared him with his tusks, and lifting him, hurled him once again. This time he landed several feet away, his face buried in a mound of fresh dung. His companions shouted, another called for a gun, but Amigo was on him again. Raising his leg, he brought it down with all the force he could muster. As I watched I recalled the image of the old bull crushing the poacher that had murdered my mother, and for a moment I wished it was my foot crushing the young man.

It was then I noticed Don Tejón. In his hands was a rifle. Without thinking, one of his men tried to grab it, but he pushed him away. Ignoring the rain, he stood at the fence and watched Amigo for several minutes. His men were excited, all talking and shouting as one, but Don Tejón remained silent. When he spoke he said that if anyone deserved to be shot it was the idiot who'd entered the pasture of an elephant in musth. Then he turned and walked away.

The day after he killed Don Tejón's young bodyguard, Amigo tried to smash the gates of our fence, forcing Don Tejón to sedate him. When Amigo awoke he found himself chained by his leg to the enormous oak. For the next six weeks he spent his days trying to free himself without success. Then, just as suddenly as it began, Amigo's rage disappeared, his secretions ceased, and his chain was removed.

Weeks later I was again brought out to be displayed to my master's guests. This time Don Tejón's female was with him. Around her neck she wore a chain of yellow gold with a single enormous emerald dangling from its centre, and from each of her ears hung a string of speckled opals, and together they reflected their colours into the eyes of their female guests.

Doña Tejón was very proud of her jewels. She twirled the emerald in her fingers while she spoke and tossed her head from side to side so that her ear-rings glinted in the sunlight, and all the while she looked at the other females for their approval. They smiled and flattered her, but I could see that they were jealous, and they looked to their husbands as if to say, *Why her and not me?* But their husbands were afraid of Don Tejón and ignored them. Don Tejón was the alpha male, and their wives knew this. And so, like kittens, they purred their admiration.

It was hot that day, and as I watched them the uncertain memory of a cool sea and a shallow bay came upon me. I saw a young orca beckon to me, and behind him his mother called out, *Come, come with us and you'll be safe.* I entered the water and straddled the young orca, and off we sailed across the bay and into the open sea. His mother led the way, and we followed across a vast and unfamiliar ocean to another shore where large grey boulders rose from the sand on sturdy legs and beckoned to me with their trunks. As I struggled ashore they greeted me with caresses and low rumbles, and their matriarch suckled me until I was full and fell into a deep sleep. I slept for a long time thinking only of my mother and knowing that when I awoke she would be there to greet me, and I would be safe and free.

But it wasn't a memory. It was only a dream.

MRS BOSS

Well, my my, if it ain't the Beckham boy, and dead on time at that.

Those were his exact words. It wasn't hard for Boss to get that little sonuvabitch round here. All he had to do was give him some guff about wanting to get rid of two more runts. Kid fell for it like a tree to a saw. Boss told him to come straight to the farrowing shed, not to stop by the house. Didn't want anyone, including me, to see him or his pickup parked out front.

I was standing in the shadows in a far corner of the shed when the kid came in. I knew Boss was up to something because I'd heard him talking to Hank on the phone. When it came time I made an excuse about going to town to fetch some shopping and headed out of the drive onto the main road. Soon as I was clear I doubled back to the farrowing shed, parked behind a thick stand of trees and walked the rest of the way. I didn't want nobody knowing I was there – not those two comic-book villains snickering like a coupla twelve-year-olds ogling their daddy's dirty magazines, and not Boss, all two hundred and fifty pounds of glowering hatred.

When Billy came in Boss didn't waste any time getting right to the point. Just came straight out with it.

What was it that crazy bitch of a pig whisperer said? Y'all remember? Hank? Gordo? Something about airplane seats and such.

And Hank answered. *She said keeping a pig in a sow stall is like asking a human to spend its life strapped in an airplane seat.*

That's right, said Boss. *Well, I reckon we oughta put it to the test. Whaddaya think, Billy? Shall we put it to the test?*

He didn't wait for Billy to answer, and truth be told the kid was too confused to know what the hell was going on. He just stood there watching as Boss motioned to a big rectangular-like lump covered with an old blanket. Gordo waited for Hank to close the shed doors, and then he snatched off the blanket and, lo and behold, standing there in all its worn glory was a vintage airplane seat. Vintage my backside. Just another fancy word for a junked piece of crap. God knows where he got it. Probably from Jim Gowdy who collects all kindsa weird and useless stuff nobody wants. Stores it all in a barn with a big old 'Antiques' sign painted on the side and suddenly something nobody wants becomes something every sucker wants. Nice work if you can get it.

So like I was saying, Boss turned to Billy and smiled and said, *Watcha waiting for, boys? Strap him in.*

And that's when Billy woke up and bolted for the shed doors, but by then it was too late. The boys were all over him and they dragged him kicking and screaming to the airplane seat. He put up a helluva struggle and made a fierce racket on top of it. They slapped duct tape over his mouth and bound his wrists and ankles with zip ties and pushed him down into the seat and strapped him in. They didn't just buckle his seat belt neither, but tied a nylon cord around him just in case 'til he was as snug as a bug in a rug, but not nearly as content, I reckon.

Finally, Boss walked over and grabbed a chain rigged to a pulley hanging from a girder and began to haul him up, and before you knew it Billy was dangling from the ceiling like a side of pork. Only difference was no pork I've ever seen come trussed like that. Least not while it was still alive.

I drove back to the house well before Boss returned. When he came in he didn't say a word and neither did I. There wasn't anything unusual about this. We hardly spoke at the best of times. I put his dinner on the table and then went back up to my room. Soon as he was finished and seated in the living room in front of the TV I came back down. I went straight to the calendar and counted five days. That was how long I was going to leave it before I called the police. I figured as long as he had water the boy wouldn't starve, and the longer he was kept against his will the worse it'd play for Boss. I'd done my research. If things went well for me he could get up to four years. I knew he wouldn't because he didn't have any prior convictions, but even if they only kept him locked up for four days it'd give me enough time to gather up my things, empty our bank accounts and hightail it outta there.

And that's exactly what I intended to do.

On the third day the police came round. They were asking all the neighbors if they'd seen Billy. They didn't stay long. Asked a few questions, said to call if we heard anything and left. I watched Boss while the cops were chatting with him. Cool as iced tea on a summer's afternoon. He even managed a joke, and I smiled in spite of myself. But then he was a practiced hand at lying.

It was in the early hours of the fifth day when I discovered Billy was no longer in the shed. I'd been visiting him every night, clandestine and all. I like that word. Clandestine. Makes me feel like an undercover agent. I knew Boss was giving him water because I'd seen him take a bucket and ladle with him that first afternoon that Billy was strung up and every day afterwards. He'd go in the morning after breakfast and in the evening after he ate his supper, so I wasn't worried. As long as the kid had water he'd last easy five days.

Like I said, I went checking on him every night. If you want the truth, I was making sure he was still breathing. Even with the ventilation system running at full blast the air inside that damn shed wasn't exactly Alpine fresh. I'd wait for Boss to fall asleep. Then I'd wait some more. I knew exactly when he was least likely to wake up. It was always the same – about an hour after he went to bed and before the clock struck four. I can tell by the way he snores. At first it's like listening to a cement mixer making hay with a hurricane. Around midnight it trails off to a tolerable volume, and then nothing – not God or the apocalypse itself – can wake him.

That night I got up about one, and quiet as I could I got in my car and drove down to the sheds. I went in a side door behind where Billy was hanging because the sheds are always lit, and I didn't want to risk Billy seeing me. But that night he wasn't there, and at first I couldn't believe my eyes. I'm thinking he's escaped, but then it dawns on me that there isn't any airplane seat neither. The only thing left is the pulley hanging from the girder. And that's when it hit me – he'd let him go. But no, Boss'd never let the little sonuvabitch go, not because he'd be afraid of the consequences, but because he's too damn murderous and mean. Don't know why this hadn't occurred to me before. Maybe I just didn't want to admit it. It's possible. The plain truth is Boss'd rather hang than forgive somebody a slight, never mind an outright theft.

I got in my car and drove back to the house. There was no moon that night. It was as dark and cheerless as a widow's frown. I got into bed and lay there as quiet as I could, because if Boss found out I was snooping around there'd be all hell to pay. Around three he stirred. Normally, you can set your watch to his sleeping pattern. But that night he'd set his alarm an hour earlier than usual, and he got up and said, *Guess I'll make an early start. Got that sow auction up north.*

May as well as you're up anyhow, I said.

And realising I was awake, he said, *May as well get your skinny ass outta bed and make me some coffee.*

So I did.

He didn't bother taking a shower that morning. Didn't even shave. Unusual for him, and a sure sign he was less easy than he was letting on.

I made a fresh pot and sat drinking a cup and waiting 'til he came downstairs. Without looking at me he went straight to the cupboard, grabbed a cup and poured himself a coffee. He stood by the sink, his back to me, staring out the window as if trying to make up his mind about something, and all the while slurping his coffee in great loud gulps and ignoring me like I wasn't there. Okay by me. I was used to it.

When he was finished he put his cup in the sink, grabbed his coat from the hallway, and as he was leaving he said, *I'll be back after lunch.* As if I cared one way or the other. Soon as he shut the door I got up and stood by the window. I watched his red pickup head down the drive, but instead of turning right toward the main road he turned left to the sheds and the slurry pits. And that's when everything fell into place.

I didn't bother to get dressed. I just threw on a coat and a pair of boots, ran outside and got into my car. I made my way down the drive and turned left, using just my parking lights to guide me. I took it slow. I didn't want Boss to know I was following him. All told, I doubt I was gone more than twenty minutes.

Soon as I got back I went straight into the kitchen, picked up the phone and dialed.

MY COUSIN ZHEN

I visit my cousin most evenings after work and every weekend. Often my boyfriend comes with me. He says hello to her and then he waits in the hospital cafeteria so that I can visit with her privately. Her mother also comes once a week. Sometimes her father comes too, and I wonder if Zhen knows this. I hope so.

I start by telling her all about my day. About the bears and the sanctuary and especially about Tiáopí. It's obvious Tiáopí misses her. Every day she comes out at the usual time and waits for Zhen to appear. She waits and waits, and when Zhen doesn't come she goes back into her den looking dejected and confused.

Everyone at the refuge always sends Zhen their love, and I tell her what everyone is doing. Then I tell her about our visitors, especially the schoolchildren. It was her idea to focus on the children. *The younger the better,* she said.

Often when I arrive Zhen's professor is sitting at her bedside. When he sees me he looks apologetic as if what happened to her was his fault. But mostly he just looks sad. Deeply sad. Like he's lost his best friend, and it makes me wonder if he's fallen in love with her. How could he *not* fall in love with her? She's smart and beautiful and dedicated and strong. He'd be lucky to have her.

If I tell you something, will you promise not to laugh and think me a stupid, silly girl? I can't put it out of my head, and I keep thinking that if I tell someone then maybe it will stop tormenting me. It's just that, if I'd told someone about what Zhen said to me the night before the attack, and about the man known as Uncle, then maybe none of it would have happened. It was obvious she was worried. Why else would she have said to me what she said?

When I speak with the doctors they say they've not given up hope. Far from it. As for me, I know she'll wake up. I just know it.

Like Zhen said. Never give up. Never.

GRANDMA

It was Diana and Bristles that first raised the alarm. What I mean to say is they raised such a ruckus when their breakfast was late they woke the whole darn house. My granddaughter was the first to go into Billy's room. As soon as she saw her brother was gone she came into my room asking, *Where's Billy, Grandma?*

I went into his room to have a look-see and I could tell, in spite of the usual mess, that he hadn't come home. But I didn't tell this to my granddaughter. We chased those two piglets downstairs and got 'em fed, and I remember thinking it was high time they slept in the barn. Sooner or later a piglet turns into a pig, runt or no runt.

After this my granddaughter ran outside and started calling for her brother, and by this time my son and his wife were up and wondering what all the hoo-ha was about. Nobody was all that bothered at first 'cept for my granddaughter, but for the most part we ignored her. At that moment we had no reason to be alarmed. Wasn't as if somebody had broke in and kidnaped him. So we ate our breakfast and tried to calm her best we could.

It was while my son's wife was getting my grand-daughter ready for school that I said to my son, *Did Billy mention he was staying out last night?*

Right away he shook his head and said, *Nope*. But a moment later he looked at me all quizzical like and said, *Why? Didn't he come home last night?*

Well, there it was, and there was no ignoring it now.

Guess he stood over at his friend's house, I said. *Think he mighta mentioned he was going over there after work.*

But even as I said it we both knew he woulda called if he wasn't coming home. Soon as the little one climbed into her mom's car and was gone, my son got on the phone and called the store where Billy works, but there wasn't nobody there. Too early. After that he called Billy's friend. It was then we learned he never showed up, and his friend hadn't seen or talked to him since he left work the day before.

Long story short, we started calling round. We're a small community and everyone knows everyone, so we were fairly certain someone'd know his where-abouts, but by lunchtime we still hadn't heard a word. We knew he wasn't at work, and we were all starting to get worried. My son put in a call to the sheriff. A formality really. They said there was nothing they could do for forty-eight hours, and to call 'em back in the morning if we still hadn't heard from him.

That was the longest afternoon and evening of my life. Of any of our lives.

My granddaughter came home on the school bus that day, and the first thing she did when she came into the house was to shout out her brother's name. When I told her he hadn't come back she burst into tears. Yep, kids are funny that way. When her brother's around she spends most of her time annoying the heck out of him, but as soon he's not around she's missing him.

It was her first mentioned Boss. In the beginning none of us took much notice. As far as we were concerned that dispute was settled, and not one of us had seen or heard from him since. Not that we expected to. We weren't what you'd call friendly, but we didn't go out of our way to avoid him neither. The fact is our paths rarely crossed. The only time I ever saw his wife was on those rare occasions she and I happened to be at the beauty parlor at the same time. Even then we barely nodded to one another. It was her more than me. She never spoke to nobody. Always with her dark glasses hiding the latest evidence of her husband's fondness for contact sports. Poor woman. I pitied her. That's the truth, though I'd never say as much to her. Everybody's got pride no matter how battered and bruised. And she had plenty. I thought to myself more than once that when that woman blows it's gonna be felt all the way to the Great Lakes and beyond, and look out any poor soul who stands in her way. Turns out I was right.

Next morning my son called the police again and they agreed to come round. First thing they did was ask who we'd been speaking to. That was easy because we'd rung practically everyone we knew. Then they asked was Billy upset about something, did he seem fussed or anxious. All of us agreed he seemed the same as always.

One of the officers said, *Well, you know how teenage boys can be.*

And my son looked at him and said, *Well, I know how* our *teenage boy can be, and it's not like him to walk out of the house in the morning and not come back.*

Then they asked to see Billy's room. My daughter-in-law took 'em upstairs and they poked about looking for what I don't know. His room was the same that morning as every morning – like a tornado had passed through a yard sale. Don't know what they hoped to find in that mess 'cept a month's worth of dirty socks and underwear, most of which ended up in a pile and served as bedding for the two runts, but they poked about all the same.

It was fall and the leaves were turning. Always was, for me, the happiest and saddest time of the year, and the most beautiful. All those colors. Like the whole world's been painted tropical sunset. That's the happy bit. The sad bit is my husband passed in the fall. Never mind. That's life.

So the police poked about, and when they left they said to give 'em a call if Billy showed up. He didn't. Not that day or that evening or the next morning.

By this time his mom was frantic. So was his dad. So was I, but I was busy calming my granddaughter. I told her she had to concentrate all her energies on Bristles and Diana, and this kept her mind off her brother 'til bedtime. After that it was all the tears none of us dared shed. I told her he was likely stood over at someone's house and would be back in the morning, and she said in this case the police oughta go and check-see. After a while she fell asleep, and I closed the light and went downstairs, and it was then the rest of us could talk freely. Before we went to bed my son said he was going to the police as soon as the sun was up and make 'em file a missing-persons report, and if they refused he'd write it up himself. None of us slept much that night. I know because you could hear every one of us tossing and turning and getting up to go to the bathroom and such even more than usual.

The next morning my son was up before daybreak and out of the house at first light. He didn't come back 'til close on ten o'clock. He said the police were sending out a patrol to visit all the neighbors. It was then I remembered my granddaughter mentioning Boss. Once I had the thought I couldn't let it go. It bounced around in my head like a startled bat, and I made the mistake of saying his name out loud.

Straight away my son looked up and said, *Whaddaya mean, Mom?*

Nothing, I said. *Just thinking out loud.*

I regretted it right away, but it was done, and I could see that he wasn't gonna let it go. So I told him I was heading over there the next morning to pay Mrs Boss a visit because I had a magazine she'd left behind at the beauty parlor and I'd been meaning to return it. It was a pure lie, and he looked at me like I was crazy.

Jeez, he said, *what the heck is the matter with you? Worrying about a damn magazine at a time like this?* And it was crazy, on the face of it. Then he said, *Okay, why're you really going?*

I said that I'd promised to take my granddaughter to school and thought I'd drop it round on the way back. He looked hard at me, trying to decide whether I was telling the truth. Then he asked if I wanted him to come with, but I told him no, I wanted to go on my own. Mrs Boss was tricky at the best of times, and given what had passed between me and her husband I thought it best if I went alone. Truth was I thought my son might hit Boss if he showed his face, and I didn't want things heated up 'til I had a chance to talk with Mrs Boss in private.

That night, after I went to bed, I lay awake listening to my granddaughter tossing and turning, and at one point in the early hours she woke up and started to cry. Her dad went in to calm her, and soon as she was back to sleep he went downstairs and put up the fire.

Wasn't long afterwards I got up. When I came downstairs there was coffee ready. We sat at the table. Neither of us said much. Then my son's wife joined us. She poured a coffee and the three of us sat there silent as snow on a winter's night. Neither I nor my son said a word about me stopping by Boss's farm later on that morning after dropping my granddaughter to school. No point. We just sat and sipped our coffee and avoided looking at one another. I'm sure we were all thinking the same thing, about trying to say something to break the silence, but not a one of us could think of anything to say.

I got up to put my cup in the sink when the phone rang. By then it was close on four or five in the morning. All three of us froze. I don't know if we were waiting for the other of us to answer or what, when my son jumped up like a jackrabbit with his tail on fire and crossed to the phone. He didn't say hello. Just listened for a second or two and then turned to me and said, *It's for you*.

I took it, but before I put the phone to my ear I knew who it was. Don't ask me how I knew. I just did.

The Poacher's Daughter

The sisters have been good to me. I share a room with another girl. She is older than me by one year and has lost both her parents. Killed by government soldiers on their way to the market that comes once a month to her town. She was supposed to go with them, but that day her Auntie Flo came and so she stayed at home.

Since three months Auntie Flo comes to visit me also. The sisters tell me, *Now you are a woman and you must take care to behave and not to send wrong signals to men.* But I don't feel like a woman. I feel angry, because the other girls tell me my father laid with my mother when it was her moon-time, and this is how I came to be an albino.

The priest comes to visit with me every week. He is a kind man. I tell him that since my first moon-time what the others say to me, and he tells me, *They are wrong. Do not listen to them. They are silly girls who should know better.* So I don't say to him that I have heard some of the younger sisters talk among themselves the same thing.

When he comes he tells me news of my father, and each time I ask him when my father will be released. He smiles and reaches out a hand to put on my shoulder and says, *One day, my child. One day.* I know he means well, but I am not his child. I am my father's child, and I want my father to come back to me.

On weekends I work at the elephant orphanage not far from my school. Two of the sisters walk me there in the morning, and in the evenings, when I am finished my work, the man and his wife who made the orphanage walk me back. They are my bosses, my *sonkos*, and they are good to me and teach me many things.

Last week I said to Lady Sonko, *I want to find out about one elephant that my father captured and sold before he went to prison.*

And she answered to me, *Tell me what happened and I will see what we can find out.*

So I told her everything, and that's how it began.

She teaches me computer, and I have learned to search many things. When I am not searching for my work I search for Little Calf. Nearly one year goes by and still I find nothing and I think I will give up when I read the story of a powerful narcotics *sonko* who lives far away across the ocean. This man is very rich from smuggling bad drugs, and when the police kill him they search his house and find he has his own zoo, private zoo, with two hundred animals. One of these animals is an elephant calf. He has no mother, like me, and no father. He is an orphan.

I keep reading until I find the thing that I am searching, and then I see, and at first I cannot believe it. I run to show Lady Sonko. She smiles and tells me that I am learning the computer very quickly, and when I finish school she and her husband will make me a proper job with a good salary. But I am interested only in Little Calf. I show her the photograph the police make and when she sees it her eyes grow wide and she says to me, *Albino, he's an albino just like you*. She smiles, and when she does I smile also, because I am more happy than I can remember to know that Little Calf is alive.

After this Lady Sonko and I follow the story of Little Calf very carefully. We learn that the police who killed the narcotics *sonko* are looking for homes for all of his animals. When I read this I go to her, but before I say to her one word she sees my mind and says to me, *We will try*. I say to her that I will help to raise the necessary monies, and she looks to me like a mother who knows her child wants to help but cannot because the child is still too young. In that moment I realise she does not know how strong I am inside, and I think to myself, *I will show her*.

In school I write how my father came to do his poaching, and what happened to him and to others who must do this evil business in order to take care of their families. Then I write the story of my hunt for Little Calf, what happened to him, and how we found him, and how we wish to adopt him now and bring him to our orphanage. The sisters help me. They make many suggestions and correct my mistakes, and I can see that they are very interested in my story.

When I finish I take it to Lady Sonko, and after she reads it she looks at me like a mother who realises her same child has grown wise under her nose while her eyes were looking elsewhere.

She says to me, *He is a very lucky little elephant. Albino elephants are very rare, and it is because of this that he is lucky.*

When I am afraid that my father will never come home, I remember what Lady Sonko said to me about Little Calf, and I think that maybe one day I will be lucky also. I hope so.

Every night when I say my prayers I think about this, and I say to God, *Is it true? Am I also lucky?*

And he answers to me, *Yes, you are albino just like Little Calf, and so I will make you lucky also.*

I remember this when Lady Sonko brings a journalist to speak with me. She writes for a very important newspaper, so I ask her, *How many* wadosi *read your paper?*

She looks at me surprised, but she answers to me, *Many. But not just rich people. All kinds of people everywhere read my paper.*

So I tell Lady Sonko it is okay if she gives my story to this journalist and she does, and the journalist prints my story in her newspaper. Afterwards, monies are donated to our elephant orphanage from all the countries of the world.

When I tell you that today Little Calf lives in our orphanage, do you believe me? Or do you think it is the fantasy of a young girl who dreams for better things? It is both. I see him every day. He remembers me from that time in the forest. It is because he knows that I tried to save him that he is not afraid of me. Now he has many allomothers to teach him. Elephant allomothers. When he is older he will go among the bulls and learn his place among his brothers, so that when it is time to live free again he will know how to behave. I will miss him, but I also know that I have rescued one elephant.

Soon after my story is told my father is freed. When he comes to the orphanage and sees Little Calf for the first time he cries so hard I think he will never stop. He will dry up like the savannah grasses in summer and no amount of rain will bring him back. So I go to him and put my arms around him and he holds me and kisses the top of my head.

You are my little calf, he says to me, *and I will never do these bad things again, these inhuman things that made me leave you.*

And I say to him, *Do not worry. God said to me that because we are albino, Little Calf and I, we are lucky.*

Now my father looks at me and answers, *Lucky. This will be Little Calf's name. From now on we will call him Bahati.*

Later I tell this to Little Calf, and when I see that he understands, I smile.

THE SOW

By the afternoon of the second day the boy stopped
crying and groaning. I expect he knew by then that
he wasn't going to be fed and was grateful when Boss
showed up with his bucket and ladle, ripped the duct
tape from his mouth, and gave him a drink of water.
Each time that Boss took hold of the chain and lowered him a look of hope came into the boy's eyes, a
look that had long since vanished from my own. It
was pi .... pitiful to see. But it was early days, and
Billy had yet to learn Boss's ways.

That second evening Boss began to taunt him. It
was awful to watch. At first the boy tried to reason
with him, but Boss ignored him and told him it
was folks like him poking their noses in where they
didn't belong that were determined to wreck his business and every other kind of farming, and it was
likely why his father had gone bust and had to sell
his farm.

This made the boy angry, and he called Boss names
telling him he was a cruel sonuvabitch, and saying
how everybody knew that he beat on his wife, and

how it was hardly surprising considering how he treated his sows. I wanted to shout out to the boy, *Hush, or you'll never get out of here*, but I have no human words. So in an effort to warn him I began to squeal, and my sisters, sensing my desperation, joined in.

It was all just so much noise. If anything, it made things worse. Boss blamed the boy for causing a ruckus, and told him if he didn't shut up he'd tape up his mouth for good. The boy went quiet. Even so Boss withheld his water to punish him. For the rest of the night until Boss returned in the morning, the boy sobbed with thirst.

Then there was Mrs Boss. From the very first night she showed up, and every night after that, a murmur and scuffling rippled through our shed as soon as she arrived. She always came in through a side door. I suppose this was to keep the boy from seeing her. It was late when she came, the darkness outside mocking the cold harsh glare that taunted us day and night. She'd make her way si .... silently up the row and stand behind him, looking up as if she was trying to make up her mind.

On the third night she lit a cigarette, and as soon as the boy smelled it he raised his head and called out, *Who's there? Is anybody there? Please help me. Help me.*

She never said a word, just stood there looking and smoking. As I watched her I wondered if the smile on her lips came from the boy's suffering or because she now had another human who shared in her own. After Boss came and took the boy away I realized it made no difference.

On the last night we were all of us, including the boy, in various stages of sleep when Boss entered. It was long past his usual visiting time. Last call was always right after he'd eaten his supper. He'd come in smelling of whatever it was Mrs Boss had cooked – usually pork – and as he stood and watched Billy he'd flick remnants of it off the front of his shirt and burp. Then he'd walk over, lower the boy, fill the ladle with water and hold it up to Billy's lips, making a point of spilling some down the front of the boy's shirt. At the same time he'd yell at him to keep still or he wouldn't get any, but the boy was as thirsty as he was hungry, hanging up there like he did near the top of our shed all day and all night where the rising heat and stench were likely even more unbearable.

That last evening it was different.

Boss showed up late and he didn't offer the boy any water. He came in quietly so as not to alert him, and taking hold of the chain he dropped him fast so that the chain jerked and the boy woke with a jolt. As soon as he saw Boss he knew something terrible was about to happen, and he screamed so loud I was sure it would bring someone, but no one came.

Boss told the boy to shut up and then tried to tape his mouth, but Billy jerked his head from side to side until finally Boss slapped him and wound the tape around his face and the back of his head. Then he turned and grabbed a chain coiled on the floor near the door and wound it round Billy's chair, and took one end of it and went outside, and all the while Billy struggled. We heard the sound of the tractor firing up, and then Billy and his chair began to move across the concrete floor and through the shed doors.

We were all of us awake by then, and we listened to the sound of the tractor fading into the distance until we couldn't hear it anymore.

THE ORCA

I'm in the holding pool waiting to perform. I don't want to perform. I don't want to do anything. I've had a bad night. Worse than usual. Haunted by memories of my capture. It was my mother who heard their engines long before I did. I thought we were safe.

That was our mistake. We should have fled when we had the chance.

Afterwards? A long journey to a small pool. Room enough to swim slowly in small circles or lie still near the surface, but no more. One year I spent in that pool. Alone. Day and night. The only sound my mechanical filtration system. The songs of the sea a distant memory.

Today my lungs are hurting and there's blood in my stools. *Ulcers,* says the vet. As if this isn't enough my tooth is killing me. Tough luck. The audience is waiting.

Let them wait.

Sharon is standing nearby. She's already been over to check on me. A cursory glance to see that I'm in position. Now she prepares for her entrance. Head bowed, she breathes deeply, bends over to touch her toes, then straightens and shimmies her body from head to foot to relax her muscles and release the tension in her spine. I've watched her go through this routine a hundred times. It never changes. Another quick glance to me. Cue the music. It builds to a frenzied pitch. An announcer's voice booms from the loudspeakers. Sharon makes her entrance, raises her arms to wave at the crowd, blows her whistle. This is the signal for her colleagues to raise my gate, and when they do I enter the performance pool.

And now, let the show begin!

I watch Sharon carefully though I know exactly what she will do. Raising her right arm she sweeps it down in a circling motion and I obey. As I hug the perimeter of the pool I pick up speed, and on my third revolution I dash into the center and leap into the air where I hang just long enough for the crowds to appreciate all twelve thousand magnificent pounds of me before I crash onto my back, unleashing a wave that soaks the first two rows of gaping spectators. The crowd has gotten their first look at me and they are duly impressed.

So they should be.

A few more tricks, and then a female orca joins me and immediately I'm distracted. We don't get on.

I look to Sharon, but she's vanished. Two other trainers signal to my companion. She ignores them
and rakes me, grazing her teeth along my flank.
No, not today. Not today of all days. Her trainers
sense her mood and try to get her attention as
together we prepare to execute a series of syn-
chronized leaps. One, then two, and on the third
she rams me as I leap from the water so that I
land on my side too close to the edge of the pool.
Now they tire of her antics. They try to coax her
back into the holding pool. She toys with them,
the slave baiting her masters. Tensions rise, and
she rakes me one last time before speeding toward
the holding pool where the gates crash down
behind her with a clang. Too late. My concentration is shot.

Sharon returns. We resume, but I miss my cues.
My tricks are sloppy, ill-timed. The whole performance lacks precision, and I can tell from the crowd's
half-hearted applause that they grow bored. *You're*
bored, I want to scream. *You're* bored? I execute a
tidal-wave splash. Take the audience by surprise.
Some get up to leave. *Good riddance.* Others laugh.
Hah! You won't be laughing for long. Sharon runs over
and catches my eye. She's going to cut the show short.
At least she has the good sense to know when the
game is up.

Wait, what's this? *No. No! Don't dive in! Don't!*
Not today! Please. I can't ... I ... Okay, but don't say
I didn't warn you. You want to play? You want to play?
So we'll play. I look for her in the water, prepare to
swim underneath her and propel her into the air when,
without warning, a trawler enters the cove where my
mother and I are resting. I hear the noise of the
charges exploding in the water and ... No, it's not
the charges. It's her. Sharon. She's screaming. Why
is she screaming? Now it's my mother's screams that
I hear. Mother? MOTHER! *Stop struggling, Sharon.*
I'm only playing. You like to play, don't you? Dive!
DIVE! My mother's cry is urgent and loud. Arm in
my mouth I go deeper. *You're not listening, Sharon.*
Stop it now. There's no need to struggle. Blood. I taste
blood. Blood in my mouth. *What's that? You're*
wounded? Well, what did you expect? What part of
'Don't dive in' did you not understand?

Mother? I can't see her. Where has she gone?
There's a boat between us. Mother? Mother, where
are you?! Nets drop into the water. She tries to reach
me. Tangles herself in their mesh. I hear her cries.
Let her go! Let my moth ... *What? Yes, let her go!*
Let her ... Wait, what's that? You mean Sharon? Non-
sense. She'll be fine. Now more boats, smaller, circling
all around. They block our exit. I thrash about. Ram
one. A rib cracks and bubbles burst from Sharon's

mouth. She goes limp. Shouts from above. What do they want? Can't they just leave us alone? We're playing, Sharon and I. That's all. It's all part of the act. We've performed it a hundred times. *NO! I won't let her go! She's fine! Look at her. Relaxed as a rag doll. I'd never hurt her. She loves me.*

Mother? MOTHERRRR!!!!!

***

They'll never let me out now. I'll die here. But then I was always going to die here, wasn't I? So what. So ho-hum, hody-hody-hum. Sharon used to say this whenever there was something she couldn't change or fix. She never got angry. She just repeated it over and over. Her mantra, she called it. Sometimes she'd even sing it. But she won't be singing it now. Not now, not ever. Poor Sharon. She meant well. And I miss her. I do.

Ho-hum. Hody-hody ... hum.

MRS BOSS

I took a chance calling that early, but then I figured with Billy gone they probably wouldn't be getting a lot of sleep anyway.

I was right. His dad picked up on the second ring. I didn't waste time with pleasantries. Just came right out and said, *Lemme speak to Grandma.* When she said hello I had the feeling she knew it was me calling before I ever uttered a word. It happens. Been times when somebody's been on my mind, sometimes for days, sometimes for weeks, and then bingo, right outta the blue they up and phone me.

No, she wasn't surprised. Not one bit.

So I said, *I know where Billy is. Call the sheriff and tell him to meet you here. Come straight to the house. Won't be nobody else here but me.*

Then I hung up.

Why'd I ask for Grandma? No particular reason other than she's the one I bump into now and again. At the beauty parlor. At least she has the decency not to stare when Boss's been practicing his fisticuffs on my face.

Don't look so surprised. I never said I wouldn't get back at him. I said I'd do it in my own good time. I had to make sure I had something serious enough to send him on an extended vacation, because sure as hell wife-beating ain't it. I reckoned kidnapping and unlawful imprisonment would do the trick. Now I got attempted murder to add, and if that ain't enough to justify what I did then there's nothing else left. You may just as well go ahead and shoot me.

The Journalist

It began with menacing phone calls. Soon men in parked cars were photographing the entrance to our offices. Then one day two men trailed me home from work. They followed me into the metro, and when I boarded the train they shoved their way into my carriage. I noticed them right away. I think they wanted me to, because they made no attempt to keep their distance. When they got out at my stop and followed me from the station to the street I turned and shouted at them, *What do you want?*

That's when one of them walked straight up to me, leaned into my face and said, *If you don't stop writing about us you know what will happen.*

And very stupidly I shouted, *Us? You mean Uncle.*

He glared at me and the other one came up and shoved a newspaper into my hands. By then several people had turned to look at us, and I watched the two men as they vanished into the rush-hour crowds. Then I glanced at the paper. On the front page was my follow-up story of the attack at the university's bear sanctuary. A sudden rush of fear overwhelmed me, and for an instant I thought I was going to be sick.

A young woman noticed me. She came over and took my arm. Not knowing what to say I said, *I'm sorry. I don't feel very well. It must be something I ate.*

She offered to walk me home, which was very kind of her because she had no idea how far she would have to go. But I told her no and assured her I was fine.

Before she left me she noticed the paper in my hand, and she looked at me and said, *Terrible, isn't it? Who would do such a thing?*

It was all I could do to keep from saying, *Did you see those two men who approached me just now? They would do such a thing.* But I remained silent and shook my head to show that I shared her revulsion. Then I collected myself and walked home. Along the way I looked over my shoulder now and again to see if I was being followed. When I arrived I stood across the road from my building before entering and heading up the stairs to my flat. I wanted to make sure no one was waiting for me. When I got upstairs I made a cup of tea. Then I went to my file cabinet and fetched all the material I'd collected about the young student called Zhen and the bear sanctuary where she worked. As I reread it I was reminded of the details of the attack.

According to the police, she'd arrived in her office early that morning before the rest of the staff turned up for the day. Once inside she switched off the alarm system, and as soon as she did her attackers cut through a perimeter fence and made their way to the enclosure of her favourite bear, Tiáopí. The police say it proves someone working at or connected with the sanctuary must have been involved in the attack, but I don't buy it. I know virtually every member of the staff, and not one of them has ever been anything but totally devoted to Zhen and her bears. The same with her colleagues at the university. Completely devastated. All of them. Especially her professor who's also her mentor and colleague. When I interviewed him he looked like a broken man.

The police say Zhen must have surprised her attackers just as they were getting ready to shoot Tiáopí. She put up a terrific struggle, because when the doctors examined her they found she'd suffered a severe concussion and a broken arm and rib. Her struggle also upset the other bears because a terrific racket ensued. As it happens another member of staff also arrived earlier than usual that morning, and when he heard the commotion he sounded the alarm and went to investigate. This sent the attackers running. He found Zhen slumped in front of Tiáopí's enclosure and called an ambulance. By the time she arrived at the hospital she'd slipped into a coma. That was a month ago.

It's unclear whether or not Zhen recognised her attackers. During her time at the sanctuary she made quite a name for herself, and there are those who think they must have known her. Otherwise, they reason, why would they have chosen Tiáopí as their target? One of those who believes this is Zhen's cousin. Despite her shock and grief, she was able to give the police the description of a man. A few days later she participated in a police line-up and identified the man she described as the same man she'd seen at Zhen's seminar the week before the attack. She also told them that he'd been the principal buyer at her father's now defunct bear bile farm. The police interviewed the suspect, but to date no arrest has been made.

Getting to Zhen's cousin was not easy. It took me several weeks. In the end I think it was her frustration at the lack of progress in finding Zhen's attackers and bringing them to justice that persuaded her to meet with me. Poor girl. She's like a person caught in a nightmare. Since we spoke she's been placed under police protection. I have my doubts about the motive for this. It seems to me it's more about keeping the press at bay than keeping her safe.

When I was finally able to speak to her I persuaded her to tell me about the man she identified. To my surprise he's the same man I've been watching for weeks. How could I have been so naive? Until his thugs approached me, I thought he was unaware of my presence. Now I'm sure he's been following my reports, starting with that day when I saw him stop in the street and stare at my front-page story.

Yesterday I went to the police and told them about the men who threatened me. Both were stocky and muscular, and both had tattoos, though one tried to hide his by pulling up his collar. When I told the police about the tattoos they looked at each other and then away, and I thought, *What are they hiding? Do they know these men?* The more I discover the more I'm convinced that this goes way beyond Zhen and the bear sanctuary and involves more than just a few individuals. It's about an entire industry; one that is protected and facilitated by powerful people. How else can it operate with such impunity?

Meanwhile, I'm being watched and threatened. I should tell my editor, but I know what she'll say. *It's too dangerous for you now.* And then she'll reassign me and give the story of the bear sanctuary and Uncle and all that goes with it to another journalist. I don't want to hand over this story to someone else, but if I tell her she'll insist, and if I protest she'll look at me and say, *What good is a dead journalist?* And I know already what my answer will be.

No, I'm not about to quit. Not yet, anyway.

GRANDMA

I didn't want my son to go with me. I had a bad feeling, but there was no way I could convince him to let me go on my own. Not at that hour. Billy's mom called the sheriff while we threw on our coats and boots. Neither one of us bothered to get dressed. Then we hurried outside and got in the car.

It was a chilly morning in late October, black as a crow's breast, and there was a bitter wind blowing in from the north. I think we both took it as an omen, though we never spoke of it then or after. Omens are one of those things you only think about later. A lot of life is like that. You figure it out after the fact. Like watching a film for the second time when all the things you missed the first time suddenly fall into place, only you can't rerun your life.

We drove in silence to Boss's farm, our brights on the whole way. But even in the pitch dark you could find your way to his spread just by following the smell. Soon as we turned off the main road onto the drive we saw the lights in the house were on, and at the sound of our car Mrs Boss stepped from her house onto the porch. She stood there watching us, not saying a word as my son cut the engine. He hadn't seen her for some time yet, and I knew this and stole a sideways at him. No doubt about it, he was shocked. He remembered her from when he was a kid fresh outta college. She still had her looks back then. But that night she looked like she always looks now. Like a woman who's been wedded to her husband's fist for thirty years.

Like us she hadn't bothered to get properly dressed. She was wearing an old coat over a faded pink terry-cloth robe that I swear hadn't been washed since the day it left the sales rack at Walmart, and her hair was pulled back in a ponytail. She used to have beautiful hair when she was young, but now it's thin and scrappy like a dog with mange. She had a half-smoked cigarette dangling from her left hand, and as we climbed the steps to the porch she brought it to her mouth. I was standing right next to her when she exhaled, and the smoke mixed with her breath which was still sour from sleep. She hadn't bothered to brush her teeth. Funny what you remember.

My son didn't waste any time. *Where is he?* he said.

She dropped her cigarette onto the porch and stubbed it out with her foot before saying, *I reckon the sheriff'll be here any minute now.*

I thought he was going to grab her and shake her, but just then a pair of headlights swept up from the road onto the drive, and I turned to see the sheriff's car coming toward the house.

I'll get my keys, she said, and headed back inside.

We turned and waited for the sheriff and his deputy to cut their engine and join us on the porch. When they did the sheriff said, *What's this all about?*

And my son answered, *We're waiting to find out, and now that you're here I expect we will.*

Just then Mrs Boss came back out holding a set of car keys and said, *Follow me,* and headed down the steps to her car.

The sheriff turned to my son and said, *Why don't you two ride with us?*

And so we did.

The drive to the slurry pits took some few minutes, but it seemed like it took forever. It's hard to describe the smell when you're standing next to 'em. It's enough to take the paint off a barn a mile away. Just five hundred pigs can generate two hundred and sixty-five thousand gallons of waste a year. Boss had a thousand. None of us thought to bring a handkerchief with us, so we had to pull the collars of our jackets over our noses and breathe through our mouths. Even so the backs of our throats burned.

The sheriff and his deputy had flashlights, and soon as we stopped they stepped out of their car and turned 'em on. Mrs Boss also had one, and right away she switched it on and started to sweep it round the perimeter of the main pit. Wasn't more than a few seconds before her beam hit on a red pickup.

Isn't that Boss's? said the sheriff.

But Mrs Boss didn't answer. Instead she swept her flashlight further along the rim of the pit until it picked up a tractor parked right near to the edge. The sheriff and deputy followed her beam, and now all three flashlights were focused on it. Its arm and bucket were raised in the air, and in the bucket was an airplane seat, and chained into it was Billy.

Nobody said a word. We just stood there staring with a mixture of wonder and horror, like little kids at a fun park seeing a roller coaster for the first time. Billy's dad ran to the tractor, climbed in and switched on the engine. He backed the tractor away from the pit, lowered the arm, and climbed into the bucket. By now the sheriff and his deputy had joined him, and between 'em they managed to get Billy free. He was so weak he could hardly stand, and his dad and the deputy had to carry him to the sheriff's car and lay him on the back seat.

When Billy was settled the sheriff went over to Mrs Boss and said, *Any idea where Boss has got to?*

Yep, she said, and then she pointed her flashlight back at the slurry pit and said, *Put him in there myself,* before turning and heading back to her car.

According to Mrs Boss he was supposed to be heading north to the main highway on his way to an auction, so when he pulled outta the drive and turned left toward the pits, she became suspicious and decided to follow him. When she got there he was sitting on the tractor about to unload Billy – airplane seat and all – straight into the pit, but when he saw her he climbed down and made a beeline for her car. He told her to go back to the house, and if she ever said a word to anybody he'd kill her.

Well, everybody knows what he's capable of, and wouldn't nobody put it past him, including and most especially Mrs Boss. So right away she backed up her car to leave, but changed her mind and rammed him straight into the pit. She claimed she was only acting to save the boy. The police charged her with manslaughter. Course the only witness was Billy, and he testified that she was telling the truth, but even so the judge imposed the minimum sentence of twelve months. In the end she only served three.

Mitigating circumstances, said the judge.

Still three months too many if you ask me.

It didn't take Billy long to recover. He's a strong boy. But after the trial he refused to talk about it again. His parents let it be, but I had a hunch there was more to it than he was letting on.

Months later we were sitting on the porch. He was home for Easter vacation or some such. I'd made a jug of fresh lemonade because Easter'd come late and it was warmer than usual. I was pouring him a glass, when all of a sudden he looked up at me and said outta nowhere, *Grandma, I didn't tell the whole truth like I swore.*

And I looked at him and said, *I know yet. But if you want you can tell me now.* And he did.

Turns out Boss did climb down off the tractor like Mrs Boss said, and he did make straight for her car looking mad as a bull in heat. But before he ever opened his mouth she put her foot on the pedal and drove right at him. When he bounced onto the hood of the car she kept on going, slamming on her brakes just shy of the pit's edge and hurling him straight into the slurry.

Then she backed up and made her way real slow over to Billy, and leaning outta the window said to him, *You awright?* And when he nodded she said, *Good. Now you saw how he came for me, hollering and threatening to kill me and all, didn't you, boy?* Again Billy nodded. *That's right,* she said, *because the police are gonna be wanting to talk with you and hear your side of the story.* And when he nodded again she said,

Okay, then. Don't you worry now. Just sit tight and I'll be right back. And then she turned round and headed back to her house.

And that's when she called me.

Can't say as I blame her for what she did. After all those years of beatings and Lord knows what else, he had it coming to him. Nobody misses him, that's for sure. Not Mrs Boss, and not his neighbors, and not his pigs. Since then she's sold the farm with the condition that the pigs live outside like pigs are supposed to, and because of it she didn't fetch nearly as much as she could've. But credit to her, she doesn't complain.

After Billy told me the truth of what all had happened he said to me, *Grandma, are you going to tell the police?*

I said, *You want me to?*

He didn't answer straight away. Just sat there dead quiet. Finally, he said, *Grandma, I reckon even when something is the law it doesn't mean it's necessarily right or fair.* And right away I told him I reckoned there's a good number of folks everywhere that would agree, me included.

That was the last we ever spoke of it.

THE FOXHOUND

Come in, come in. *Make yourself at home* as my mistress likes to say. But perhaps best not to sit on that chair. It's a bit delicate for a chap with your build. May I suggest the sofa? I've sat on more than a few in my day, and I can vouch that it competes with the best. Just ignore the upholstery if you can. Hideous. No accounting for taste.

Well, then, if you're comfortable, I'll begin.

For weeks after my former tormentor brought me home I barely ate a morsel, just enough to keep me alive, though there were many days I wondered why I bothered. Then I would think of Mac. What would he have done? Why, he would have kept going. Kept going for the sheer joy of being alive. That was Mac. He had *joie de vivre* in spades.

The first day, when I awoke, I had no idea where I was or how I'd arrived here. It took me quite some time to recall it, and when I did I was anything but grateful. Too little too late, as the saying goes. My new master heard me stirring and came into the kitchen where he'd made a bed for me by the cooker to keep me warm. The moment I saw his face I tried to get up and make a run for it, but he'd closed all the doors. Whenever he approached me I bared my teeth and growled. I still had some fight in me, though how I haven't a notion. Sheer stubbornness, I suppose. He'd put out water and a plate of food for me, but while he was watching I refused to touch it. Of course I was thirsty and hungry, but even in my miserable state I managed to retain a touch of the old dignity. I like to think Mac would have been proud of me.

During this time my new master remained, for the most part, at home. I assumed this was to keep an eye on me, but I soon learned that he'd quit his job at the lab and had nowhere else to go, so we spent the days together. He would chat, mostly about his time at the lab. Why he'd done what he did, what he was thinking at the time, how sorry he was for all of it. I listened, though I never let on that I understood a word or cared a farthing for his confessions or his companionship. I'd wait until he left the room before I ate, and when I needed to relieve myself I stood by the kitchen door, refusing to look at him. He'd clap a collar and lead on me, and off we'd go for a tour round the garden.

After a time the garden became the neighbourhood, and the neighbourhood the local parks, and

soon people recognised me, though I never acknow-
ledged their greetings or my master's long-winded
explanations of how I came to be in his care. The
children annoyed me most. Their hands all over me,
their arms around my neck trying to squeeze the life
out of me. I knew letting my guard down in the
company of these bothersome brats was a slippery
slope towards accepting all humans, and I was determined to die before I let that happen again.

One day my master brought home a female. Her
name was Emma. She was unlike any other human
female I'd ever known. In the beginning she kept
her distance, but she would speak to me. Nothing
important. Mindless chit-chat, almost as if I wasn't
there. It was her voice that first caught my attention.
It was like a favourite blanket. Warm and soft and
familiar. And she had the kindest eyes I've ever
seen. I found myself meeting them in spite of my
best efforts to look away, to look anywhere but into
her eyes.

It was many weeks before I understood why. They
reminded me of Mac's. He had eyes like hers. Eyes
that understood you before you uttered a word. Eyes
that forgave you in spite of yourself. She seemed to
have an uncanny understanding of what I'd been
through, how I felt, how much the loss of Mac meant
to me. I could tell that my new master was fond of

her, too, and the more time they spent together the fonder he became. Soon Emma moved into our house, and from that moment things, for me, began to change rapidly.

The first thing she did was put a small camp bed in the kitchen. She would sleep one night in the kitchen with me and one night with my master. At first he objected, but she ignored him and he soon backed off. This musical-beds routine lasted for several weeks. It was hard to say which of us it annoyed most, but, in retrospect, I think it's fair to say it was my master. Emma's ritual was always the same. She'd come in wearing her dressing gown, make a cup of tea, sit at the table, open a book – she was always reading something – and sip her tea until it was finished. Then she'd stand, cross to the sink, place her cup in the washing-up bowl and turn off the lights. If there was no moon she'd feel her way to the bed, invariably crashing into the table, a chair, a counter on the way, pull back the covers and climb in. Many a time I thought the bed would collapse beneath her. It was an old foldout that my master kept for those rare evenings when it was warm and dry enough to sleep in the garden. Every time she made the slightest movement the springs jangled and creaked like a wind chime sparring with an ill-fitting window, but she never complained. I'd wait until I heard her

breathing become even with sleep before I closed my
eyes. I didn't want to give the impression I was too
comfortable with her presence.

One night I had a dream. I had many dreams, but
this one was unusual. From the moment I first arrived
at the lab until Emma's intrusion into my life, my
dreams had consisted almost entirely of nightmares.
On those rare occasions when my nightmares gave
way to a night of blessed oblivion, I would wake
relatively rested. When Mac was alive he could always
tell when I'd had a good night's sleep, probably
because he was invariably awake before me. Or perhaps he never slept. He would look at me and say,
Feeling rested, Major? There was no use denying it.
He could read me like a foxhound can follow a scent.
And with no small amount of guilt and shame I would
admit that I was. Then he would smile and say, *I'm
glad for you, old chap.*

On this night I dreamt that I was leading a hunt.
As usual I'd picked up the scent of the poor blighter
we were chasing long before the others, and I tracked
him to his earth. For some reason my pack refused
to follow me, and I found myself alone. When the
fox realised this he poked his head from his den,
looked me straight in the eye and said, *Well, well,
Major, it appears your pack has deserted you. Care to
join me for a spot of supper?*

He'd nicked a chicken from a local farmer and was on his way home when I nearly spoiled his spoils by giving chase. As was the custom my pack and I had been deprived of breakfast in order to focus us more keenly on the hunt, and I was more than a bit peckish. I readily accepted his invitation and followed him into his den. Without a moment's hesitation he laid out his plunder, inviting me to tuck in. We took no time finishing it off – it was hardly a mouthful or two between us – and yet I think it's fair to say it was one of the tastiest meals I've ever had the pleasure of.

Afterwards we chatted, and he invited me to stay the night. When I objected he insisted, reminding me that as soon as the sun set he would be off to continue his foraging, and I would have his earth to myself. Foxes are nocturnal creatures, and after considering, I accepted. We spent the rest of the day in pleasant conversation, and to my amazement my host never touched on the subject of fox hunting. In this he was a true gentleman. When evening approached he set off, but not before making sure I had everything I needed. The next morning at daybreak he woke me with a gentle tap of his paw, shared with me a hare he'd caught for breakfast, and when we'd eaten he bade me farewell. As I turned to say goodbye he told me to drop by any time – should I be passing – and then he turned and disappeared into his earth.

In the morning when I awoke I found myself lying on the end of Emma's camp bed. In one hand she held a cup of tea, and with the other she stroked my ears. I lifted my head, and when my eyes met hers she smiled and said, *Feeling rested, old chap?*

Not long afterwards the camp bed disappeared, and ever since then the three of us have slept in my master's bedroom with me curled up on the foot of their bed.

MY COUSIN ZHEN

I like the young journalist that came to see me. And yes, I've seen her articles. I've read every one. And so when we met I asked her to tell me about the man known as Uncle.

Was it the same man I pointed out to the police? I asked.

Yes, it's him, she said. *They call him the Ivory King. He's also known as the Bile Baron. He has many other names as well, but to his loyal customers he's simply Uncle.*

Have you met him? I asked.

Yes, she said, *I've met him.* And then she fell silent.

I waited a moment or two, and then I said, *Tell me, what's he like?*

He's very powerful, she said, *and he has many powerful friends who protect him.*

I asked why they protect him if they know that what he does is illegal. She smiled and said, *That's easy, because the answer is nearly always the same.*

Then she rubbed her fingers together in a gesture that means money, and I thought of my parents and how they were forced to sell their farm in return for the promise of good jobs – jobs that never came in a factory that was never built.

And the men who threatened you? I asked. *Were they the same men who threatened me? The same men who warned me not to speak with the police? The same men who warned me not to speak with you?*

She said she was certain they must be.

Since that meeting the journalist has left. She didn't want to leave. She told me so herself. She said her newspaper had another assignment for her some-where abroad. I think this is a lie. Many people have read her articles, and I think she was made to leave because it's no longer safe for her here.

You know that our president announced a ban on ivory? Craftsmen are no longer supposed to carve it and shops are no longer allowed to sell it, but still I see many shops offering ivory trinkets and bangles and all manner of expensive carvings, and I wonder how this is possible. I wish our president would also make a ban on bile farming, and I told this to the journalist. She told me not to expect too much, because it takes a long time for people to change their ways. *A single thread cannot become a chord, and a single tree does not make a forest.* She said Uncle told her this, and he's right. But it's also true that a single spark can create a blaze.

The good news is that Zhen is awake. She doesn't remember what happened. The doctors say she might never remember. I hope they're right. When she asks me I tell her she had an accident and she must get better quickly, because her bears miss her very much, especially Tiáopí, and this pleases her. I tell her everyone at the sanctuary is waiting for her to return. In the meantime, all of us do everything we can to make sure the bears are well looked after. All of this makes her determined to recover quickly, but what will happen when she learns the truth?

Zhen needs to get her strength back, and I worry the truth will be too much for her. Uncle walks free, and there's nothing we can do about it, so what's the point of her knowing? When she recovers, then we can talk about it. Maybe make a plan. Decide what to do. For now, she has many visitors, and she's grateful and pleased. Even her father comes, and though he doesn't say much, she's happy to see him.

But nothing makes her happier than seeing the professor.

He comes every week. Weekends, too. Sometimes he brings her flowers or cakes or games they can play together to pass the time, but mostly they just chat. He tells her about his work, and she listens like a child being read her favourite story. Often when I arrive he's still there, and when he sees me he looks embarrassed, like he's been caught somewhere he's not supposed to be. He's in love with her, that's for sure, even if he doesn't realise it. But Zhen does, and I'm happy for her, because this more than anything will help her to recover.

The Gorilla

Switzerland is a clean place. The humans are clean, the animals are clean, the towns are clean, the landscape is clean, even the air is clean. The Swiss Tourist Board describes it as a country of 'pristine lakes, towering mountains and vibrant skies', and I suppose it is. Its snow-covered peaks brush against a sky that is as clear as the lakes that lie beneath it. In spring and early summer its meadows are rainbowed with wild flowers drawing humans from all over the world who come to gawp at the colours and suck in the air and marvel at the nature that lies all around them. In winter more humans come, strapping boots and wooden boards to their feet and hurling themselves down white-powdered slopes for something they call the thrill of the sport. But for all this one thing was always missing, and for me it was the only thing that mattered.

I was the only gorilla.

As soon as we landed I was transferred to a waiting truck and taken to my new home. In the evenings and on weekends this consisted of a large, well-equipped enclosure. The rest of the time I was confined to a section of laboratory encased in a vast, imposing building. From the windows I could see a lake curved like a scythe before a range of mountains as implacable and imperious as a Bengal tiger. It was here that I spent the next twelve months subjected to endless examinations and questioned by a multitude of humans dressed in long white coats who could not sign.

Dr Sadiq translated. She rarely left my side. In this she was true to her word. She called herself my personal assistant, seeing to all of my needs, comforting me, quieting my fears, and explaining all the things I did not understand. I am certain this was exhausting for her, for there was much that I did not understand. But gradually, with her help, I began to appreciate why these humans that surrounded me were so keen to study me. It was simple really. I could communicate with them, and it soon became clear what they wished to know. Namely, what animals and humans have in common. This seemed so obvious to me that it was all I could do not to lose my patience, but I knew this would get me nowhere. Instead, to amuse myself, I began to observe each of them closely just as they were observing me. They stood about clutching notepads, clipboards and pens, huddling and whispering among themselves while they studied my every move. No matter what I did, however trivial, someone wrote it down. After several weeks I concluded that their interest in me was far greater than my interest in them, though I judged it best to keep this to myself.

It was during this time that my training began. As part of it Dr Sadiq aimed to increase my vocabulary. She did this by reading to me from a variety of books. I liked the stories about humans and animals most, and in this way I learned just how pivotal to human development we are. We figure in every aspect of your lives from medicine, science, mythology and the arts, to philosophy, religion and ritual. From the moment you evolved you have depended on us for everything – from transportation to agriculture to the food on your plates and the clothes on your back. Your first tools, the very instruments you claim define your species, were made from our bones. And though some of you may consider me presumptuous, I think it is fair to say that without us you humans would not have survived. But while all this was a revelation to me, I remained focused on Dr Sadiq's promise that, in exchange for my help, I would be allowed to return to my mountain home. It was this that made me apply myself, and apply myself I did. By the end of my training I understood exactly what was expected of me. Furthermore, I was confident that I could deliver it, for as far as I could tell the art of diplomacy relied upon rarely speaking one's mind. For me this was easy. I had been doing it for most of my life. When I told this to Dr Sadiq, she laughed.

True, she said, *but because you are a gorilla and not a human, you have a chance to do things differently. To make a real difference.*

How? I signed.

You can communicate with animals and *humans and so help us to understand how we are, well, you know, alike.*

I thought she was joking. If she didn't know this by now then she would never know it.

What I mean is, you can help us see the world through your eyes. Tell us what you and your fellows are thinking and feeling and—

I felt a surge of anger, and before she could finish I interrupted her.

You ask how we are alike, and I will tell you that in every essential aspect we are exactly alike. We want to be safe, to raise our young, to have enough to eat and a place to call home. We are animals just like you. Nothing more and nothing less, and we have as much right to these things and to be here on this earth as you.

Then I fell silent. I thought about all the effort and activity that surrounded me. All the questions and experiments and games. The endless poking and prodding. The countless lessons in etiquette, diplomacy, politics and public speaking. And all of it for something so simple and obvious even a human could figure it out.

You're right, she signed. *As always you are right. But if you do this then perhaps many things will change for the better, not only for you, but for us humans as well.*

I could hardly believe it. It had never occurred to me that with all the power humans wield they should need help from a lone gorilla.

But we do, she signed, *more than you could ever imagine.*

***

By now it should come as no surprise when I tell you that we animals – from the greatest to the least among us – are, in varying degrees, capable of a wide range of thoughts and emotions. Joy, grief, fear, desire, gratitude, empathy, loyalty and regret are all familiar to us. We lie, steal, cheat and deceive. We can be altruistic and yes, cruel. We know the difference between what is right and what is wrong, and we feel aggrieved when we are wronged and ashamed when we transgress. Like you, we are aware of ourselves and others, and because of this we respond to our names. Sometimes these consist of a signature call or other sound to which only a particular individual will answer. The point is that when we recognise our names in whatever form they take, we react. And if we can identify ourselves as unique from those around us, are we not self-aware, and therefore, by your own definition, intelligent?

Above all let me assure you once and for all that it makes no difference whether we are fish, birds, reptiles, insects, crustaceans or mammals – we feel pain. That you ever doubted this is testimony to your ignorance and arrogance. There is but one emotion we do not share with humans and it is this: we are not sentimental. We leave this to you, for as your philosophers have noted – life is solitary, poor, nasty, brutish and short.

But sometimes, if we try, it can be so much more.

***

You're not going to like this.

So began the preparations for what Dr Sadiq referred to as 'my return to the wild'. When she first told me that I would be returned, as promised, to my ancestral home, she said, *It will not be as easy as you might imagine. The gorillas you'll encounter in the forest are wild. There's no guarantee they'll accept you. They may even be violent towards you, and you must be prepared for this.*

She described for me gorilla hierarchy, and the chances of me – a single male silverback and a stranger at that – being integrated into an unfamiliar troop. We both knew that aspects of my behaviour, despite all of Dr Sadiq's best efforts, were bound to be strange to my brothers and sisters unhabituated to human contact. None of this worried me. The only thing that mattered was the chance to be back among my own, and for this I was willing to risk my life.

There's something else, she said.

I waited.

When we return to the land of your birth and before we release you, you'll have to be quarantined for several weeks.

Explain, I signed.

Isolated, she said, *in an enclosure. You'll have no contact with any other wild animals, and it will be many weeks before you'll be free.*

I thought she was kidding, a practical joke as humans say. But I have learned that practical jokes are rarely funny or practical, so I changed the subject.

What do you mean when you say wild? I said. She looked at me like she often does, with a mixture of surprise and amusement.

Wild is the opposite of tame.

Define tame, I said. Humans like to define things and sometimes I am grateful for this, but not always.

Well, you are tame now, she said. *But once you were wild.*

At that moment a colleague entered and she was called away to consult on what she called an emergency. I never found out the nature of this emergency, nor did I ask. But while she was away I considered this concept of wild and its opposite – tame. What is wild? What is tame? It was then that I remembered hearing another member of staff use the expression 'reverted to the wild' when describing a chimp that had mauled his trainer – a human female who had cared for him from the moment he was abandoned as an infant until he reached adolescence. One day this chimp attacked his trainer, causing severe injuries. When asked what might have provoked him, the trainer and her colleagues suggested various hypotheses, but all concluded that, whatever the cause, the chimp had reverted to the wild.

As I recalled this I began to realise that the chimp had not reverted to this thing called wild. He had simply remembered his nature. And in the moment that he remembered it he must have experienced overwhelming feelings of confusion and rage. Naturally, the humans responsible for the chimp did not agree. They felt the chimp had betrayed them. He had behaved badly. Very badly. So badly that he could no longer be trusted. Now the problem was what to do with him. It was then I understood that reverting to the wild was merely another way of saying that the attempt to subdue his nature, his very essence, had failed spectacularly, and for none more so than for the poor chimp himself.

Shortly afterwards he was put down.

***

Once I completed my training I began my career as a goodwill ambassador for the International Union for the Conservation of Nature, commonly referred to as the IUCN, the first non-human animal ever to hold such a prominent and important position. With Dr Sadiq acting as my translator, adviser, colleague and companion, I have given speeches, toured wild-life parks, advised governments and politicians, lent my name to conservation societies, visited schools, and posed for my photograph with a human child on my knee more times than I care to count.

But by far my most important mission has been conducting and collecting the interviews you find within these pages. My human colleagues tell me they are invaluable, that without them all the goodwill in the world will have little effect. Yet I don't see much evidence that humans are getting smarter, not in the numbers and with the urgency and speed that is required. Nevertheless, I carry on. I mustn't give up, they tell me, or all of my kind will be lost, and those of us who are left will be confined to a handful of zoos and nature reserves to live out our days.

And if so, if it comes to this, what then? Will future generations ever know what they have lost? Perhaps. Or perhaps the make-believe world you call virtual reality will be enough for you.

My human friends tell me that their hope lies with their children. I wonder, and like them, I hope.

I have several more interviews to do and still more in files waiting to be translated and transcribed. Some days I question why I bother, but then I think of the captain and Bowzer and Karim and Dr Sadiq. I hear of a human who has given his or her life to save one of ours, of others who have rescued countless numbers of us, of teachers who teach their students and parents who teach their children why we, and not just you, are important. Dr Sadiq tells me that the more I reveal to humans about the inner lives and minds of animals the more humans will respect and care for us. Again, I wonder and hope.

In many ways I am learning as much as my human colleagues. But the hardest lesson for me is to understand how your species can at once be so brilliant, so creative, so innovative and adaptive, and at the same time so wilfully, blindly, unimaginably stupid. In this you humans are truly unique.

Meanwhile, I carry on. When I am asked how I find the strength in spite of all the pain and suffering I have endured, in spite of all the obstacles that remain for all of us, I think of my lost family and of all those with whom I have spoken and whose stories you find in these pages. It is because of them that I am able to meet your eyes and say to you the words the poacher spoke to me so many moons ago.

Because I have no choice. No choice.

Epilogue

Dr Sadiq

By the time Einstein boarded a jet for the last time he was used to travelling by air, though for him each time was as terrifying as the first, and none more so than his flight home.

The jet in which we travelled was specially fitted with a custom seat built for him. On his left was a window. I requested that his seat be positioned as close to it as possible, so that during our flight he had an unencumbered view of the landscape below.

I was sitting opposite him, not a metre away, my medical bag at my feet. Behind me stood his cage liberally strewn with straw. Water, food and certain other indispensables were provided. Altogether there were four of us on board: our crew consisting of a pilot and co-pilot, and us. I had already given Einstein a very mild sedative, just enough to relax him. Even so, he was firmly strapped in his seat because, as any flyer knows, take-offs and landings are often the most dangerous and nerve-wracking episodes of any flight.

Over the course of our journey we reviewed again the events of the previous few weeks. As a goodwill ambassador for the IUCN Einstein's fame was widespread, and for his services he had received numerous accolades and awards. In short, he was a celebrity. Humans from all over the world knew his name. Many millions more knew him by sight, some firsthand, some from the many photographs taken during our tours of duty. His appointment as the first non-human animal ever to hold an official position with an international organisation made him not only famous, but infamous, and along with his many awards he received a fair number of threats. It was because of the latter that it became necessary to provide a security detail whenever he travelled in his official capacity. It seems there were – *are* – many humans, too many to count, who view him as a direct challenge to their religious and philosophical beliefs, and one they cannot countenance. Because of this there was an element of real danger in returning him to his mountain home. Word was put out simply that he was being retired due to ill health. When asked for further details it was announced that any post-retirement plans depended entirely upon his recovery and left at that.

As expected, every media organisation carried the story of Einstein's failing health. The news was met with an equal amount of sadness, wishes for a speedy recovery, and a kind of frenzied glee. Because of the latter the humans that knew the truth were kept to an absolute minimum. Apart from myself, the head of the IUCN, and a carefully selected team of indispensable facilitators, no one was any the wiser.

EINSTEIN

The decision to keep me relaxed, but aware, is granted at my request. Though I have travelled hundreds of thousands of miles by air, not one image from a single one of my flights intrudes upon my memory. Until now I have always travelled in a crate placed in the hold of a cargo plane, but this trip will be different. After months of viewing photographs and films of my ancestral forest I am determined to approach it with my eyes, mind and senses alert.

***

We are now boarded, and I have been strapped into my seat. As we taxi down the runway Dr Sadiq reaches out a hand and lays it on my arm, and with her free hand she signs to ask me if I am all right. I grunt. I am already feeling the drug's effect. Dr Sadiq reads my mind and begins again to sign.

Don't worry, she says. *The sedative I've given you is very mild, and it's a long flight. If you fall asleep, I'll wake you.*

Again, I grunt. I want – need – to see my home for myself from every possible angle, and when I do I am not disappointed.

***

Morning breaks as we approach our destination. Below us subsistence farms give way to endless savannahs, soggy marshlands, tangled jungles, jagged massifs, unlikely glaciers, and montane forests that look from the air to be impenetrable. Although my eyes never stray from my window, I know that Dr Sadiq is as enthralled as I because she never utters a sound. We skirt an active volcano, its rim ringed by a circle of clouds. As we bank I stare into its crater where a molten soup criss-crossed with spidery red veins, like the capillaries on an old man's nose, simmers. I am at once reminded of kindly Old Man who nursed me at Circus so long ago, and of my friend, Joey. I hear myself grunt.

Spectacular, isn't it? replies Dr Sadiq.

And in spite of the memory of my departed friend, I have to agree that it is.

***

There's one final detail we still haven't discussed, she signs. *You'll need a new name.*

I agree.

Any ideas? she says.

Mpendao, I reply. *It means 'loved one'. It is the name my mother gave to me.*

She smiles and her eyes fill with tears. It is the last thing I expect, and immediately I begin to sign.

Is something wrong? Tell me.

Nothing's wrong, she says. *It's perfect.*

She turns away. I watch her wipe the tears from her cheeks and wonder if the females of my own species will be as curious.

***

Before we land I enter my cage and sit down in a self-induced stupor. Dr Sadiq laughs.

No one can play dumb better than you, she says.

I do not dare to sign a reply. It is not the time to exchange jest, for already the plane has come to a standstill and the co-pilot is on his feet and approaching the cargo doors at the rear of the plane. As soon as he opens them a surge of hot humid air enters. Within seconds Dr Sadiq pulls her shirt away from her body and wipes her face with her sleeve.

I don't know how you'll manage in this climate, she says. *It's like wearing a fur coat in a steam bath.*

It is true. We have come straight from the sub-zero temperatures of a Swiss winter only to find ourselves in an equatorial rainforest. But we could have landed in the steaming fires of hell for all it matters. I am home.

We are met by a smug government official whose bulging eyes, squat legs and stout body remind me of a hippopotamus. He takes no notice of me and I return the courtesy. Accompanying him is the park's director – a human of aristocratic ancestry, or so I am told. I suppose this is meant to impress me, but what impresses me is his manner. He is polite and confident, his speech spontaneous but never frivolous. He looks at me without staring and introduces himself without condescension. We are, at least in his mind, equals. I have yet to make up my mind and I think he senses this, but to his credit he does not take offence. On the contrary, I think my reserve is exactly what he expects.

Once the formalities are over I am loaded onto the back of a truck. In the cab sit the aristocrat and Dr Sadiq. It takes us many hours to arrive at the park's headquarters. As we climb the air grows cooler, and in an effort to warm herself Dr Sadiq rubs her arms.

***

On arrival we pass the administration building and head immediately to a long, low compound which serves as the park's orphanage. At that moment it is empty, its previous occupants having been released back into the forest in the weeks preceding my arrival. In the interval no new orphans have arrived to take their place, and so I am alone once again. But I do not complain. I am expecting this.

Dr Sadiq reminds me that I will experience a period of acclimatisation before I am freed. This is necessary to ensure my best chance of success, by which she means my survival. For myself I have no such fears, but I do not protest. Foods I will encounter in the wild are introduced into my diet, and I am vaccinated and monitored for a variety of diseases lest I unwittingly introduce a pathogen into the forest to which its inhabitants have no natural immunity. All of this takes time, and Dr Sadiq, as ever, remains by my side.

***

A full two months pass before I am judged fit for release, and they are, without a doubt, the longest two months of my life. To be so near to my ancestral home and still confined to a cage is almost more than I can bear. It is made more difficult by the fact that

Dr Sadiq and I rarely sign, and when we do it is only at night. She waits until everyone is asleep before she ventures out to speak with me. Not even the park's director has been informed of my true identity. Even so, I often wonder if he suspects. If he does he keeps his suspicions to himself, and I never doubt that my secret will be safe with him.

***

Tonight is my final night in captivity, and Dr Sadiq comes one last time to visit me. It has been raining all day and the air is cold and heavy with moisture. She waits until all the rangers and their alpha male, the aristocrat, have gone to bed before slipping through the dark to my enclosure. I hear and smell her long before she stands before me, and I rise and come forward to meet her. Immediately, she begins to sign.

How are you feeling? she says.

Impatient, I reply.

She smiles, but there is sadness in her eyes.

I'll miss you, she says.

And I will miss you.

I wait. I want this conversation to be over as much for her as for me.

Will I see you again? she says.

This is the question I have been dreading most. I cannot bear to lie to her, and so I say the first thing that comes to mind.

Never say never.

I bare my teeth, hoping she will interpret this as a smile, and wait for her reaction. To my relief she changes the subject.

There's something I need to say to you, she signs.

I am listening.

She turns her head and gazes in the direction of the forest. It is a moonless night and nearly impossible to see where the compound ends and the forest begins. Through the darkness unfamiliar sounds drift towards us from every direction. Night after night I spend hours listening to these sounds, memorising them, trying to form a picture in my mind of the creatures from whom the sounds emanate. Some are familiar from my days at Circus, Fairground and Zoo, others are new, but in among them I hear several of my brethren. It took less than a week for them to discover me. Though they keep their distance they can smell me, hear me, and I cannot help but wonder how they will receive me when at last we meet.

The poachers that killed your family have not gone away, she says. *Others have taken their place. This is a problem that will not end soon, and I'm afraid for you.*

I look at her long and hard. Why is she telling me this? What does she expect me to say? That I will remain imprisoned behind these bars? That I will spend the rest of my days in the company of humans instead of among my own? Both of us know that this is not an option, yet her eyes demand an answer. Under cover of the blackness that conceals us, I raise my hands.

And I am afraid for you, I sign. *If you humans do not change your ways your children will wake up one day and find their world emptied of all the abundant life that once thrived. They will pore over their picture books and read their stories and look about them and wonder what happened to this paradise you call Earth. And then they will look to you, their parents and grandparents, demanding answers you cannot give. Do not worry for me. Worry for them.*

It is a long time before she answers me. She stands, as still and heavy as the air around us.

As always you are right, she signs.

She tries to smile, but her sadness makes her whole face quiver. She reaches her hand through the bars of my cage, her palm open, her fingers spread. I raise my own hand and press it against hers, and we remain like that, palm to palm, animal to animal, ape to ape, until she turns and disappears into the night.

Dr Sadiq

I didn't accompany Einstein on the morning of his release. I was afraid one or both of us might give away his true identity with a telltale signing, a gesture, a well-meant but too familiar farewell. I think he was disappointed, but not surprised. In a way I suspect he was relieved. It was hard for the two of us not to be too familiar, because by then we were the best of friends. A final goodbye was the last thing either of us needed.

I watched from a distance as his keepers opened the gate to his cage. Behind them stood the park's director, and next to him a detail of armed rangers whose job it was to escort Einstein into the forest. Dawn was just breaking. It was time to get moving, and Einstein needed no encouragement. He loped across the flat red-brown earth of the compound. Behind him the rangers struggled to keep up. At the forest's edge he paused and took a deep breath. It was the first breath of freedom he'd tasted since he was an infant, and I'm sure he wanted to savour it, to remember that moment for as long as he lived. As the air filled his lungs he paused and tilted his head as if listening to a distant sound, and at the same time I imagined I heard a voice – faint, yet somehow strangely familiar.

Come, Mpendao. We are waiting for you.

He must have heard it too, because he stretched like a giant arising from sleep. The muscles in his arms flexed and of their own accord rose to beat his chest, and he seemed to lift and rise like a great bird of prey. As I watched him I felt a joy I have rarely known, but at the same time a profound feeling of longing and loss. Perhaps he sensed this, because for the briefest moment he hesitated, and in that moment I heard myself whisper, *Goodbye, loved one.*

And then he was gone.

ACKNOWLEDGEMENTS

For their help and/or encouragement my thanks to Lizzy Attree, Sally Burnett, Mary Chamberlain, Jo Dwyer-Butler, Henry Eliot, Ceara Elliot, Celine Ernest, Ferdi Ernest, Benjamin Evetts, Julie Fallon, Stephen Fry, Anna Ganev, Marsha Glenn, Sheila Hayman, Jane Howard, Brij Kar, Himesh Kar, Denny Kaylor, Miriam Kutschinski, Peter Littell, Troy Luster, Dominick Lynch-Robinson, John Kuria Ngarega, Patrick Olden, Michael Palin, Charlie Peters, Juliet Pickering, Isabelle Ralphs, Ane Reason, Sam Rees-Williams, Elena Roberts, Roya Sarrafi-Gohar, Martin Scurr, Steve Smith, Jeffrey Thomas, Lydia Weigel, John Weiley, Ruby Weiley. To my husband Richard Loncraine for his love, endless patience and support, and for preparing hundreds of delicious dinners while I was writing this book; to my agent Isobel Dixon for taking a chance on me; to Koko for her inspiration and example; and, last but not least, to my editor Selina Walker, whose patience, wisdom, skill and tact made this a much better book.

ABOUT THE AUTHOR

Felice Fallon was born in Los Angeles, California, and worked in advertising in New York before moving to London to marry and raise a family. In her mid-fifties she read History, Politics and Philosophy at Birkbeck, University of London. *Interviews with an Ape* is her first novel.